I0544096

THE SCARAB EATER'S DAUGHTER

A SISTER WITCHES URBAN FANTASY NOVEL 3

CORALIE MOSS

Copyright © 2020 by Coralie Moss

All rights reserved under International and Pan-American Copyright Conventions.

No part of this book may be reproduced in any form or by any electronic or mechanical means, including information storage and retrieval systems, without written permission from the author, except for the use of brief quotations in a book review.

This is a work of fiction. All names, characters, places, objects, and incidents herein are the product of the author's imagination or are used fictitiously. Any resemblance to actual living things, events, locales, or persons living or dead is entirely coincidental.

Published internationally by Pink Moon Books, British Columbia, Canada.

ISBN 978-1-989446-14-0

Editor: Michelle Meade

Cover Design: Elizabeth Mackey

Proofreading: Lillie's Literary Services

❀ Created with Vellum

ABOUT THE AUTHOR

Coralie Moss loves everyday heroines and complicated witches, layered magic and earthly moments, and will always believe in the power of love. She lives on Salt Spring Island, British Columbia with her family and two globe-trotting rescue cats.

Join Coralie's mailing list for book news, giveaways, and the occasional homage to sisterhood.

 facebook.com/CoralieMossWrites
 twitter.com/moss_coralie
instagram.com/authorcoraliemoss
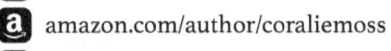 amazon.com/author/coraliemoss
bookbub.com/authors/coralie-moss

ACKNOWLEDGMENTS

Massive thanks to my editor, Michelle Meade, for working with me on this book through the very trying times of early 2020.

Massive thanks to the Beta Belles, for always, *always*, catching things others didn't!

CONTENTS

AUTHOR'S NOTE: THE SISTER WITCHES & OTHER SERIES

The Scarab Eater's Daughter is book #3 of the Sister Witches Urban Fantasy Series. Alderose Brodeur stars.

- **Once Blessed, Thrice Cursed** (book 1)
- **Demon Lines** (book 2) is the continuation of Clementine's story.
- **The Scarab Eater's Daughter** (book 3) gives us the sisters' continuing adventures from Alderose's point of view.
- **Beguiled, Bewitched, & Broken** (book 4) completes the first Sister Witches series and features the middle sister, Beryl.

Readers first meet the sisters' aunt, Maritza Brodeur, in the Calliope Jones series:

- **Magic Remembered** (book 1)
- **Magic Reclaimed** (book 2)
- **Magic Redeemed** (book 3)

- **Magic Restrained, a novelette** (book 3.5)
- **The Magic Series: Box Set #1 of the Calliope Jones novels**

———

Join Coralie's mailing list for news of upcoming book releases.

GLOSSARY

Alderose Brodeur: Witch. Unbinder. 34 years old. Trained by her father. Prefers knives and daggers. Works in Convention Security. Based in New York City. Nicknames: Rosey, Rós

Heriberto del Valle (deceased): Witch. Unbinder. Bounty hunter. Nicknames: Berto, Tío Berto

Needles and Sins: Moira Brodeur's shop, where she sold sewing supplies and paperback romance novels. The shop was also a front for her other businesses and contains hidden rooms accessed by an emerald and gold ring. Located in Northampton, Massachusetts.

Moira Brodeur (deceased): Witch. Binder. Nickname: Tía Momo

Beryl Brodeur: Witch. Spellcaster. Wand. 32 years old. Middle sister. Nickname: B

Clementine Brodeur: Witch. Binder. Seer. 28 years old. Youngest sister. Nicknames: Clemmie, Sissy

Sidan: Fae. Girlfriend to Alderose. Nickname: Sid

Jadzia/One-Becomes-Three: Fae who murdered Alderose's father.

Kostya Arkadi: Fire Demon. 34 years old. Nickname: Koz

Serena (deceased): Witch. Unbinder. Divorce Lawyer. Cousin of Moira Brodeur. Former manager of Needles and Sins.

Maritza Brodeur: Witch. Binder. Professor of Necromantic Studies. Nicknames: Mari, Tía Mari

Alabastair Nekrosine: Necromancer. Portal Keeper. Beloved of Maritza Brodeur. Wears capes all the time. Nickname: Bas

Malvyn Brodeur: Sorcerer. Master Jeweller. Specialty is collars that restrain wearer's magic. Enforcer for the Board of Magical Governance. Nickname: Mal, Papa

James Brodeur: Botanist. Half-Witch. Husband to Malvyn. Father to Leilani. Nickname: Dad

Leilani Brodeur: Witch. Binder. Imbuatrix. Daughter of Malvyn and James Brodeur. Cousin to the Brodeur sisters. Nickname: Lei-li

Rémy Ruisseau: Water Mage, Elemental. Husband to Gosia. Father to Zazie. Former client of Moira Brodeur (*see Once Blessed, Thrice Cursed*).

Gosia Ruisseau: Melusine. Wife to Rémy. Mother to Zazie. Former friend and co-conspirator of Moira Brodeur.

Zanthe 'Zazie' Ruisseau: Melusine. 13 years old.

The Demesne: Family curse for the Brodeur family that causes one to fall to their knees at first sight of the fated mate. Has variations. Has been known to be wrong.

Laszlo Arkadi: Ice Demon. Mate to Clementine. Oldest of the 3 Arkadi brothers. 38 years old. Nickname: Laz

Fentress: Will-o'-wisp. Was rescued from captivity by Moira Brodeur. Nickname: Fen

Felicia: House Manager to Malvyn & James Brodeur.

Carlos: Majordomo to Malvyn & James Brodeur.

Lionel Vigne: Fae. AKA The Collector, The Imperator. Resides in Chamonix, France. Would never allow anyone to call him by a nickname.

INTRODUCTION

My name is Alderose Brodeur. I'm a witch, an Unbinder. My magic comes from my father's side of the family. He put a set of small knives in my hands when I was four. And died before he could finish my training.

I'm going after the fae that murdered him. And though he let my youngest sister know that he's happy in his ghost form because it means he's finally reunited with our mother, that doesn't excuse what happened.

I don't care what anyone says. I'm going after that fae.

THE SCARAB EATER'S DAUGHTER

1

Magic. Mine had shattered into millions of brittle, misshapen flakes. My legs moved on autopilot as I stumbled down the interior stairwell of the Hotel Northampton, leaving rust-colored prints on the industrial carpet.

I exited the side door into the blue-black dusk and veered to the outer edge of the sidewalk. Every step felt stilted and off-kilter. I was hyper-aware of headlights glowing like oversize fireflies, and the clicks and jangles of shop and restaurant doors opening and closing as I moved against pedestrian traffic. A few humans with vaguely familiar faces paused, started to raise an arm or say something, then kept going when I didn't slow down.

Only one person's voice would bring me to a full stop, but he belonged to the newly dead. When a random man's fatherly admonishment sounded at my back, I faltered. The weight of the duffel bag slung across one shoulder pulled me off center. I landed hard against a metal bike rack, tamped down a string of *fucks*, and waved away the father-and-son duo who offered to help straighten the tipsy bicycles.

I didn't need help. I needed to do penance.

Much earlier in the day, when I realized my father was being attacked by the three-faced fae, I'd hollered at him to *move*. My sisters had yelled. Everyone gathered with us high above the abandoned quarry had yelled, screamed, while our bodies froze in disbelief.

And in that prolonged, surreal moment, Dad said *nothing*.

His face registered his utter surprise. He flailed one arm in the air and tried to swat away the cluster of slender blades protruding from one side of his ribs. He opened and closed and opened his mouth and said...nothing. Not help. Not good-bye. Not I love you. Nothing.

I set the bicycles to right, inserted myself into the flow of oblivious humans, and snapped every one of my emotions tight against my chest. Grief compounded by guilt was a much heavier load than the knives and daggers in the duffel, and public Alderose aimed for self-containment.

Digging the heel of my palm into the side of my tender hip, I limped the remaining four blocks to the building that housed my mother's shuttered shop. Behind windows recently refreshed with magical wards that blocked the truth from curious humans, I could make out carousels of faded paperbacks and a haphazard arrangement of shabby chairs. I knocked the sides of my boots against the granite half wall and dug into my pocket for the worn brass key. Flickering streetlights made it hard to see the lock plate.

This is what happens when you neglect your training. You dropped your guard, Alderose, and you must never, ever drop your guard on the field of battle.

The last thing I wanted dredged up from a lifetime of lectures were my father's impromptu thoughts on battle strategy. Not when he'd been dead less than twelve hours. Not when I blamed myself for paving the way for his murder. I should have manacled the fae we captured with...something. Anything. Instead, I left her on the ground, unconscious and unshackled, while I turned my attention to those we had rescued. My thigh muscles tensed at the memory of my sister Clementine shouting, of looking over my shoulder as the resurrected fae triumphantly lifted my father until his feet dangled above the ground and dark red blossomed across his waterlogged jacket.

I knew I would replay that scene in my head over and over and over. And that no matter how many times I relived those moments, nothing I could do would change the outcome.

Because you know what happens when you let down your guard? People get hurt. People die.

"Shake it off, Alderose." I choked back a sob as I crossed the threshold into Needles and Sins and bolted the door. My voice, scratchy and unconvincing, dissolved within the unlit space. I leaned against the door jamb and fidgeted with the emerald ring weighing down my middle finger.

I'd come here for solace, and for inspiration. If I had any hope of getting through the coming hours and days without falling to pieces, I would need more than reflexive rage to fuel me. Going through the process of re-forging and restoring my magic would help. There had to be abundant supplies here; my parents were both witches, for Goddess sake. Shuffling toward the checkout counter, I plopped onto a stool, hugged my bag to my chest, and took the weight off my shaky legs.

From the moment my father planted his hands on his hips in the middle of our backyard and announced he was going to train me, he'd insisted on sessions where I wasn't allowed to call on my magic. Which didn't seem all that weird to a seven-year-old kid who barely knew she *had* magic.

Those sessions got really hard once Dad deemed me old enough and big enough to smack the grips of real weapons into my little-girl-sized hands. Whether it was swords or knives—or later, in hand-to-hand combat—he pounded into me the importance of knowing how to wield my weapons without the help of spells and other enhancements.

Because magic could be blocked.

Magic could be countermanded.

Magic could be drained.

Tonight, with callouses and random bruises affirming I continued to train hard, I would make a ritual circle and charge my body and my blades. Surely Mom had a stash of the things I'd need. I could unlock the doors to her underground potions laboratory and her sewing room on the third floor with the help of the ring she bequeathed me. And if I put the right tools and ingredients into my hands and let kinesthetic memories flood my body, I would remember what to do.

How to cast a circle.

How to call on my power.

How to recharge my blades.

If my mother had a dedicated ritual space, my sisters and I hadn't come across it. And keeping my ass on the stool wasn't getting me any closer to making room on the floor in front of me. I slid off the stool. Dirty plates and cups from Friday night's pizza and champagne dinner rattled against the surface of the first cutting table as I dragged it to the side wall. I shoved the other table toward the back of the shop then scanned the shelves and racks.

Salt was the standard material for circle-making, but my mother didn't sell salt at her shop. She sold sewing supplies and there, at the bottom of a pegboard display, was a selection of tailor's chalk. I poked my finger through a square plastic bag and removed one of the small rectangles. This compressed version was too waxy for drawing a circle, but it could come in handy for making runes or sigils. I pocketed the package and rifled through the other choices.

I found what I needed hanging on a lower rack and pulled

bags of the pourable, powdered talc used to mark skirt hems off a hook.

Candles and matches were next.

The three stubby beeswax candles we'd used during Friday night's dinner sat on a porcelain saucer in the middle of one of the tables. I had a lighter somewhere. I crouched by my bag and unzipped the main compartment. Stuffed on top of a pair of leather pants was a smattering of knives and daggers and random pieces of soft armor. I shoved aside gauntlets, shin guards, and a long vest with flexible metal inserts that protected my internal organs, located my favorite hip pouch, and found the lighter.

Before you begin any journey of importance, Alderose, know your starting point.

I faced the interior of the shop and hoped the compass my father had set into a floorboard was still intact. He'd installed it as a symbolic gesture, a reminder about the value of home and family. At least, that's what he said. I tapped on my phone's flashlight and swept the beam across the slugs of dust and forgotten sewing pins filling the spaces between warped boards.

The sight of a pancake-sized, tarnished brass disc made my heart thud extra hard. I dropped my duffel nearby and rubbed a fingertip across the compass's surface. I could barely see the lines of the rose.

Do it right the first time. A worthy opponent rarely hands you a second chance.

The compass deserved to shine. I grabbed a canister of powdered cleanser and a dampened rag from the bathroom and attacked the dulled surface.

The metal gleamed when I finished. I rinsed my hands in the sink and looked up to where Clementine had ripped the medicine cabinet out of the wall. Four hemp ropes as thick as my fists hung behind the gaping hole in the horsehair plaster. I turned my mother's ring so the emerald was flush with my palm, swept my hand across the wall, and heard the same portentous click as before. Facing the door, I braced my hip against the sink and waited for the pulley system hidden in the wall to activate, transforming the bathroom into a one-stop elevator going down.

Had my father known this room existed? Mom kept secrets from her daughters—did she keep secrets from him too? They'd sold the family home while Clementine was in college and had turned this building's second floor apartments into one big living space for themselves.

The tiny elevator creaked to a stop. I waved my hand across the mottled surface of a corroded metal door, unlocking the entrance to the lab. It had been so long since I'd seen my parents together that the whole dynamic of their relationship was about as clear as the inky darkness that greeted me. Coaxing a flame out of my lighter, I held it to the stubby candle in the nearest wall sconce and whispered *lucerna lumen*. Beryl had used the phrase a lot over the weekend. I waited for the rest of the candles to light for me as they had for her.

They didn't. The continuing darkness was a harsh reminder that spell casting required more than simply mouthing specific words. Intent was essential, as was rote practice. Beryl had been drawn early on to using a wand as a tool for her spell-based magic. Me, not so much. I liked my pointy tools to come with a molded grip and at least one sharpened edge.

I used the lighter on two more candles and set one on the ground, then ventured deeper into the room to gather dirt. Bits of my mother's excess magic would have seeped into the soil through all the years of her working and living here. That magic had had nowhere to go, and no one to extract it, for at least seven years.

Also, this room had gifted Clementine with tubes of magical mascara she'd put to good use over the weekend. The mascara had enhanced her ability to see moments from the past. I wanted the room to offer something similar to me. Rifling through a pile of magical implements, eyes open for the glint of possible treasure, I palmed a pair of rusted scissors and grabbed a wide-mouthed beaker. Crouching, I hacked at the oily-textured soil with the scissors' dulled tips and stopped collecting the loosened clumps when the beaker was two-thirds full.

The tip of the scissors came in handy again. I used them to pry a squat red candle off the worktable's uneven surface, plucked another candle from the wall, and paused to scan the room. The pressure to set up the circle and get this done was entirely mine, not some memory of one of my father's training sessions. I took a deep breath. Closed my eyes. Half-heartedly hoped that if I asked for something reasonable, the building would respond.

Help me out a little here. Please?

I waited in silence until the musty odor made me sneeze into the crook of my elbow. It seemed the laboratory had nothing more to offer beyond what I'd already chosen. I palmed the scissors and a similarly rusted athame, along with the filled beaker, then blew out the remaining candles, stepped into the bathroom, and closed the door. The room shuddered to a start and returned me to the ground floor.

After depositing my haul on the floor near the compass, I collected the plate of beeswax stubs and removed my boots. The daggers strapped to my lower calves went into a neat pile near the duffel. I was ready to begin.

There is beauty in displaying an economy of movement, Alderose. Every word, every object, every gesture in its place.

"I know, Dad. I know," I muttered, carefully snipping a corner on the first bag of powdered talc and rising to stand. I measured out four feet from the compass, then another foot for good measure, and reaffirmed the locations of the cardinal directions. I started at East, spreading an unbroken circle of talc in a clockwise direction. Once I finished and set four candles at the cardinal points, I opened a fresh bag of the powder and began to draw the pentagram. This time I started at Spirit.

As each point of the star met the circle, something inside me clicked into place. And as I was about to draw the fifth line of the pentacle, joining Fire to Spirit, I could swear I felt a tug on my leg.

Clothes. Right. I stripped off my pants, shirt, and bra, and quickly folded everything. The floor was cold and unclean—socks and underwear would stay on. Going skyclad was a variation I'd learned in college, where a slip of the tongue revealed my friend Eleanor was also a witch. During the casting of our first circle, she taught me to work naked, and it was within the sacred confines of that circle that we went from friends to friends-with-benefits. One night with Ellie confirmed I liked guys *and* girls.

"No lovers here, Rosey." I shivered. I'd neglected to turn up the thermostat before going to the cellar. I'd also neglected to update my new-ish girlfriend on what had happened over the weekend. Once I had completed the ritual of replenishment, I would get in touch with Sidan and tell her everything.

Because honesty was going to be one tenet of my new relationship policy. Honesty and transparency. Plus, Sid was fae. And I was going to need her help to enter the fae lands and go after my father's killer.

2

Focus. The words that would seal the pentacle within the circle as I drew the final line eluded me. I undid the thick braid hanging down my back and shook out my hair. Goosebumps marched up my legs and arms. I squatted, arranged my hair over my shoulders for warmth, and searched hard for the invocation I wanted to use.

It would help if I knew what I wanted beyond *Make me powerful enough to defeat the three-faced fae.*

I took in a long, slow breath through my nose, released it through my mouth, and did the adult thing. I tempered my need for revenge with discernment and patience and let the words of invocation flow along my raised arm to the tip of the athame in my hand. I drew a small pentacle in the air as I recited each line.

Powers of the East. Rising sun. Illuminate my path. Light
    me from within.
Powers of the South. Rising waters. Draw me into your
    flow. Guide my steps.
Powers of the West. Rising winds. Sweep away clutter.
    Grant me clarity.

Powers of the North. Ever-present Earth. Ground me.
Connect me to my roots.

Light from the candle sitting at east spread around the circle, kissing each of the next three flames clockwise in unhurried succession. I sucked in a breath at the beauty of the rising magic. The five lines of the pentacle began to glow too. I forgot about my chilled skin, centered my butt over the compass, and crossed my legs. After placing my mother's ceremonial knife in front of me next to the beaker—which would do double-duty as the chalice—I slowly, deliberately, withdrew my blades from the duffel bag. One by one, I arranged them in a circle around me, their points facing away.

I became the center of a metal-petalled flower. The glowing circle of activated talc sent its light upward, not out, building a translucent wall. Reflections wavered across my blades. Lifting my chin, I could barely make out the patterned tiles of the pressed tin ceiling.

Focus. I un-stoppered the beaker, gathered bits of crumbling soil in my fingertips, and scattered them in between each blade. From earth, I went to air and to my breath, using the brass compass below me as my focal point. I drew my breath up my spine and exhaled it down, touching my awareness to the polished bit of metal, to the fanned out blades, and to the bits of dirt. Within a few more breath cycles the latent power of the metal under and around me coursed through my vertebra, sending a warm stream of power flowing through my bones. That flow continued into my pelvis and chest, down my legs to my toes, out my arms to my fingertips. I leaned right, then left, forward then back, touching one fingertip to each of my blades and drawing blood each time. I flicked my fingers, scattering crimson droplets over my blades and my skin and the bits of dirt.

As my intentions solidified, the magic that was always present within my cells, even when I was running on empty, became visible underneath my topmost layers of skin. Radiating from the inside out, I called on the fire of the forge and I called on my blood to act as flux.

I called on the metals bonded to my magic.

I called on my ancestors.

Like my father, I reclaimed Unbinding as my base skill.

Like my mother, I vowed to use my skill in service to those who needed me most.

Clasping a dagger in both hands, I raised my arms above my head, piercing the floors above until my awareness danced across the rooftop, witnessed only by the starlit sky. The next exhalation drew me down, down, into the soil far below my seat. I took another breath, which shot me back up to the rooftop. Circled by light, infused with fire, grounded in the combined magics of my parents' lineages, I freed the words collecting in my throat.

"I hold the dark.

I seek the light.

Let my blades strike true.

Let me seek what's right."

I wasn't sure where those words came from. They weren't my father's words; these were *my* words and they felt right for *me*. *True* for me. All day long, I had been too close to the edge, too eager to open the door to my murderous intentions, and I'd let myself be guided solely by revenge. I needed this magical, spiritual grounding.

"So mote it be," I whispered.

My awareness flitted across the rooftop. The tip of my blade sought the stars. The wind picked up velocity and blew across my weapon, honing the blade's edge and adding its own magic. Though my arms grew numb, I couldn't lower them. Because inside the vacant, unlit part of me, I knew I was searching. I knew I had to hang in there, reach higher, dig deeper, wait longer.

Alderose.

Mom? Dad?

My heavy eyelids had sealed shut but my eyes felt open. The faces of my parents flickered in the wall of light in front of me, then disappeared. Hands—cool and weightless—placed themselves over mine where I gripped the dagger's handle. Another set of hands cupped the back of my head and my forehead.

Find your third eye. Use it.

For one brief, brilliant moment I knew where every part of my body was in space. I knew each of those parts was seamlessly connected and capable of reacting instantly to external conditions and internal commands.

I was calm. I was centered.

I knew my parents loved me. And I knew my parents were together, wherever they were.

I sucked in that moment of bliss like a desiccated sponge dropped into a bucket of water, and the moment I did, my parents' spirits left. The force of their departure dropped me like confetti from the stars to the rooftop to the hard wooden floor of the shop.

"Alderose. *Alderose.*"

I opened my eyes. My spine was on fire and the world was tilted on its axis.

No, I had fallen over. And my girlfriend was crouched outside the circle with a very worried look on her epically gorgeous face. Clutching my dagger in one hand, I pushed up to sitting and waved feebly at Sidan. "How long was I out?" I asked, rubbing my other hand down my face and wiggling my jaw.

"You literally just fell over. I was watching you from outside the door and I wasn't going to interrupt but your hair is perilously close to that candle." She pointed to my left. The wick in the candle in question was also close to setting fire to the wooden floor.

I stared at Sidan. She'd dropped the glamour she wore in the human realm and was dressed in her travel uniform of body-hugging leggings, suede boots, and a long-sleeved shirt. Every article of fae-made clothing was close to her natural, faintly purple-gray skin tone.

"What are you doing in Northampton? How did you get in here? I double-bolted that door."

"We had a date," she said, settling back on her haunches. "And those bolts are human-made."

"Oh." I'd forgotten we were supposed to meet at my apartment in New York City. Which meant Sidan didn't know about the past weekend going off the rails, or about my father. I dropped my gaze to the blood-dappled petals of my blades and to the clumps of dirt on the floor and in the beaker. Small balls were moving around inside the glass.

I stared, unsure what magic had been triggered by the ritual and while I tracked the balls as they tumbled about, I told Sidan everything.

I started with the meeting on Friday afternoon with the estate attorney that had brought me and my sisters to Northampton in the first place. She reminded me I had let her know about the trip beforehand.

I told her about our demon friend, Kostya, sent by my uncle to investigate the death of the shop's caretaker, Serena. And the arrival of Alabastair, the necromancer and portal keeper tasked by my aunt to deliver my mother's emerald and gold ring. And then most startling of all, Rémy, the elemental water mage whose appearance triggered a series of events, starting with the delivery of a forty-eight-hour deadline to find his beloved.

"There's so much more," I added, "and the worst of it is that after everything that happened, while we were celebrating bringing Gosia and Zazie and Rémy together...my father... My father was killed right in front of us." The retelling of that last chapter sent waves of grief up my body, from my gut to my throat. I realized the fire in my spine had cooled. I was shaking.

"Rosey, close the circle and come here."

I rolled onto my feet, blew out the candles in reverse order, thanked the elements, and scrubbed a doorway in the line of powdered talc. I left my weapons where I'd placed them. As soon as the low wall of light dropped to the floor and flickered out, Sidan stepped into the circle and picked up my clothes.

"Let's get you dressed first," she said, gently leading me out. My fingers were icy. I fumbled with getting my legs into my pants and tucking in my stretchy sweater evenly, and then with the button fly. When I finished, Sidan took me in her arms, and finally, *finally*, I cried. "Shh, shh, sweet Rós. Tell me more."

"I want your help. I need to get into the fae realm."

"Why do you need entrance into my lands?

"Because it was a fae who killed my father." I told her what I knew of One-Becomes-Three. How she'd beguiled Gosia into thinking they were allies and confidantes. How she'd used that trust to gain access to Gosia's daughter, Zazie, in order to snatch her. How the mother and daughter were a rare kind of Magical known as the melusine, and that the three-faced fae worked for someone who was collecting those rare Magicals through kidnapping and other means.

I was exhausted by the time I finished. Sidan wrapped me tighter in her embrace. "Alderose, can you listen to me?"

"Mm-hmm."

"You cannot go into the fae lands in the state you're in. You're radiating grief and anger and other intense emotions and you stink. Literally." I sniffed my wrist. I thought I smelled like me. Maybe a certain amount of rage was my baseline.

"Also," she continued, "there's only so much you can hide when you're relying on temporary glamour spells like the one I put on your favorite pants to camouflage your daggers. Those spells have to be fed constantly. True fae will see behind my work within seconds, so you can just forget about going undercover in my land unless I'm with you every moment."

She tightened her grip on me, as if to ensure her warning had sunk in and stayed.

"I'm debating what to tell my sisters," I said. There had been talk of meeting at the hotel and doing something for dinner.

"You can't tell them the truth, that you want to go after the one who killed your dad and that you want to leave like...now?"

I shook my head and shrugged my shoulder. "I don't know, I feel like we should talk about what to do with...with his body and organize a memorial service and..." A fresh wave of sorrow cut off my ability to speak. Sidan rubbed my back.

"Is there a chance either of them would want to join you?" she asked.

"Uff," I said. "Probably? But I'd feel responsible if anything happened, and my guilt load is already critical. And on top of everything, Clementine got zapped with the family curse and now she's got her own deadline to deal with it."

"They may be your younger sisters, Alderose, but they're grown women too. They can decide for themselves." Sid popped her butt onto the table, hooked her toes around the back of my knee, and drew me closer. "And what do you mean about Clementine getting zapped?"

"The Brodeur Family Curse," I said, crossing my arms. "A long time ago, an ancestor on my mother's side wanted to find her true love, a shaman intervened, the witch had to make a promise—which she might have forgotten—and all I really remember is that each of her descendants has the potential to be cursed by the Demesne."

"And what is this Demesne?"

"You recognize your true love the moment you first meet and supposedly you both fall to your knees and are consumed by passion and live happily ever after."

Sid stared at me and said nothing. The reason for the loquacious fae's silence sunk in. Neither of us had gone to our knees the first time we'd met. That had come later, in turns, when we were peeling off each other's clothes.

She finally said, "Looks like I'm not your one true love."

I wanted to close my eyes. Go to my numb place. Sidan's intense gaze challenged me to stay present to this fledgling thing of *us*. "Do you want to keep seeing each other, Rosey?" She continued to speak as I fought the urge to shut down. "Or do we call it quits right here, right now? I'll still help you, but—"

"Neither of us has said the M word, Sid."

She looked taken aback. "Whoa. *Marriage*, Alderose?" Embarrassment—or maybe it was anger—added a flush of magenta to her cheeks.

"No, *monogamy*."

"Oh!" Sidan laughed. The tension between us dissipated. "Come here, witch. You *know* how I feel about monogamy and *I* know you don't want to hear me rant on about humans and patriarchy and outdated relationship structures."

Relieved, I melted into Sid's embrace. She planted a friendly kiss on my cheek, shifted her weight, and lifted me onto the table beside her. "You're going to have to deal with your emotions before I bring you into my land. Either that or figure out how to bottle those feelings up nice and tight. We're talking industrial strength lockdown. You've got enough stuff stewing in here"— she tapped the center of my chest—"to unleash a plague of locusts. Take all that anger and sorrow and guilt and distill it. When the situation calls for you to release it, do it with precision. And when you do, I hope I'm not on the business end of whatever weapon is in your hand."

My body had gone still. Sidan and I hadn't been together long, but her ability to read me was both terrifying and a turn on. I was about to plant a kiss on her mouth when my phone vibrated inside my hip pouch. I slid off the table and dug through the duffel bag.

Beryl had sent a text. "HELP NOW"

"Where are you???" I typed.

"At the hotel. Bring your knives. HURRY."

I hit the call icon and held the phone between my shoulder and my ear. I needed two hands to buckle the pouch around my hips. Sid slipped her finger through one of the belt loops on my pants and drew me closer. Beryl picked up on the first ring. "Alderose," she said, "are you on your way?"

"Almost. What's going on?"

"It's the girl. Zazie. She's going into her change and everyone's freaking out. We need to get her to the biggest bathtub we can find. Or a protected pool. Tía says Uncle Malvyn has both of those at his estate and—"

"B, slow down. Why do you need me there?"

"Because Zazie needs a bodyguard while they transport her through the portals."

Yeah, they needed me alright. "I'm on my way."

"What's happening?" Sidan asked once I set the phone down.

I paused pulling on my jacket. "I apologize for switching gears so fast. I was really hoping we'd get to kissing when my phone rang."

"We'll make time later. Fill me in."

I did, while tightening the laces on my boots and stuffing my weapons and the things I'd collected in the laboratory back into the duffel. "I'm not sure how long this will take," I added. "At least twenty-fours, maybe longer." I strode back to the circle, brushed the clumps of dirt into the beaker, and pressed the rubber stopper into place.

"Alderose. Stop a sec and listen to me. You've had a really hard couple of days. You're in a rush to take your revenge, when what you need to do first is just be there for Beryl and Clementine, for the rest of your family. Physically, like you're about to do now. And emotionally."

I nodded while I packed. Sidan paced behind me. "Don't even *think* about entering fae land without me. Bury your father, grieve with your sisters, sharpen your blades, strengthen your magic. Gather whatever iron tools you can find. I'll ask the kinds of questions that'll get us information, not trouble. And I promise I will do everything I can to help you find who murdered your father and bring them to justice."

"Thank you, Sidan."

"You're welcome, Rós. You know how to get in touch with me. Unless I come across something vital, I'm going silent. Don't take that to mean anything other than the best way for me to help you right now is for no one to know that I'm connected to you or your sisters."

I stopped what I was doing, stood up, and brought Sidan's face to mine. For a moment, I smelled the rage and grief she mentioned rising off my skin, along with dirt from the cellar, candle wax, and molten metal. Around all of that floated her particular scent. She'd mentioned the name of the flower she often wove into her hair, but it didn't grow in the human realm and I forgot it. Lifting my heels, I threw my arms around her neck and found her generous lips.

When Sid was done kissing me, a sliver of doubt almost pierced my resolve to leave. She was the one to disentangle our tongues and arms, say it was time, and wave goodbye. I savored the sight of her striding across the street, glamoured to look like she was just another college student meeting friends for pizza and ice cream.

I hefted the filled duffel bag and locked the door behind me. Getting the thirteen-year-old daughter of a water mage and a melusine to British Columbia had become my top priority.

3

THE STAFF at the Hotel Northampton gaped as I jogged through the lobby. Unsheathed knives and daggers clanked around in my bag, making it sound like I had raided the restaurant's cutlery drawers. I ignored the odd looks and focused on my sister. Beryl had her bare knee jammed against the door to the elevator and her back to the annoyed couple glancing at their matching smartwatches.

"Medical emergency," she said, hauling me next to her and hitting the button to the third floor.

"I could have taken the stairs." I settled against the paneled wall, patted my pockets for an elastic, and wrangled my hair into a braid as we passed the second floor.

"I know, I know. Right now I'm fueled by grief and anger and not enough food or water. Just like you."

I dropped my bag and grabbed my sister. "I love you," I said. "I know I haven't told you that enough, but I love you. And I'm so mad about Dad. Mad, and sadder than I've ever been. About anything. I messed up, B."

"Rosey, I love you. Always have. Always will. We can talk about Dad and Mom later. If we start now, I don't think I'll be able to stop crying, and Rémy and Gosia don't have time for our tears. Not until Zazie's safe."

A muted ping sounded our arrival. It took forever and a day for the doors to open. Beryl held my elbow and steered me past the room we'd stayed in on Friday night to one at the end of the hall. The door opened as we neared. Kostya, our demon friend, pressed himself against the wall and waved us inside. I noticed his investigator's badge was displayed prominently on the front of his leather jacket.

I didn't see the family we'd reunited earlier in the day. Or Kostya's brother, Laszlo, and my youngest sister, Clementine. "Fill me in," I said, setting my bag between the wall and the nearest single bed.

"Rémy and Gosia are in the bathroom with Zazie. Gosia said the kid's on the cusp of letting out her tail for the first time, but she's traumatized and...and she's stuck and Rémy's—" The bathroom door opened inward and the water mage squeezed out, closing it behind him.

"Gosia needs a special, spelled cloth to wrap around Zazie's legs," he said. "She thinks that should help delay the transition long enough to get our daughter to a safer location." He'd gone from being the extremely threatening man we'd first met three nights ago, to the extremely concerned and protective parent of a teenage girl.

My aunt uncurled herself from one of the room's two upholstered chairs. "Would any spelled cloth do?" She rubbed at her upper arms. She looked physically wasted. The battle earlier in the day and everything she'd done to keep us alive must have depleted her store of magic. The tray set up beside her chair held bowls of nuts, dried fruits, and cubes of cheese. I was surprised Alabastair hadn't insisted on adding intravenous fluids.

"Rémy?" A trembling, heavily accented voice sounded from

behind the bathroom door. "We need filaments de la mer. The cloth is so rare, I fear no one on these shores knows of it."

"Moira had some in her workroom," Kostya volunteered. "Or something like it. I noticed the label when Beryl had me open every roll of fabric."

Beryl bounced off the corner of the bed and pushed her way to the door. "Kostya, with me. Tía, you too if you're up to it. Alderose, give me Mom's ring. Alabastair, you fill Rosey in on what's been happening. We'll take good care of Maritza. And please, for Goddess's sake, keep your eyes on Fen. We don't need a repeat of this morning."

I twisted the ring off and gave it to Beryl. Alabastair insisted my aunt wear his thigh-length velveteen cloak. His concern was palpable as he emptied the bowl of nuts into one of the pockets and implored her to keep snacking.

The door closed behind Kostya, leaving me and Alabastair standing and a young woman asleep on one of the beds. Just what this day needed. Another mystery guest.

"What's the plan?" I asked. "And I assume that's Fen?" A magic-dampening collar of square, metal pieces circled her neck and felted wool garments two sizes too large encased her waifish body.

"Yes, that's Fentress, the will-o'-wisp. She slipped into the shop earlier today as your sister and Laszlo were leaving to come here to change their clothes and pack."

"Hold on a sec." I massaged the headache brewing across my forehead. "Did Clemmie and Laz leave town already?"

Alabastair nodded. "You just missed them. Clementine needs an opportunity to recover and the two of them need time for the Demesne to take hold. She and the demon are headed to Boston where they'll take the portal to the Reformed Realm."

Clementine's sudden departure was—well, it wasn't a shocker. At the quarry, she was the one who'd watched the fae rise from the presumed dead, stab our father, and take him over the cliff. Clementine was the first one of us to jump back into the frigid water and the first one to reach his body. Pushing back the tears threatening to overspill my dammed up grief, I had another look at our visitor. "And what's her story?"

"Maritza found her in the shop. Fen said she was rescued by your mother close to the time of Moira's death and that she checks on the shop whenever she's in town."

"Her story seem plausible?" I asked.

Alabastair said it did, adding, "Plausible, and compelling enough for Mari to introduce her to Clementine. At some point during their conversation, Fen's corporeal form began to dissipate. Mari had one of the Enforcer's collars with her and used it to restrain the little wisp."

"She looks like she's sleeping."

"She is. Your aunt added a slumber spell to back up the collar. Wisps are notorious for disapparating."

"Is her appearance a coincidence? Or is she somehow relevant to all this" —I waved my hand to indicate the bathroom —"and to what happened?"

Alabastair gave the sleeping Magical a look between frustration and distrust. "Fen claims your mother made it possible for her and her mother to escape their captor. She didn't say where they had been kept, but she did mention that Moira also helped them financially. Here's the curious thing." The necromancer settled into the chair Maritza vacated and crossed his legs, never taking his gaze off the delicate-looking creature curled atop the bed. "Fen's been living in a marsh on Salt Spring Island, the same island where your uncle Malvyn resides. The marsh is located on a parcel of land owned by a witch Maritza and I have become well acquainted with. And that witch possesses a clutch of melusine eggs."

Talk about a plot thickening. Gosia needed to give us the

rundown on melusine physiology as soon as her daughter was past the immediate crisis. "Let's set aside Fen and her complications for the moment. Tell me about Zazie."

"It's clear the girl has inherited her mother's genes," Alabastair said, re-crossing his legs. "From what Gosia has shared, melusine first release their tails around the same age human girls begin to menstruate. Gosia thinks the stress of Zazie's abduction precipitated the changes in her body. Though thirteen is an absolutely normal age for either of those events."

Alabastair took a deep breath and let it out slowly. "This situation has gotten infinitely more difficult with Fen's appearance. Your aunt has suggested we take Rémy, Gosia, and their daughter to your uncle's home on Salt Spring Island. If Fen was sent here to spy on the shop, then it's possible she has information that could lead to further harm for the girl."

"Why are we taking Zazie to Uncle Malvyn's? He's on the other side of the continent. Wouldn't it be safer for Rémy and Gosia to just take their kid home?" I had no idea where the family lived, other than knowing Rémy's territory was the entire Eastern Seaboard of the North American continent.

"Zazie needs to be in an absolutely secure, completely defensible body of water. Rémy feels the location of their home has been compromised and he doesn't want anyone in their circle to know Gosia has returned. There's a real possibility one of them is an informant for whoever's behind the kidnapping.

"Your uncle is a prominent sorcerer. And as the Enforcer for the Board of Magical Governance, he has resources at his disposal should additional measures need to be taken to protect the girl—and her parents. One of those resources is Malvyn's estate. It has its own portal, which is in excellent working order and which I have taken the precaution of sealing off to everyone but the members of our group.

"He also has an indoor pool the perfect size for a melusine, and his staff is willing to accept magic-bound gag orders. According to Gosia, no men are allowed to witness the melusine change. Ever. Not fathers, not husbands or lovers or friends. Plus, there are trustworthy witches on Salt Spring Island. I believe it is imperative those witches meet Gosia and Zazie *and* Fen."

"Are we *all* going?" I asked. The evening was turning into a logistical nightmare.

"No. Beryl and Kostya volunteered to stay in town at your parents' apartment and remain on alert for other magical activity. Beryl will keep the emerald with her, in case access to the portal in the cellar is needed. I shall lead our group to Malvyn's through the safest and most secure route I can devise," Alabastair said. "I'm working on mapping the sequence of stations right now."

I leaned against the wall. "The fewer bodies traveling the portals as a group, the easier it will be for me to defend Zazie." The necromancer agreed.

Rémy stepped out of the bathroom, closing the door behind him. "I will not be separated from my wife and child again."

I tried to picture how I was going to protect a young girl going through one of the most profound changes of her life while accompanied by stressed-out parents, one of whom had a hair-trigger on his magical response systems. "Can Zazie still use her legs or is she already transitioning?"

"Her legs are working. The spelled cloth will reinforce what strength and control she has left."

"Then let's hope the fabric Kostya saw is the real thing."

Alabastair agreed. I told him I needed to think and left the room to pace the hall. By the fourth loop I was ready to hash out a plan.

"Alabastair, what if you and Tía lead the way. Plan the most direct route possible. You two take each portal first then text me the all clear. I'll follow with Zazie and Gosia. Rémy travels third, right behind us." Portal stops were usually located in clusters of trees, often in public spaces like parks. Boston's famed Emerald Necklace was the closest major portal hub and would be the most practical choice for a starting point. Plus, it was the hub I knew best. "We have two rental cars to get us to Boston. We'll leave from there once the morning commuters have thinned out."

The rustle of bodies and clothing in the hall announced Beryl and the others had returned. My sister rushed past me and tapped on the bathroom door. "Gosia, it's Beryl. We found some fabric. Can you have a look?"

I hadn't seen Gosia since the morning, in the minutes before my father was murdered. My belly clenched at the sight of the melusine, with her extraordinary light brown skin flecked with opalescence, and her waist-length hair the color of oxidized copper. She was a physically stunning woman. And she—and her daughter—had been through so much. A different kind of sorrow swelled under my breastbone. This one tasted of hurt and resentment. Gosia and my mother had worked together. Why hadn't Mom thought to ask *me* for help?

"Rémy? Can you sit with Zazie?" Gosia asked.

The two changed places while Kostya placed the rolls of fabrics on the empty bed. I darted a glance at Fen. She was out cold. I wouldn't be able to forgive myself if the wisp turned out to be involved in the weekend's events only to somehow slip out of our collective grasps. My aunt bent forward, curled her fingers around Fen's slender wrist, and whispered into her ear.

"Alabastair, if you could again take my place?" Maritza waited for the necromancer to settle on the chair before turning her attention to Gosia and the rolls of fabric.

"This one has a blend of filaments de la mer along with other natural fibers." Gosia flicked the deep green piece off the cardboard tube and watched it settle on the bed. She assessed the fabric with the speed of someone who knew exactly what she was looking for. "It will do, especially if you can stitch one or two spells into the seams."

"What would be the purpose of the spells?" Maritza asked.

"Zazie's skin is very, *very* sensitive right now. The filaments de la mer create a viscous barrier that protects the melusine's flesh or scales, depending on where they are in their transition. A spell to hold the moisture in would be helpful, as would a spell to deflect attention."

Maritza nodded and held the fabric up for Alabastair's approval. "The witches should have some of this." He agreed. She turned to Gosia. "Describe the garments. Please."

"Mm, the most important item is what covers her body from the waist down. I think a simple pair of leggings with feet will do. Also, a big sweatshirt with a hood to keep her identity hidden."

Alabastair pulled an oblong case from his satchel and handed it to Maritza. She perused the contents before swooping her hand in the air like an orchestra conductor. Three needles and a spool of iridescent green thread floated upward. The needles threaded themselves, one after the other, as my aunt snipped the thread, then she motioned for her tools to wait as she cut into the special fabric. Laying the pieces in three stacks, she directed one threaded needle to each stack and issued instructions through a series of hand gestures, finger flicks, and murmurs.

While the garments took shape, Maritza folded the remaining section and the leftover pieces of the special cloth, tucked the bundle into the satchel with her supplies, and kissed Alabastair's cheek.

"I need some exercise," I said, pointing to the door. "I'll stay inside the hotel. I've got my phone. Call or come get me if anything changes."

Forty minutes later I had a text from Alabastair saying the garments were finished. Sweaty from running up and down stairs, I tapped on the door. Rémy answered, then blocked me from entering. He held a finger to his lips, gestured for me to enter quietly, and whispered, "Zazie should have as little stimulation as possible."

"Then how's she going to manage the portal station?" I asked. "Does anyone have a pair of noise-canceling headphones she can use?" Every teen I'd seen lately, both human and Magical, wore a set while traveling public transportation.

The mage actually smiled at me. Then he grabbed my cheeks, squished my face, and kissed my forehead. I tried not to squirm. I got how anxious he was. But this sudden effusiveness was way out of character. "Give me one minute," he said. "We're almost ready to go."

Standing in the doorway a little after midnight, I watched as everyone lined up inside the room. Alabastair cut a dashing figure in one of his ubiquitous cloaks. He handed me my duffel bag, lined up his and Maritza's two suitcases, and went to gather Fen into his arms. She was so slight, they'd swaddled her in a shawl, allowing Bas to carry her across his chest like a baby. The wisp wasn't going anywhere. Maritza snuck around Alabastair, tucked the shawl over Fen's face, and waited with me.

Gosia herded her daughter into line. A hood covered the girl's head and a set of cream-colored headphones bobbed in time to music only she could hear. Rémy brought up the rear.

"We ready?" I asked. At their nods, I turned toward the stairwell and led my ragtag collection of Magicals out of the building and into the night.

. . .

THE RIDE to Boston was subdued. I had Rémy and his family in my car. He rode up front with me, with his arm draped over the back of his seat and his hand in Gosia's the entire time. Alabastair drove with Maritza and Fen. I tried to ask Gosia questions about her time with my mother, but she made it clear she needed to rest, and Rémy was adamant I could—and would—be saving any and all questions for some point in the future.

The remainder of the ride was quiet. We parked our rental cars side by side in the return lot and staggered our arrival times at the portal tree without incident.

Alabastair decided Toronto would be our first stop. As he explained at the hotel, the city was his home and if anything happened, the scope of his family's resources was at least as wide as my Uncle Malvyn's Vancouver circle.

Toronto was crowded. Though I didn't get a whiff of danger, winter's bite kept lifting handfuls of dried leaves and slapping them against our legs as we waited out turns. Our next stop was Vancouver. I'd forgotten how wet the Pacific Northwest was this time of year. Damp cold and stomach pangs had me longing out loud for an order of poutine. My aunt assured me her brother's cook would have a hot breakfast waiting for us.

The final leg gave us the only bit of trouble. Maritza'd had to subdue Fen again, which raised a few eyebrows and led to mutterings about calling the police. We left Vancouver just after dawn and landed at the base of a gnarled fruit tree in my uncle's landscaped front yard. The proximity to the ocean elicited a deep sigh from Gosia.

"Mari, Bas, honored guests, we are so relieved you made it."

I tore my gaze off the water and turned to greet my uncle. My cousin, Leilani, was right behind him, yawning as she tugged on a bulky, oversize sweater. Rémy let loose a low growl, planted himself in front of Gosia, and called for his powers to rise. Thick, gray clouds swirled around him and his family, obliterating the sky.

"I smell fae," he roared. "Alderose, your knives. *Now*."

Leilani patted her father's elbow. "I can explain," she said, opening her arms to the mage. "There are no fae on our property. You probably smell my friend, Sallie. This is her sweater." She peeled off the offending garment and dropped it on the ground.

Beside me, Zazie whimpered, calling for her mother.

"You lie, you die." Rémy waved away the stormy shreds of his cloak, swept his daughter into his arms, and strode toward the house. "Show us to the pool."

4

MALVYN and a female member of his staff escorted Rémy, Gosia, and Zazie into the house. The rest of us stood around, exchanging quick hugs with Leilani. Seeing my one and only cousin made me happy. And sentimental.

"Been a long time," I said. "And when did you get so tall?"

"Rosey, I'm only five-four." She bent to pick up the sweater Rémy found offensive and shook it out. "Height doesn't run in our family."

"I know, but you seem—"

"Older? More mature?" she said, shoving her arms into the sweater. "We haven't seen each other since Tía Momo's memorial service. I was eleven. I'm eighteen now."

At the mention of my mother's pet name—Momo—I was slapped right back into the emotions I had sidelined for the portal trip. I almost lost it right there under a branch lined with rotting pears. "But I've seen Tío Berto a lot," Leilani continued. "Well, maybe not a *lot*. He visited us this summer, when the grandparents were in residence. Maybe he'll pop in while you're here!"

Leilani's hopeful smile cracked my chest. She didn't know

her Tío Berto was dead. I swung my gaze back to where the water and the horizon were bisected by the zig-zagging peaks of a far-off mountain range. Thank Goddess my aunt was there to intervene. "Lei-li, come inside with me. I have some news to share with you and your father." She slipped her arm around Leilani's waist and guided her to the grand front doors.

That left me, Alabastair, a conked-out Fen, and a pile of luggage. The necromancer didn't seem to be in any rush to follow my aunt and cousin inside.

"We got everyone here, safe and sound," I said. "Thanks for doing your part."

The possibility of rain wafted off the ocean. I welcomed the cold, damp air against my exposed skin. Alabastair drew his hood over his bald head, readjusted the shawl around Fen, and cleared his throat.

"I think it would be prudent for you to stay, Alderose," he said. "Your family needs you, and you all need time to process this loss together."

"I've got things to do, Bas. My knives are redundant here."

"You're planning to go after Jadzia," he said, using the name we'd first heard the fae give herself.

"I didn't say anything about going after her." Actually, I'd said a lot of things under my breath when I was deciding where I would go and what I would do. I didn't realize anyone had been listening.

"Yes, you did, Alderose. And by the time Beryl called you back to the hotel, your entire attitude had shifted. I must surmise you did something to strengthen your magic—which I applaud. Now is not the time for any of us to let down our guard. Should you choose to pursue Jadzia on your own, you will need every ounce of your magic, and every advantage your family can give you. There are objects your aunt and uncle and I can provide, but their creation will take time."

When I asked if he was trying to sidetrack me with the lure of shiny objects, all I got was an enigmatic smile.

"I could see staying through Zazie's change," I said, finally. Though I was itching to put myself in Sidan's hands, Alabastair had piqued my curiosity. "What kind of objects?"

"Have you ever been to the fae lands?" he asked.

I shook my head, noticed one of the staff waving to us, and suggested we take our conversation inside. I had been promised food and my growling belly reminded me I hadn't eaten in a long time. "Let's talk after we eat."

A woman named Felicia led me to the guest wing of my uncle's estate, showed me to my room, and added my fingerprints to the house's state of the art security system. "There are rooms you won't be granted access to unless you're accompanied by Malvyn or James," she said. "Don't take it personally. Your uncle and his husband limit who can enter their labs and workshops."

"Afraid a guest will get in there and blow stuff up?" I asked.

Felicia arched one eyebrow. "You have no idea. Breakfast is buffet-style. It will be out in ten minutes. Here's a map of the estate to help you find your way round."

Needing a map to get to breakfast was new for me. First, a shower was in order. Though I had bathed at the hotel, I could smell the mucky waters of the quarry in my hair and every time I did, I had to fight to not drown in the replay of yesterday's events.

Uncle Malvyn and his husband, James, lived a very comfortable life. I relaxed into the designer dining chair's curved back and let my gaze wander past the rain splattered, floor-to-ceiling windows. My belly was full and I swore I heard the massive sectional couch calling my name. Atop a long credenza, I had been thrilled to find the poutine I'd been craving—French fries topped with crumbled cheese curds and coated with gravy.

I could allow myself an hour of lethargy, of feeling warm and safe within the embrace of family. Once I'd digested I could go back to organizing my weapons and seeing what my aunt and uncle could offer by way of magical implements and accessories.

Light hands settled on my shoulders. "I'm so sorry about your father, Rosey." Leilani leaned forward, wrapped her arms around me, and snuggled her head into the crook of my neck. "I can't imagine losing either of my parents."

"Thanks, Lei-li." I put my scheming on hold. I loved my much-younger cousin so much, and I hardly knew her. That needed to change.

I needed to change.

"I have something for you." She released me from the hug and returned with a freshly brewed cortado and a dessert plate topped with a slice of frosted cake. The coffee had a heart drawn through its dark brown foam, and the cake consisted of four pink layers interspersed with thinner layers of fruit jam and custardy filling. "I'm making a cake to celebrate Zazie's first change," she whispered. "This is from the practice cake."

"When did you make this?" I asked. I was not a baker. I believed in the power of water and heat to transform dried powders into a myriad of meals.

"Just now." She set a dessert fork alongside the plate. "Baking helps me process my emotions. And it's an expression of my magic. Tía says I'm on my way to becoming an imbuatrix." The pride in Leilani's voice was unmistakable. Imbuatrixes were a sought-after type of witch, especially when it came to love potions, and there weren't many of them practicing this demanding, esoteric art. I sliced off a bite of cake with the edge of my fork and popped it in my mouth.

I had to close my eyes. *Love. Hope. Welcoming. Sisterhood.*

Nothing out of a box ever tasted like this. And through the layers of flavors and emotions, a tart, slender thread.

"Why the sorrow?" I asked, putting down my fork and opening what I knew were tear-filled eyes. Leilani pulled out the chair beside me and sat, pressing her hands between her knees.

"Because I'm sad about my uncle. And because the same changes that welcome us into womanhood also sever us from childhood. I'm happy-sad for Zazie."

I took another bite and continued to savor the experience. I didn't even try to stop the tears dropping off my cheeks. It was safe to eat my cousin's cake and let her ability to access her own grief guide me into releasing some of mine. "I think you should consider an apprenticeship with whichever one of my sisters takes over our mother's matchmaking business. You could do well with selling potions and charms because I have a feeling yours would actually *work*."

Leilani cocked her head toward the kitchen and gave me a bittersweet smile. "I'd like that. Maybe next summer, after I've graduated high school." She watched me take another bite, then stood and pushed the chair back under the live-edge wood table. "I'm going to go finish making Zazie's cake. Are you staying with us tonight?"

"Yes. Maybe longer, if it's okay with your dads."

"It's okay with me and that's all the permission you need, Rosey."

Those few minutes with my cousin pushed me into accepting I could handle a short respite with my extended family. I finished the treat to the sound of rain and was debating going for the couch versus a tour of the estate when the chair beside me was again claimed, this time by the towering necromancer.

"Is this a good time to talk?" he asked, and when I nodded he withdrew a slender box from within the fold of yet another cloak, then slipped the garment off his shoulders and draped it over the chair. He had changed into charcoal slacks and a dove-gray dress shirt, and his head gleamed.

"What did you do with Fen?"

"Wrapped her in the cape I was wearing earlier. Mari's stitching her into it right now."

"The cape that's spelled to repel attacks? And did you say there's a marsh on this island, and that's where Fen has been living?"

He nodded. "Yes, that cape. As to Fen, I'm not sure if we'll take her to the marsh today or wait. Keeping a wisp in custody in no easy task, but both Malvyn and Maritza would like to further debrief her."

"I can imagine," I said, adding, "Do you always wear capes?"

My non sequitur made Alabastair fidget with the crease of his dress slacks. "I have been an aficionado of the cape for a good many years. It provides armoring in social situations and pockets for everything I carry, which leaves my hands free.

"And lucky for me, your aunt rather likes how I look in them. A specialty shop in Seattle makes mine. Their work is impeccable and each cape is spelled to my specifications." He ran his hand over the fabric. "I'm debating ordering one for Maritza."

"She could just make her own. And yours."

"Mm, not necessarily. Not every witch can replicate every spell to the same degree, and Mari's skills are leaning more and more toward the necromantic. Which is why she's putting Fen in my cape. The will-o'-wisp propensity to disapparate under stress is similar to the way ghosts can suddenly manifest and just as suddenly disappear. Your aunt knows of many ways to get Magical beings back into their bodies and have them stay there."

Alabastair was growing on me. Knowledge and skill aside, he was exquisitely attentive to my aunt and took obvious pride in her abilities. I sat up straighter and examined the fabric brushing my shoulder. I hadn't kept up with my sewing or needleworking skills, but my eyes had been trained to notice a garment's construction. "This is all hand-stitched," I marveled.

"That is correct. The sisters who run the shop are gifted stitch witches. Because of the nature of my work as a portal keeper, I've had to ask them to line my work capes with fibers spelled to deflect magically imbued weapons."

The more Bas described his capes, the more I wanted one. "Being a portal keeper is dangerous?"

"It can be."

"I'd like a cape like this," I said.

"It would be handy for moving amongst the fae, but I'm afraid there's quite a wait for these garments."

"What if I dropped your name?"

He smiled. "The witches might move you up." He cleared his throat and opened the box. "But capes are not the reason I'm here. I want to offer you portal stones I designed for use in emergency situations. They'll get you out of wherever you are and bring you to the nearest safe portal. There's a cost to your magic whenever one of these stones is used, and there's no way to predict where you will land. Take as many as you'd like but know that you should never use more than three in quick succession."

I poked at the stones. "Why no more than three?"

"Because that is the most emergency jumps a Magical can make without risking illness, dismemberment, or other extreme reactions."

I gave a low whistle. "How do I activate the stones?"

"First, I key them to you. Which we have to do because these are worth..." He shook his head while palming one of the mottled turquoise balls. "Let's just say they're worth a lot on the dark market."

My father had started to take me on buying trips to the physical dark markets once I'd achieved two black belts and had completed a firearms training course with the local police. Which was yet another thing my two sisters knew nothing about.

I pulled the box closer. "How will you key these stones to me?"

"Draw your blood and use it to mark each one. The only other Magicals with the ability to use the stones once they are keyed to you are other Portal Keepers and specially certified guides—and we're only allowed to do so under extreme duress. Say, to save a life."

Alabastair cleared his throat and continued. "When *you* have need to activate the stone, you hold it like this" —Alabastair placed one in his palm and made a soft fist— "and squeeze. The composite enters your skin. Confirmation is instantaneous. Choose your stones, then all we have to do is give them a taste of your blood."

I picked three kumquat-sized balls at random and handed them to Alabastair. He withdrew a lancet from a container inside the box, swiped my fingertip with an alcohol-soaked pad, and punched the needle into my skin.

"The next step is a sigil." Alabastair pinched the first stone to keep it steady on the table. His other hand was poised to write. He closed his eyes. His relaxed features took on a slightly agitated look. "Hmm, the sigils that come to me are usually far more...complicated."

Using my blood, he drew a fletch-less arrow on each. The brownish-red trails soaked in and disappeared. "This is the rune, Teiwaz. A good one for warriors going into battle. Tip up, the arrow speaks to alignment with your purpose—external and internal—and discernment. Knowing when to pull the trigger, metaphorically speaking, and when to hold back.

"Tip down, like I have drawn on your stones, Teiwaz

cautions against haste, or ill-timed actions and urges introspection before action."

"Are you making that up to discourage me?" When Alabastair gave me another noncommittal *hmm*, I thanked him and gathered the three stones into the small pouch he pushed toward me. Mulling over his explanation, I startled when the immense doors to the combined dining and living room opened. James and my uncle strode in, waved, and veered toward the buffet.

"We'll join you two in a moment," Malvyn said. "We have good news."

James was a half-witch, botanist, and former university professor. He and Malvyn took the chairs across from me and Bas, putting their backs to the windows and the increasingly stormy sky. "Alderose, my condolences on your father's passing. We sensed his end drawing closer when he made his annual pilgrimage here in July on the anniversary of Moira's death." James rested his arm on the table, palm up. "I can only imagine how hard these days have been for you and your sisters."

I squeezed his hand and thanked him. "How is Zazie?" I asked.

The botanist flicked open his napkin and settled it on his lap. "Gosia decided it would be best to delay a complete change until her daughter's anxiety has lowered and they've had a chance to get their bearings. From what she described, a melusine's first change can be physically agonizing. We've made a place for them in my tropical greenhouse. It's warm and humid and there's always something beautiful blooming. I think it's helping."

"It'd probably be good for Rémy if he stayed there too," I offered.

"Oh, we've got him on a massage table deep within a section of blooming *Passiflora incarnata*," James said. "We have a fantastic massage therapist and our island does *not* need an unexplained weather phenomenon sending us into code red. The passionflower vines doubled their blooms and we booked a two-hour session. Rémy should be out until supper."

"Alabastair, my sister is resting in your rooms," Malvyn added. "We checked on her on our way here."

"Has she eaten?" Alabastair asked. "With all the magic she's been expending, I'm worried she's not getting enough calories."

"I had Chef make up a tray for her and deliver it when I saw you were busy with Alderose," Malvyn said.

"Thank you. As you both witnessed, the Demesne took hold almost three months ago and during that time I've noticed when I deploy more of my magic, she is similarly affected."

The two men across from us nodded in sync. "I think James would agree the Demesne affects both partners."

"Have you and James come up with any strategies you would be willing to share?"

"We had to devise something we could wear all the time. I came up with these collars, which monitor the balance of our magics and let us know when we're drawing too heavily on the other." My uncle tapped the bit of gold that flashed below the base of his throat. I'd caught glimpses of the necklaces both he and James wore. His was made of squares of hammered gold, and James's had delicately tooled leaves linked with gold rings.

"I think the benefit is skewed toward my husband, due to the fact that I rarely tap into what little magic I have," James said. "You're a powerhouse, Mal. Keeping your battery charged is a full-time job. And it's one I was more than willing to take on once we understood the dynamic of the Demesne."

"Did you know it happened to Clementine over the weekend?" I asked.

"Oh my, the poor girl. To be hit with that, and then what

happened to Berto." James planted his forearms on the edge of the table and leaned in. "Is her partner worthy?"

"I think so," I said. "His name is Laszlo Arkadi. He fought well yesterday. And his brother works for you, Uncle Mal."

Malvyn nodded. "I recently promoted Kostya. He's young. However, I sensed something in him was ready to settle down. When I sent him to Northampton, I had hopes he would uncover useful details about the death of the woman to whom your mother bequeathed the shop."

"We actually uncovered a lot, but I think you should debrief Kostya. I'm—" I shook my head and used my fork to rearrange the congealed gravy on my plate. "I'm not in a good place to talk yet."

"I understand," Mal said. The warmth in his voice backed up his words.

"I'm going to see Maritza." Alabastair turned to me. "Do you have any further questions about the stones?"

"Two. How will I know if I've portaled someplace dangerous or inhospitable to me, and what do I do if that happens on the third try?"

Alabastair considered my questions. "Trust your senses, always. And if the third try is less than charmed, pray."

5

MY UNCLE SPEARED the last of his scrambled eggs onto his fork. James excused himself and collected his dishes and mine.

"Would you like some water?" I asked, still wrapping my head around the necromancer's advice that I pray. An emergency incantation was the more acceptable Magical response. At Malvyn's nod, I filled two glasses and set them between us. He wiped the corners of his mouth and moved his placemat and dishes to the side. The butler asked if either of us wanted more coffee. I declined. Malvyn put in an order for an espresso.

Once the little movements between the end of a meal and the beginning of a conversation had been completed, my uncle leaned back in his chair and looked at me. He and my mother and my aunt shared the same eye and skin coloring, and the same thick eyebrows. Tía Mari's hair was a light brown that leaned toward blonde in the summer. My mother's hair had been like my own, dark brown and somewhat more unruly. Malvyn's wavy hair, cut close at the sides and longer on top, was beginning to show a few streaks of dashing silver at the temples.

"You're hurting, aren't you?" At my reluctant nod, he added, "And right now you're thinking that nothing would taste sweeter than exacting a brutal revenge for Berto's death. You can feel yourself delivering the coup de grace, smelling the blood of your enemy as you watch the life-force drain from their eyes."

"It's like you read my mind," I admitted. I wiped the condensation off my water glass with a clean corner of my napkin and took a long drink.

My uncle interlaced his ring-laden fingers on the edge of the table and steepled his thumbs. His gaze was on me, but his thoughts had taken him somewhere else. "When someone is taken from us in such a way, Alderose, there is almost nothing we can do to erase the memories of that moment. And when that death is compounded by guilt over the actions we know we could have—*should have*—taken to prevent it?" He stopped. His eyes refocused into the present. "It's a heavy burden to carry, especially when it is pressed upon our shoulders at an early age."

"Something similar happened to you?"

"My first husband was a sorcerer. We were young and together we were going to conquer the world. I already knew I wanted to follow the path of law and order within the Magical realm. To prove myself, I went after an elder sorcerer whom others had accused of mistreating his apprentices—badly mistreating, as in abusing his position of authority by requiring his students to participate in acts of torture against Magicals awaiting processing within the legal system. The acts were completely unwarranted but designated mandatory in order to qualify for a place in the sorcerer's permanent court. He justified his actions by saying he was working on experimental spells.

"I wanted to set a trap. My husband volunteered to be the bait—he was a beautiful man, and so very talented. He was also reckless. Damien veered from our plan and, to make a painful story short, the sorcerer overreacted and killed him."

Our shared pain housed itself deep in the walls of my chest

cavity. It seemed I had a lot of empty space in there. "I'm so sorry."

"As am I, Alderose."

Grief-filled silence rose between us. The muted sound of cupboard doors being opened and shut emanated from the kitchen.

"Are you saying I shouldn't go after the fae who murdered my father?" I asked.

"I'm counselling you to make your decisions only after you are as well-prepared and informed as you can possibly be. More importantly, to think long and hard on what losing you would do to your sisters, should your plans go awry."

"I'm not planning to die, Uncle Malvyn."

"That's your youthful hubris talking, sobrina. And now that I've pre-emptively admonished you, I would like to offer to help you, starting with a history lesson. It's time you learned more about your families' lineages."

"Families, as in Brodeur *and* Del Valle?" I asked. "Shouldn't Beryl and Clementine hear this too?"

"My sister and I will make sure they are given the same information I share with you."

The double doors to the kitchen swooshed open. "Papa?"

"Yes, Leilani?"

"Where's the cake stand? You know, the one you spelled to keep Dad from eating too many desserts?"

Malvyn laughed and stood. "Let me help my daughter, then I'll introduce you to my collections and to my workshop." He started toward the kitchen and paused. "Why don't you go get any weapons and such that you've brought and meet me in the foyer."

. . .

I FOUND my way back to my room using the map and carefully dumped the contents of my duffel bag onto the wood floor. The glass beaker tumbled out, along with the rust-coated athame and scissors I'd grabbed off the grimy table in my mother's cellar laboratory. Luckily, the cork stopper stayed intact, but dark orange rust flaked off both tools.

The beaker called for closer inspection. I held the container up to the window, fascinated by the ongoing transformation of clumps of dirt into uniformly round balls. I chalked the change in its contents up to my mother's magic and set it aside.

Surveying the jumble of metal weapons, leather clothing and armor, and more personal stuff, I debated what I would pack. Every single thing going with me had to fit into something smaller and less cumbersome than a duffel.

"Betty, make a list." I'd renamed the note-taking app on my phone. "Backpack. Leathers, one full set. Underwear, three pair. Socks, three pair. Bras, two." I patted the places on my body where knives were easily stashed and accessible: thighs, boots, lower back, forearms. "Eight knives. Pouch with portal stones. Verre de mer glasses. Deodorant, toothpaste, toothbrush."

Leaving my toiletries behind wasn't an option; neither was going without my phone. Sidan warned me about human-made electronics not working in fae lands. What if I had to use the emergency stones to escape, and landed somewhere with cell service?

Ugh. My pants felt too tight. This room felt too tight. I wasn't used to taking in so much good food and so much kindness and compassion from anyone in such a short span of time. I wiggled out of my leathers and my bra, donned the only pair of sweat-pants I owned, plus a sleeveless T-shirt and a loose sweater and padded outside. Under my bare feet, the wet decking was slippery. I held the rail with both hands and leaned back, lifting my face. A cool, heavy mist formed a film over my eyelids and cheeks.

In that moment, I balanced in an odd, in-between place. It wasn't at all like me to crave rain on my face and wood under my feet, to take in big gulps of fresh, salty air and wish I could take off like the pair of ravens chatting overhead.

Your magic is Unbinding, Alderose, just like your father's.

What's your magic, Mom?

I'm a Binder. I bring things together. Like these pretty pieces of fabric, see?

But I want to be like you.

You can be like me in other ways, mija.

"It's because of you that I keep secrets, Mom." Rain formed two rivulets and trickled into my ears. Or maybe it was rain combined with tears. I stuck my pinky in my ear to pop the watery seal and closed the sliding glass door behind me. Beryl had texted. Instead of texting her back, I called.

"Hey," I said. "I'm worried about you." I didn't tell her I was also worried about the version of Alderose being exposed by rain and proximity to family.

"Funny, I'm worried about you, Rosey. Thought I'd check in."

"I think you should come to Uncle Malvyn's for a couple of days," I said. "It's kinda nice here. Cozy. Food just magically appears."

Beryl snorted. "Kostya and I were just talking about that. He'd like to debrief Mal in person, plus Mal sent a photo of Leili's cake. You know how I hate missing out on a good dessert."

"So you'll come?"

"We've got a couple of things to take care of first, but...can you hold on a sec?" While I waited for Beryl, I opened the drawers in the tiny closet. I was looking for something to carry the knives and such to my meeting with Malvyn. "Okay," she said. "We'll be there by dinner your time. Is there anything you need us to bring?"

I pinched the bridge of my nose. "Dad always carried a black backpack with him, very military-looking. If it's not too much trouble, could you pop into their apartment and see if he left it there, or if he had an extra one in his closet?"

"Sure, Sis. I'd do anything for you."

"Thanks, B. I'd do anything for you too."

UNCLE MALVYN, dressed in pressed khakis, a button-down shirt, and a knit vest, eyed my sweatpants, droopy sweater, and shoeless feet. "Feeling at home?" he asked, not unkindly.

"Very," I said. "And thank you. You and James have built a beautiful place and being here is exactly what I didn't know I desperately needed."

"Kostya informed me he and Beryl will be here for dinner."

I nodded, padding after him in my double-layered socks. "I'm glad they're coming."

"Maritza provided us more details about Clementine's situation. I hope your sister and her demon will consider a visit once their bond has been confirmed." My uncle cast a glance over his shoulder. "What's in the pillowcase?"

"Weapons. And some dirt from the floor of my mother's laboratory."

"You brought dirt all the way from Massachusetts?"

"I did."

"Interesting. I'd like to have a look at it."

He led me up a short flight of wide stairs lit from underneath. The hallway we entered was paneled with slabs of dark, fragrant wood and lined on both sides with niches. Recessed pin lights illuminated statues of mythical figures, some large enough to sit on the stone tile floor, others perched on rectangular display boxes.

"We're here." Malvyn pressed his hand, fingers spread, to a panel set into the wall. A soft click was followed by the sound of suction breaking, and the door in front of us opened a sliver. He pushed against the wood. "Come inside."

I was awestruck. The foyer swept in a half moon shape to either side, setting up a pattern of curving lines in the floor, walls, and bookshelves. I managed to gawp out something articulate like, "This is beautiful," while continuing to follow my uncle as he made his way deeper into the windowless room toward another distinctive door.

"This is my sanctuary. It's climate controlled," he said. "You'll find my book collection in here, as well as heirlooms and relics from the Brodeur side of the family. James keeps his family's items in his personal library. I assume your father kept his in Massachusetts." He slowed his pace when he noticed I wasn't keeping up. "There are cabinets and display cases you won't be able to open on your own. If you want to know about anything or need access, all you have to do is ask."

Malvyn stopped and faced me. "I know your mother kept secrets from you and your sisters. I suspect she kept the details of at least some of her work from Heriberto, as well. My sister was an enigmatic woman and superbly skilled witch." He threaded his fingers through his hair, never taking his gaze off mine. "Do you even want to hear about this?" he asked.

"You mean, my parents' relationship? Uncle Mal, I left home for college fifteen, sixteen years ago when I was eighteen. A lot has happened to me, and I imagine a lot happened to them—and between them—so any insight you have is welcome."

He scrubbed his hands across his jaw. "Come," he said, leading me to a set of chairs and a round table inlaid with black and white squares and set up for a game of chess. "This is better shared sitting down."

I picked up the carved figure of the Queen and rubbed my thumb over her smooth curves as I waited.

"Like you, your mother was the oldest of three siblings. She was headstrong, innovative, and when she began to work with trafficked Magicals, she distanced herself from our family. I understand the reasoning behind her decision much more now. She had to create space, to protect those who helped her and those she loved the most in this world—you and your sisters."

"Did she ask *you* for help?"

"On occasion, yes. My specialty is restraining collars. The more decorative neckpieces James and I wear are based on a similar principle, that of redirecting magic force. The ones I provided for Moira allowed her to bind herself to those whom she saved, which was essential when she was in the middle of an extraction. Whomever she was rescuing had to stick with her, without question."

The mental image I carried of my mother was rapidly changing into something more heroic, mythic. "And my dad? Were you two close?"

"Your father was a complicated man, Alderose. He loved Moira, he loved the three of you, and he loved the thrill of the hunt. We often argued. The man was relentless when it came to trying to get everyone to see things from his point of view." My uncle turned his head. Paternal concern washed across his gaze as he continued. "He asked too much of you before you were of an age to give your informed consent, and that has always bothered me."

"Do you know why he started my training when I was only, like, seven years old?"

Malvyn crossed his legs and interlaced his fingers over his knee. "You were the firstborn child. Your Unbinder magic, which occurs far less frequently than Binder magic, was very clearly inherited from your father's side. Heriberto wanted an heir, and by the time you were seven, your sisters' magics were also clear. Moira trained the Binders, Berto trained you."

I told my uncle that after spending the weekend with both Beryl and Clementine, they might beg to disagree on his assertion that my mother taught them much at all.

"Oh, her lessons were subtle, Alderose. All the groundwork is there, in your sisters' genes and in the recesses of their minds and the marrow in their bones. The knowledge will show itself as they are ready."

"Speaking for the three of us," I said, "I think we would have preferred both parents were upfront and open about their methods and reasoning. Dad told me about Mom's work with Magicals in abusive relationships and then he swore me to secrecy." The secret had been thrilling at first, then become burdensome as the years passed.

"Childhood is a precious thing, Alderose. James and I share the opinion that it is manipulative and ultimately unhealthy when a parent requires a child keep secrets related to the other parent."

The more I matured, the more I agreed. "Leilani told me you and James didn't force any magical training on her."

"That is true. We outlined a watch-and-wait approach to our daughter, after observing the changes in you due to your father starting your training when you were so young."

"Did no one think to intervene on my behalf?" I asked. I hit a nerve, and watched as my uncle's face reddened.

"Heriberto's methods were a frequent topic of conversation, and one of the reasons why James and I were not as much a part of your lives as we would have liked."

I let that sink in only so far. "Was my father an assassin?"

"No." Something flitted across my uncle's features.

All through our exchange, I had been debating whether to keep or share *my* secret.

I decided to go for broke. "I killed someone. Once," I said, stumbling over the words now jostling for elbow room on their way out of my mouth. "I mean I killed one person, once. Only once." Knowing my uncle was the Enforcer had kept me from seeking his counsel at the time.

"Was it an accident?"

I chewed my lower lip and pressed my fingertips into the sharp points of the Queen's crown. "A friend of mine was attacked by someone who had been stalking her for a long time. My friend's fae, and her name is Sidan. Actually, we're seeing each other now. Back then we weren't. We had an opportunity to deliver what felt like justice when her stalker followed her out of fae lands and into the human realm. I might have wanted to show off my knife skills, and—"

My uncle held up his palm. "Let me ask you once again, was this fae's death an accident?"

"Yes," I whispered. "I only wanted to teach them a lesson. I got slash happy. I thought they were wearing armor, only it was glamour. I hit their femoral artery."

Malvyn uncrossed his legs and propped his elbows on his knees. "Could you have helped this fae, gotten them medical care that could have saved their life?"

I swallowed hard. "I could have and I would have, if they'd stayed. They blinked out. Sidan discovered later that they had died in fae lands."

"Who knows about your connection to this death?"

"As far as I know, only Sid. Though Clementine knows I killed someone. I told her this weekend when we were tied up in that cavern. I didn't tell her it was an accident, I didn't give her any details, I just blurted it out. I was angry with her and we were both so stressed at that point. Death was on my mind. Our deaths." I set the Queen back on her square.

"I'm relieved to hear it wasn't premeditated murder, Alderose. In my role as Enforcer, I would have to order an investigation and then recuse myself, had the death occurred here. I have no jurisdiction within fae's borders. But I will contact my counterpart there. These things happen—she and I know it, and now you know it too. We've had an ongoing conversation about fae using glamour in the human realm.

"Your misstep is not the first, and it won't be the last. Maybe your experience will tip the scale in the direction I would like to see."

I nodded. "I understand."

He didn't speak for a few moments. Instead, my uncle moved chess pieces around the board, playing both sides of the match. "We all want to help you and your sisters," he said, placing a white pawn and settling back into his chair. "*We* being me, James, Maritza, and Alabastair. We're ready to extend our assistance, be it financial, emotional, whatever each of you needs and wants. And it doesn't have to be right now. The offer stands as long as we're alive."

He eyed me like the investigator and interrogator he was. "Another thing, Alderose. I would guess the need to pursue your father's killer and avenge his death is more acute for you than for your sisters. Heriberto trained you. He mentored you. And now someone has taken him away from you. I want to make it crystal clear that though I am family and I support you, I am in no way advocating the course of action I believe is uppermost in your thoughts.

"I will always advocate for justice. The Magical system isn't flawless, but it works. If you find the killer, please, bring them to me. Alive. Do not, under any circumstances, take the meting out of punishment into your own hands."

"I promise I will stay within the bounds of Magical law," I said. I couldn't stop my lips or my entire upper body from trembling as the implication of his words and my promise sank in. The route I wanted to take had very real consequences.

"Ready to change the topic?" Malvyn offered me his hand and when I nodded, he wrapped his arm around my shoulders to steady me once I stood. "Grab your pillowcase. I want you to show me this dirt you've brought."

He didn't speak again until we'd passed through his library and into his jewelry-making studio. I dropped my jaw at the sight of row after row of tools, glass-fronted cases of supplies, and chests with narrow drawers labelled with the names of precious and semi-precious gemstones. Behind more glass, modern, finished pieces twinkled alongside antiques.

"Set your things here." He indicated a smooth, clean tabletop and pulled up two stools. I set down the pillowcase and took out the beaker of soil. I added the athame and the scissors because they were my mother's and Malvyn might be able to do something with any residual magic. I wiped the rust off my hands with the rag he provided.

He surprised me by reaching for the beaker first. He lifted it, then brought over a high-powered lamp. While waiting for the bulb to reach its full glow, he gently rolled the container. The balls of dirt made soft sounds as they tumbled over each other and against the glass. "I thought they had all died," Malvyn said, his voice tinged with awe.

"You thought what had died?" I asked, sliding my stool closer to his.

"Your mother's dung beetles." He handed me the loupe. "Put this on, then wait. If they're ready to reveal themselves, you'll see them once your eyes adjust."

Dung beetles. In the cellar. Crawling around in the dirt when I was there. Not creepy at all. I snugged the loupe against my eye socket and rested my chin on my hands. I was rewarded with the sight of a couple of balls unfolding shiny, spindly black legs and clambering over the other balls. Malvyn un-stoppered the beaker, opened a nearby drawer, and used an Exacto knife to spear the largest ball. He set it on a flat piece of fire-scarred wood and carefully slid the point of the knife over and over the same spot until the ball broke apart.

"*Chrysina gorda*." Malvyn poked at the beetle's metallic, emerald-green backside. "From central México. One of the species of scarab beetles your mother collected on her trips throughout the country."

"Why did my mother collect scarab beetles and—" I shook my head. Questions were piling up.

"The Del Valles are known to consume scarabs. Their magic comes from the ground they walk on, build their homes on, grow their food in. Your mother raised the beetles in soil they carted up from México, so she would always have ingredients on hand to make the concoctions Heriberto needed to sustain his magic." My uncle took the dead beetle between his fingers and handed it to me. "And this is why you, Alderose Brodeur, are known as the Scarab Eater's Daughter."

6

THE SCARAB EATER'S DAUGHTER. I rolled the moniker around on my tongue as I examined the beetle's structure and coloring with the help of the powerful magnifier.

"I imagine you have questions."

"I do. But since we're here in your workroom," I said, sitting up straight and setting the loupe on the table, "maybe you could start with explaining how beetles fit into my father's magic. One of the building blocks of his training method was to constantly stress I should know how to use each of my weapons, including my body, without the assistance of any magic whatsoever. No spells. No charms, no potions. *Nada*."

"Ah. Well, he learned that lesson the hard way, before you were born, by almost dying during a fight with an opponent who drained him of his magic." My uncle spun on his seat and reached for a Mont Blanc fountain pen and a sketch pad. He opened to a fresh sheet of paper and sketched the outline of a beetle. "When your parents moved to Northampton, they assumed they could use local beetles. Turns out they couldn't. Berto's magic required the *Chrysina gorda*."

One side of his mouth twitched as he finished drawing a stylized scarab. "Your mother took over raising the beetles and once they died, she dried and ground them into fine powder. I know she experimented with different carriers for the infused powders and settled on gel capsules. Berto could easily carry them with him, pop them into his mouth, bite down or swallow, and his magic was instantly boosted."

I'd never witnessed my father popping pills. Then again, he never took me on any big assignments when he was hired as a magically enhanced bounty hunter. I got to accompany him when he was contracted to go after humans. He felt that was safer.

"There is another aspect to your father and mother and their magic that you and your sisters should know as it will affect each of you in time." My uncle cleared his throat and capped his pen. "It begins with the Demesne. And this aspect of the Demesne was something I had to discover for myself. Well, with James's help and his astute powers of observation. A few months after we were struck by the Brodeur's blessed curse, he began to notice surges in his magic. I noticed dips in my own.

"James broached the subject one evening while we were dining. Following that discussion, we designed a series of experiments which led us to conclude that the Demesne had somehow entwined our magics, which caused them to constantly seek balance by giving and taking."

"Did the same thing happen with my parents?" I asked. I planted my elbows on the table and rested my chin in my hands. "I bet you're going to tell me my parents' magic fed on each other's and that they became that much stronger individually because of the Demesne."

"That's exactly right. Which also meant that when one of them was drained, the other was equally depleted." My uncle finished his sentence with what could only be categorized as a penetrating stare. When I didn't respond, because I couldn't respond, not with the wave of stomach acid burning up my throat, he continued, his fingers worrying over the golden links of his collar.

"Seven and a half years ago, Heriberto was on a mission in Costa Rica. It was the rainy season and all the roads on the Osa Peninsula were washed out. He was trapped, and then he was found."

"Who found him and what did they do to him?" I asked, all too ready to add their name to my list, right underneath Jadzia's.

Malvyn shook his head. "It wasn't a who, it was a snake. Heriberto's target turned out to be a snake shifter, a boa constrictor. The snake captured your father and carried him deep into the coastal jungle. Played with him for days, until Berto developed a fever. For reasons the shifter never explained, he took pity on Berto and brought him to a clinic. The medics were able to see him through the worst of the fever.

"When he finally got to a phone and could call your mother, he found out she had died."

"Why did you tell Kostya you suspected my mother and Serena had both been murdered?"

"Because I didn't have that crucial piece of information about Heriberto's whereabouts at the time of Moira's death until he visited us this past summer.

"He made his seventh attempt at ending his life in the dining room. Alabastair revived him. Afterward, I think your father finally spilled it all so we would understand the profound nature of the guilt he carried over not being able to keep his magic viable, which led to Moira losing hers—and then losing her life. In the end, all he wanted was to reunite with your mother.

"He didn't want to live without her. And I am so sorry to be the bearer of this news, but you deserve to know everything, or as much as I know, as do Beryl and Clementine. To circle around to my suspicious mind, I still find it hard to believe that my sister died from a lack of magic. She had resources beyond most Magicals. To do this day, we don't know what, or who, finally did her in."

"Did you ever talk to my parents when they were alive about using what you and James discovered, maybe offer to create something that would mitigate their bond?"

"I did. I made multiple sets of bracelets for their wrists and ankles with alarms that signaled if their magic dipped too low. Did they wear them?" He shrugged. "I'm working on a similar array of choices for Maritza and Alabastair. The Demesne affects their magics the same way it does for me and James, though their situation is complicated by the differences in their physical sizes. You've seen how cautious Alabastair is about making certain Maritza gets enough food? He's a much bigger man, and it appears he burns through his store of magic just by breathing and moving. They have to be very careful.

"I plan to offer mitigation to Clementine and Laszlo, once they've discovered how—and if—the Demesne affects their magic."

I twisted the cap off his elegant pen and filled in sections of the beetle. *Knowledge is power* was a phrase I'd heard a lot growing up. The knowledge that my father wanted to be with my mother in death was doing its best to empty my well of guilt with a demitasse spoon.

At the same time, another equally insidious emotion was sneakily adding to the well with a garden hose.

"It hurts a *lot* that my sisters and I weren't enough to keep him here. I got more of his time and attention than both of them combined and I...I think none of us ever understood his long absences. I mean, I sort of did, once he decided I was old enough to handle the truth about the dangerous part of his work." I'd completely colored in the beetle until it was all black and now I was ringing it with tiny daggers.

"Tell me about your magic, Alderose. How you experience it, how you maintain it."

I appreciated my uncle's deflection. I was about to set his pen aside when I realized I could draw it as well as I could explain it. "I hadn't performed the ritual of rejuvenation in a long time. I made a circle last night, in Northampton, in my mother's shop.

"When Dad was around, he used to bring me there to practice on nights when we couldn't use one of the local dojos. I found the compass rose he embedded in the floor." I drew the compass and outlined my knives and daggers in the flower petal pattern as I continued. "I spread the dirt from the cellar in between each blade. At the peak of the ritual, I raised one of my daggers overhead, like this" —I drew a seated stick figure with its arms raised and a sword pointed upward— "and I made a connection into the ground below and the sky above. It's just something that has always felt right to me. Right and true.

"When I have any of my weapons in my hands and I'm practicing on my own, I do this thing I call earth-dancing. I practice feeling rooted to wherever I am and then I call on the magic in the earth to charge the metal in my body, which also charges my weapons."

My uncle deftly stood and started to open drawers and cases. He gathered a few items and placed them on a velvet-lined jeweler's tray which he set in front of me. "Like the scarab, you both dig into the ground and fly above it. It's an apt magical and mythological symbol."

I nodded, gulping, stunned by the beauty of the scarabs littering the black velvet. Carved out of dull stone, sparkling gemstones, bones, and wood, each was unique. "Go ahead, pick them up," Malvyn said, "they won't break. Your mother and your grandparents gathered some of these for me on their travels. Is there a metal you prefer? I would like to create something for you."

"I've always liked twenty-four carat gold," I said. "Could you take a look at the athame and the pair of scissors I found in my mom's laboratory too? They're iron, and as pretty as gold is, I'd like to carry iron with me when I...if I..."

"If you decide to pursue One-Becomes-Three?" My uncle's voice radiated kindness, understanding, acceptance—and resignation.

"Yes."

I LEFT my pillowcase of things in Malvyn's workshop, took my time exiting through his library, and returned to my room. Exhaustion clamored to be taken seriously. I undressed down to my underwear, drew the heavy curtains on the gray sky outside, and curled into a ball under the cold sheets. I fought the urge to process everything I had learned and let my empty place take me into sleep.

I DREAMED I was belly down in the dirt underneath the table in my mother's laboratory, watching dozens of dung beetles rolling ball after ball after ball. In the background, I heard my mother's voice and the clink of the glass stirrer against the rim of a beaker. Her feet shuffled across the ground as she stood in front of her cauldron and listed off ingredients.

I lay in the darkened guest room, warm beneath the blankets, and tried to recall my mother's words.

I couldn't. Dreams were like that. Filled with symbols and sometimes signs that I could rarely make good use of. Stretching, I startled when the touchpad near the door chimed twice. The bell was followed by the disembodied voice of the woman who'd first showed me to this room. "Alderose, this is Felicia. Are you there?"

"Yes, I am."

"Dinner will be ready at six. It is five-forty. Your uncle asked me to pass along the message that there has been a change of plans. Beryl and Kostya will not be joining us tonight."

"Thank you, Felicia."

"You're welcome." A single chime signaled she was done. I rolled over and felt for my phone. Beryl hadn't texted. I tried calling and when she didn't answer, I hung up. Guilt, my new constant companion, urged me to call her again and leave a message. I did. I even told her I loved her. Again. Which was very New Alderose.

I hadn't packed any nice clothes. I put the sweatpants and sweater back on, brushed and braided my hair so it would stay off my face, and jogged to the dining room in my socks. Malvyn, Maritza, and Alabastair were standing by the fireplace, drinks in hand. Leilani was on the couch, reading. The table was set for five.

"Where's James?" I asked. "And Gosia and Rémy and Zazie?"

"The entire trio is quite taken with my husband," Malvyn said. "Gosia confided she thinks tomorrow is Zazie's big day and asked that James remain nearby. His floral remedies are working well on all three of them and he's getting the family settled for an early bedtime. He'll join us when he can."

"Does he have anything that helps with dreams?" I searched the drink tray and decided an aperitif would do no harm. I dropped an ice cube into a highball glass and added a splash of chilled Lillet and a twist of lemon peel.

"The en suite in your bedroom should have a selection of his products, Alderose. Check the cabinet above the sink."

"Thanks. I will." I carried my glass to the couch, sat next to my cousin, and tucked my feet under me. Carlos, who had been in and out of the kitchen during breakfast, was crouched in front of the fireplace and setting logs to light. "What's the story with Beryl and Kostya?" I asked.

Maritza came to sit beside me. "Laszlo said he needed his brother's help. It sounded like it was related to whatever social event was going on at the palace."

"The *palace*?" In all my years of knowing Kostya, I didn't think he had ever mentioned a palace. Though I knew his mother was the Queen of the Reformed Realm and, generally speaking, queens lived in palaces.

Leilani perked up. "Does that mean Clementine's a *princess* now?"

"I have no idea," I answered. "If there's going to be a demon in the family, I guess we're going to need to know a lot more about...demons." My inability to answer said a lot about how preoccupied I had been. I knew Clemmie and Laz had experienced the Demesne in Northampton on Saturday night, but I hadn't given it much thought until I mentioned it to Sidan. Added to what Malvyn had explained to me earlier in the day, I chastised myself for having no bandwidth for anything that wasn't revenge-related.

I sipped at the Lillet. Carlos finished his task, went in and out of the kitchen through the big swinging doors, and declared dinner was ready. Platters lined the center of the table, family style offerings of Caesar salad and lasagna and garlicky bread sticks. If I thought conversation would stay light in acknowledgement of it being mealtime and there being a teenager in our midst, I was wrong.

Malvyn brought up the dung beetles as soon as everyone had a filled plate in front of them. "Could you at least call them *scarabs*, Papa?" Leilani asked, rolling her eyes for emphasis. "I would like to enjoy my dinner without thinking about *bugs*."

"I'm pleased to hear you're making something for Alderose," Maritza said. "Have you figured out what she needs?"

I darted an eager glance to my uncle while wiping my mouth. Napping had made me ravenous.

"A torc, which I've created from a section of tubular gold. The torc will sit at the base of her neck with endpieces that screw on, allowing Alderose quick access to anything stored inside. I might need your help with the other object, Mari. I'm using almost-pure iron to create sections of filigree. They're coming out somewhat brittle. I think the pieces would last longer and be more comfortable for Alderose to wear if they were stitched directly onto a piece of clothing."

Maritza turned and appraised what she could see of my body, which wasn't much. "A vest. I assume you have a leather vest with protective inserts amongst your collection of soft armor? This could be worn as an undergarment, keeping the iron close to your skin and protecting you from fae. I think we can assume there are fae in your future?"

"Yes," I said. "Including my girlfriend."

7

"Ooh, I want to meet her!" Leilani said. "I keep telling Papa *all* fae aren't bad. Look at Harper's cousin, Sallie. She's one of my best friends."

"Who's Harper?" I asked, biting into a breadstick.

"My boyfriend. His mom's a witch and his dad's fae, which he kept secret from everybody for *years*." My cousin talked more about her boyfriend and his brother, Thatcher, as we ate. Harper was a gyrfalcon shifter and Thatcher was known as the Racoon Whisperer. I told Leilani I hoped I got to meet them both, as well as the other Magical teens she nattered on about.

Once everyone finished eating, my cousin and I cleared the table and brought everything into the kitchen. Side-by-side refrigerators, a wine cooler, and an eight-burner industrial stove were the first appliances to catch my eye. I twirled in place to see a wall of pots and pans and the entrance to a pantry. Generous bunches of herbs hung upside down over bowls of fruits and vegetables.

"Whew, Lei-li, this would be an amazing place to practice your magic."

She hummed in agreement as she opened a cupboard and

reached for a stack of dessert plates. "It is. Dad keeps it stocked with stuff from his gardens and greenhouses, and Abuela teaches me new recipes every time she visits." She set the plates on a butcher block section of the counter and pointed to a drawer. "Could you get the dessert forks? I have a hunch Zazie's feeling up to cake."

"Are you psychic too?" I teased.

Lei-li laughed. "I sent her a test slice and boosted it with my secret ingredient."

"Ooh, what's that?"

"Dung beetles!" At my horrified expression, she swatted my arm. "Just kidding, Rosey. My special ingredient isn't a thing, it's more of a meditation, a visualization. I know Zazie's scared. Her fear might be holding her back from letting this transition unfold. As I put together her cake and decorated it, I pictured everything happening smoothly. I amplified her innate ability to self-control the process so she wouldn't feel like it was something happening *to* her, against her will—more like the act of letting out her fish tail was as natural and as beautiful as breathing."

My eighteen-year-old cousin stunned me. I was *so* not like that at her age. I had been...stabby. Very, very stabby. "How—?"

"How did I figure all that out?" She clutched the plates to her chest. "I've had to learn about boundaries, Rosey, otherwise I make myself ill just by letting in everything around me, all the emotions and stuff and not just from humans and Magicals. Plants, animals, the ocean. Basically, everything out there has the potential to affect me in here." She patted her chest with the top plate.

Voices filtered through the space between the swinging doors, along with clapping and a call for cake as Zazie and her parents entered the room. "When did Mal and James start to teach you about all of this?" I asked.

"Never," she said. "They've been very hands-off until recently, when I asked if I could start more formal studies in witchcraft. They didn't force anything on me on purpose. Now, they're super excited. And I am too. I'm meeting the most amazing Magicals." She pushed against the door and was greeted with a cheer. I set the forks on the table near the fresh placemats and napkins added for the extra guests and went to say hello.

Gosia and Zazie were dressed in matching ceremonial dresses. My aunt's magic-imbued threads winked through every seam of the long, pale green tunics and I thought I saw my uncle's hand in the mother's and daughter's headpieces, delicate coronas of silver and gold filaments and tiny gems. Rémy had on a more formal coat too, though on closer inspection I realized it was a long caftan embroidered with raindrops and stylized waves.

Malvyn tapped the side of his wineglass with a fork and requested everyone come to the table and find their seats. "Welcome, Zazie Ruisseau, our honored guest, and your parents, Gosia and Rémy." He waited until the glasses had been filled with champagne or sparkling apple cider before continuing his toast. "May this moment of transition in your life be marked by joy and supported by the bonds of family and friendship."

We all sipped. Zazie stood, beaming, and asked for a knife to cut the cake. With James's help, Leilani set an enormous covered cake stand in front of the thirteen-year-old. We gasped in unison as the lid was lifted.

"Oh, my *Goddess*," Zazie said, handing the knife to Gosia and clapping her hands to cheeks as bright and pink as the frosting. Leilani had added swirls and flowers and fish and other decorations to the triple-tiered cake. My heart sipped at the love infusing the room as my fingers itched to swipe one of the sugary roses.

Later, after we'd eaten most of the dessert and drained the bottles of bubbly drinks, my capacity to absorb joy maxed out around the same time my fork captured the last crumb on my plate. I excused myself, citing exhaustion, and reminded everyone to wake me up if they needed a bodyguard or if Zazie's transition went into high gear. Uncle Malvyn followed me to the door.

"I'll be in my workshop all night," he said, "or until I have the torc ready for you and the iron filigree pieces ready for your aunt."

"I appreciate the rush job," I said. "I really do."

"I sense your—anxiety?" His eyebrows knit together. "Maybe that's not the right word. You're buzzing and it's not from the sugary dessert."

"I have a hard time relaxing under normal circumstances. Being here has magnified that for me, the contrast between me and everyone else in my family. But being surrounded by all of you? That's...that's been priceless. Thank you for seeing me, for explaining more about my mom and dad. And thanks for wanting to help."

"We're family, Alderose. I'll have your things delivered to your room if I finish them before I see you at breakfast."

I found James's herbal sleeping aid right where they said it would be and took the recommended dose. I managed to not dream, or at least not remember any dreams, and greeted the morning with an unexpectedly calmer head and heart.

Crawling back into bed after opening the curtains, I texted the number Felicia left with me. My body craved a workout and I hadn't packed any sneakers. "Good morning, Alderose. How may I be of assistance?"

"Would you happen to have a stash of running shoes by any chance?" I asked.

"What size do you wear? Should you need it, there is a small gym located in the wing off the dining area, one floor down" she added.

"Size eight," I said. "And thank you. For the sneakers and the gym. I don't suppose the estate has a steam room?"

"There is a hot tub on the deck you share with the other guest rooms. Go outside and you'll find it around the corner to your right. On the deck on the opposite side of the guest wing is an outdoor sauna. Would you like me to have Carlos light it for you?"

A run followed by a sauna sounded perfect. I could let myself feel spoiled for one more day. "Yes, please."

"Your footwear will be delivered in fifteen minutes."

The map of the house included a layout of the entire property, including James's greenhouse and gardens, trails through the woods, and ways to reach the rocky shoreline. I got into my sweats once again and opened my door when I heard the dull thud of something landing on the floor. A shoe box sat next to a much more ornate box. I bent to pick up both. The square wood box was much heavier.

I tossed the shoebox on the bed and plopped next to it, testing the bounce in the heavenly mattress. I was fairly certain the ornate box had come from Mal's workshop. Filling my lungs with oxygen, I held my breath and let that moment of not-knowing ramp up my anticipation.

My uncle had not disappointed the part of me that secretly lusted for more bling in my life. A gleaming gold torc sat in the middle of the bottom half of the box, kept in place by satin ribbon ties. The tubular neckpiece had fluted sections at each end, creating an opening that would span the front of my throat. I untied the ribbons and picked up the piece made for me and only me. Tilting it side to side, I felt its heft and heard the rattle of its assorted contents.

Each endpiece screwed into place. I undid one and tipped

the torc, emptying marble-sized golden balls and dried green-and-gold scarab beetles into my palm. I slid them back in, secured the end, and opened the folded piece of paper wedged into the box's lid.

ALDEROSE,

The torc is keyed to you. No one else can wear it, not even your sisters. The balls are miniature portal stones Alabastair asked me to add. Though I was able to find a few dried beetles, I'm afraid we'll have to wait on the capsules. I can't find your mother's grimoire with the recipe. I thought I might have the book in my library. I will look for it again after a short rest and will plan to see you at lunch.

—Uncle Malvyn

I SET the note and the torc back in the box and readied to go outside. Felicia had tucked a pair of cushioned socks inside the sneakers. An hour later, I'd run, jogged, and walked the majority of the estate. My sneakers were muddied, my clothes were soaked, and I was happy.

I was rarely happy. Showering off the sweat, I donned the guest bathrobe and slip-ons and went in search of the promised sauna. It was hot, and filled with the smell of toasty cedar planks. I set my open towel on one of the benches, hung my robe on an outside hook, and lay down with a view to the stormy ocean.

I spent the next hour alternating between sweating inside the sauna and standing under the cold-only shower attached to the privacy fence outside. Thoroughly relaxed and invigorated, I padded through quiet halls to my room. Another package was waiting for me. This one was soft. I pressed my palm to the keypad, lifting the package as I opened the door.

There was no waiting to see what was inside. I wiggled my hand under the folded paper. This gift had to be from my aunt. I lifted the top piece of clothing, a vest with Mal's promised filigree pieces stitched all over. Looking closer, I noticed the delicate iron pieces were joined to the ones nearby with gold rings. I put the garment on over my head and pulled on the zipper positioned on my left side. As soon as the pull reached my armpit, the long vest snugged against my body from hips to shoulders, shrinking to my exact shape.

"Tía!" I knew she couldn't hear me, or see the shaking in my hands. I could get used to custom-made clothing, and Beryl's insistence on having everything sewed just for her made sense for the first time ever. I'd always had an attitude about her quirk, but now—

So judgy, Alderose.

"Yeah, yeah, I know," I answered. I found my boy shorts then opened the jewelry box and gently slid the torc around my neck. The tall mirror in the bathroom crooked a finger to my vanity. One look couldn't hurt, and standing before my reflection, seeing the gold neckpiece against my skin and the pattern of gold rings breaking up the blacks of the vest and the filigree, I felt a sense of my own power and beauty. Briefly, ever so briefly, but it was there.

Also in the package was a pair of sweatpants and a hoodie, only these were Aunt Maritza's couture-level casual wear. I left them on the bed, showered again, and twisted my hair into a messy topknot. I had one more pair of clean underwear, thank Goddess, and when I slipped into my new clothes, I whispered, "I get it, B, I totally get it" to my absent sister and went in search of food.

. . .

THE DINING ROOM WAS SILENT, as was the kitchen when I peeked in and saw only clean countertops and a stack of washed dishes on the drainer. On the dining room sideboard was a carafe, a plate of croissants under a linen napkin, a covered glass of orange juice, and yet another note. This one was written in a different hand:

ALDEROSE,

We came looking for you but you weren't in your room. We received a call from Laszlo's parents. Something happened in the Reformed Realm, and your sisters need our help. We will get an update to you as soon as we have one.

Love,

Tía, Uncle Malvyn, Leilani, and Alabastair

AN AUDIBLE CLICK sounded from inside my chest, marking as one moment's façade of happiness switch into the next moment's core understanding: something bad had happened to someone in my family and it was my fault because I wasn't there to prevent it. My hands shook as I turned the top of the carafe and filled a mug with coffee. There was no running to armor up. Where would I go? I would drink my coffee and eat my croissant and then I would see who was here that could provide me more information.

Lock it down, Alderose. When you're on a job there's no time for tears, no time to be sidetracked by doubt. Pick a route and follow it, and if it's the wrong route, pick another one until you get to where you need to go. Process of elimination. That's all it is.

Heriberto del Valle was back in my head. I stood close to the massive wall of windows and sipped my coffee. Lines of rain poured from the ends of gutters and sluiced down the glass. I set the emptied mug on the table, slipped two croissants onto a plate, and crossed to the kitchen. Protein and carbs. I'd make sandwiches, find nuts and dried fruits to snack on later. Hydrate. There had to be refillable water bottles in the well-ordered kitchen.

I found everything I needed, set it on the wooden surface, and paused unwrapping the sliced cheeses and deli meats. Two people had entered the dining room. It took a moment to register they were speaking in Spanish. I listened as their conversation continued beyond the double doors.

"Have you called the witches?"

"Yes, the ones Maritza specified, the doctor and the plant witch."

"Do we have rooms for them if they have to stay overnight?"

"We have extra cots we can set up in the two empty rooms in the guest wing. One room for the injured girl and her demon, the other room for the other sister and her demon. You better put in an order to have groceries delivered. We don't have time to shop."

"James is staying with the fish girl and her parents. I have their shopping list here. Let me help move the cots, then I'll get everything ordered."

Felicia's and Carlos's voices faded as they left. Something had happened to Beryl and Clementine, and the two of them and Kostya and Laszlo were expected to arrive here today. James was with Zazie, Gosia, and Rémy, which meant *that* situation was close to being a go. I stabbed my fingers through my knotted hair.

Fuck. Stay on task, Alderose.

I made the sandwiches, filled a water bottle, and bagged up the makings for gorp. I even located a cloth rag and wiped down the counter. Passing the sideboard, I noticed a clipboard. On it was a printed message and a handwritten list of foods and personal items with an initial after each. B. K. Z. G. R. C. L.

Beryl. Kostya. Zazie. Gosia. Rémy. Clementine. Laszlo.

I couldn't stop myself from skimming the email. A few words and phrases burned into my brain as I read and reread.

Vampire. Attack. Needs blood. Gather the witches.

The Collector. Lionel Vigne. Chamonix. France.

My nostrils flared and the skin all over my body tightened in anticipation.

I re-prioritized my list. I knew who to hunt first.

I was going to France.

8

EVERYTHING CHANGED when I had a destination in sight and a plan for how to get there. Methodically, I folded my clothes and piled them in my duffle bag. I rolled my knives and daggers into the pillowcase and set that atop my clothes. I slid the torc around my neck and zipped up the filigreed vest. The sneakers were left in the bathroom to finish drying, along with the damp sweats.

Scanning the map, I memorized the route to the front door and the portal tree, stepped into the hall, and closed the door behind me.

Fen. Carlos and Felicia hadn't mentioned Fen. The wisp had grown up in captivity. My mother had rescued her and because Moira was dead, my sisters and I assumed her debts *and* her accounts. Fen *owed* us and now, Fen could pay me.

I again consulted the map of the estate and located the other guest wing. Maritza and Alabastair's room was easy to find. Their door was open. A wash of warm golden light spilled into the hall and a lilting voice invited me in.

"I was hopin' someone would answer me song," Fen said

from her perch. She was bundled into one of Alabastair's capes and wedged into a chair. "I dint think it'd be *you*."

"Do you know who I am?" I asked.

"You're related ta Clementine the seer witch and she be a daughter of Moira, so you must also be a daughter of Moira. Am I righ'?"

I set my bag by the doorway and stepped closer to the wisp. "My mother rescued you, didn't she?"

"Yeh, she did. Wha' of it?"

"She asked for nothing in return, did she?"

"Tha' is true."

"As her daughter, I invoke the right of reparations and ask that you tell me everything you know about who took your mother and where you were kept."

Fen started to shake her head, increasing the tempo until her hair loosened and her moss green cloche flew off. "Stop," she hissed. "I dinna want ta do tha'."

"Fen." I retrieved her hat and went to my knees front of her. I was careful not to touch the cape or the chair. "Do you know Lionel Vigne?"

The way her face paled told me she did.

"Do you know where he lives?" Her face went even whiter and her hair began to float in the air and disappear like wisps of clouds in a breeze. "Fen, stay with me," I begged. "I'm not going to hurt you, I just need information."

"Jus' *thinkin'* about tha' man hurts me. Jus' hearin' his *name*."

"I think he did something to one of my sisters."

Fen's eyes widened. Her hair stopped floating and settled back on her slender shoulders. "Guillaume," she whispered, picking at the button tacked to the side of her hat. "He makes *him* do the hurtin'. Guillaume the vampire and Arnaud the fae. An' Linette."

I shut my eyes. I had four names now and I committed them

to memory. One more piece of information would go a long way to helping me. I looked into Fen's soft gray eyes and poured as much compassion as I could muster into mine. "I know they live in France, I think near Chamonix. Is there anything else you can tell me about how to find them?"

Exiting the portal center in Boston, I was greeted by more rain and a growling stomach. I ate both sandwiches as I drove to Northampton, parked the rental car in the lot behind my parents' building, and carried my stuff to the front door.

Fen had given me her hat, and a crucial description of another front door, the one that led to her prison, thousands of miles away in the French Alps. I looked for my reflection in the cold, dirty glass. It was time to stop thinking of this building as belonging to my parents. Technically, it belonged to me and Beryl and Clementine and we hadn't had a single minute to start a conversation about what we wanted to do with the property, let alone how we wanted to divvy up my parents' businesses.

I let myself in, and set both bolts this time. I didn't want anyone—not even Sidan—entering without my knowledge. Pressing my hands against both sides of the door jamb, I spoke a spell to seal me inside and went straight to the old office.

Beryl had left the door to the stairwell propped open. I gave silent thanks and not a thought more. If I started to picture Beryl and what might have happened to her and to Clementine and why a medical center was being set up at my uncle's house, I would start stabbing the wrong things. I jogged up one flight of stairs and opened the door to my parents' spacious apartment.

Flicking the wall, I hit a switch. The electricity was working. Staying with the theme of careful and cautious, I locked this door behind me too before heading down the hall to the room that spanned the entire length of the building, turning on lights as I went. Even turned up the thermostat, flushed a toilet, and opened the faucet in one of the bathroom's sinks until it ran hot.

I could stay here.

I could stay in Northampton, set up shop, do my research, find someone to come with me to France, and pursue this Lionel Vigne. I plugged in my phone, turned the ringer on loud, and sent a text to Sidan. The message would land at a communications relay center, get coded, then sent on to her via a method that was simpatico with fae magic.

I had only my phone, no laptop. I wasn't a fan of public research and my equipment was home in New York. I surprised myself—why didn't I go there? What drew me back here to Northampton?

My father's backpack, that worn piece of equipment he took with him everywhere. Only, he hadn't been wearing it when he showed up at the quarry, ready to help us take down the fae. The pack had to be here. I forgot about the idea of going right on to New York and started my search in my parents' old bedroom.

Which was a mistake. Mom's scent was everywhere. Dad hadn't come back here after she'd died, or not much. I opened other doors and found what had to be his office. It shared a bathroom with another room with a rumpled double bed and a closet. Piles of clothes were everywhere. For a man who revered precision in his work, he was a slob at home. I went back to my mother's room. Odd. They didn't appear to have shared a bed. Her room was adjoined to another, also with a bathroom in between.

Somewhere in here, or in the laboratory, or the shop, or the workroom on the third floor, was my mother's grimoire. I hadn't sensed it in my uncle's library. If I could find her book, I could find her recipe for Dung Beetle Surprise or whatever she called the mixture that amplified my father's magic and would therefore amplify my own.

Somewhere in my father's rooms was his backpack. And inside his backpack were the kinds of secrets he trusted only himself to carry.

I hoped.

I returned to the hall. The hall felt neutral. So did the front room. I dragged my duffel forward and deposited it there. Now was the time to assess and plan. If I had a different kind of relationship with my sisters, individually or collectively, I would be running toward them to offer comfort.

But I was the Scarab Eater's Daughter and a voracious part of me hungered for something that was missing.

WHEN MY MOTHER'S friend Serena called me seven years ago to tell me my mother had died, I asked a lot of questions. Serena didn't have a lot of answers. Here, in the middle of Mom's and Dad's barely used living room, feet in socks on a plush, hand-knotted rug I couldn't recall having seen before, I realized I hadn't asked Serena where my mother's body had been found.

This room had an air of abandonment that differed from the other rooms on the second floor. A seating arrangement with wide couches and two ottomans, fronted by a long, low glass-topped table at one end left plenty of floor space in the other half for large groups of people to gather and mingle and even dance.

Velveteen curtains hung to either side of each of the four windows. I stood in front of one and surveyed the busy street. When my father started pulling his disappearing act with me five years ago, I said a silent *fuck this* to his increasingly erratic calls to help him bring in one bad apple after another and applied for a job running security at conventions. Turns out I was good at that kind of work. Now, watching streams of cars and pedestrians flowing left and right two stories below, I let my eyes soften and my peripheral vision take over.

Patterns. Traffic patterns. I could start with that. I turned my back to the wall of windows, unzipped my hip pouch, and pulled out my eyeglass case. I hadn't worn this special pair in a while; they didn't work when my magic was low, let alone depleted. Today, my batteries were charged and it was time to see what had really been going on in these rooms.

I cleaned the lenses and the wraparound frames with the special cloth and slipped them on my face. Enhanced sight didn't happen immediately. I had to coax forth my magic and renew my connection to the spell-coated shells that served as the translucent lenses.

This magic was similar to Clementine's. With the use of imbued story threads, she could see moments from other people's pasts recreate themselves in front of her eyes. That kind of magic took a toll on her body. She was the only one who could see both the threads and the images and interpret what was going on. Having to describe what she saw had the potential to be traumatic, something I'd witnessed firsthand over the weekend.

Unlike Clementine, I didn't see bodies or objects. I saw movement trails, those stirrings of dust motes in the air and above surfaces. Once the remnants began to appear with the help of the lenses, I had to wait, proceeding with stealth only if the threads called to be followed and drawing no conclusions that would interrupt the flow of information.

During my training I had to learn how to slow and control my breath enough that I disturbed as few particles around me as possible. Hooking into that breath bridged me right into my magic. The empty spaces in the living room began to fill with faint sparkles. I could get lost in the swirling motes or I could get a move on. I chose to visit my mother's rooms first.

A body lies atop her bed. Legs swing to the side, the body stands and leaves.

One closet door opens and closes, hangers shuffle to one side and the other.

Lines stream in and out of the bathroom; more lines stream through the bathroom into the room with the desk.

Drawers open and close, open and close, open and lift and unfold.

A book opens. Pages shuffle. A pen writes.

A book closes. The desk drawer swallows the book, refolds, closes, slides away.

I decided to stay in my magic, keep the glasses on, and keep going. My father's rooms were thick with movement trails. Arms slice through air. Fists hit walls. Objects are tossed.

I had to stop, quiet my heart and my breathing. I recognized the familiar ways in which my father moved when he was angry or frustrated. I stepped closer to his closet.

Door opens. Folds in half. Objects are lifted and replaced, lifted and reordered, lifted and sliced through the air.

A whirlpool of lines. Two. Bodies moving in an intimate dance, one too short to be my mother.

I backed out of my father's rooms. Talked myself into continuing. Jogged up to my mother's workroom. Saw the wing patterns and other movement trails that confirmed what Clementine had seen when she described Mom being lifted off the floor by a giant bird and flown out the tall window.

Two big worktables, heavier than the ones on the shop. Heavier, older, and filled with more drawers than could be seen by the naked eye. Again, magical motes showed drawers opening, closing. And when I identified the humanoid shapes ringing the room as mannequins, the lenses showed me they were much more than legless, mute dummies with pins jammed into their cloth bodies.

A compass, larger than the one in the ground floor shop, embedded in the floor.

Five lines make a five-pointed star. At each point of the star, a mannequin. I would never have noticed their placement without my glasses, unless I was looking deliberately for signs of geomagick.

Underneath chaotic movement paths I could easily attribute to everyone who had been up here over the weekend looking for clues to our mother and everything she had hands in, were five distinct movement paths. No, not paths...vertical walls, creating a pentagrammic prism.

Mom, what were you doing up here?

I walked around the five mannequins, giving them as much space as I could while dodging corners of furniture and trying to not trip on the rug. If the placement of the dress forms was based on a pentagram, each served to represent one of the five elements: water, fire, earth, air, and spirit. And if my mother was invoking geomagick these mannequins had to be more than simple dress dummies. The amount of shimmery particles I could see running between all five was too evenly distributed to suggest my mom used them randomly.

One of the mannequins wore an unfinished black corset. Three of the mannequins were bare. And the last, located near the hat-making supplies, was draped with a length of peau de soie. The fabric hadn't been there the last time I was here, then I remembered Beryl, Kostya, and my aunt had come to the work-shop looking for the filaments de la mer for Gosia. One of them must have draped fabric over the mannequin.

I took care lifting the silk off the dummy's armless shoulders and let it float to the ground behind me. Plain muslin covered and shaped the female form, from the upper thighs to the neck. On the back of the neck was an inverted triangle the height of my thumb. I moved clockwise to the next mannequin. This one had another triangle, point up. I continued checking the backs of the remaining three and found similar symbols on each: an inverted triangle with a horizontal line near the tip; an upward-pointing triangle, also with a horizontal line near its tip; the fifth one had a circle bisected by four lines, breaking it into eight, pie-shaped wedges.

My hunch was right.

And my questions compounded fivefold.

If my mother's magic had gone to nil while my father's magic was drained out of him in the Costa Rican jungle, what had she been doing right before she died?

I had fucked up. Serena was dead, and there would be no asking her...anything. What was it my father always said—well, one of the many things he always said? Something about asking all the questions you can before going in, because answers were information, information was a weapon, and sometimes information was more powerful than anything requiring a sharpening stone, a bullet, or an incantation.

9

I COULD STAND THERE. Be the sixth dummy.

That would get me nowhere.

I could continue through the building while the eyeglasses were synced to my magic and collect more patterns.

Or, I could stop, take a thorough look at the mannequins then go to the second floor and open all those drawers and doors and see what my parents might have hidden. And if none of that panned out, I could top off my magic, put the glasses on again, and keep looking.

Better to do this in stages or run the risk of forgetting what I'd seen. I reverse-engineered the bond to my glasses and the seal released. I folded the frames and set the glasses in their case, grateful to the sorcerer who had provided my magic with such a perfect tool. Once my eyes adjusted to the daylight and to seeing objects, not the spaces between those objects, I shook out my arms and legs and cracked my neck.

I examined the black corset more closely. Nothing about it screamed "Killer Corset" or that it had a magical purpose; it simply looked like a beautifully made intimate garment for a person about my size—five-foot-two and curvy. I unlaced the cords and slipped the corset up and over the top of the headless dummy. The inside showed off how detailed my mother's work had been and when I held it up to the light, the stitching along the many seams glinted. Was it metallic thread? Spelled thread?

I rolled the corset inside out and tucked it in under my arm. Magic or not, it was going with me. I went over each of the other mannequins thoroughly, running my hands over their shapes, checking their metal stands, even knocking on the bodies to see if they were hollow or filled. Nothing seemed out of the ordinary. Not until I stepped into the middle of the pentacle and felt a low vibration of magic. Each mannequin turned on its three-legged stand to face into the center of the five-pointed star—to face *me*. The brass compass, elaborately decorated with more symbols than the standard E, S, N and W, clicked under my feet.

Pentagrams. The magic of invoking and of banishing.

Did Mom use them to help her find mates for her clients? Did she use them as portals? I had walked in a circle behind the mannequins, which could have been construed as me drawing a circle to contain the pentacle. I hadn't walked the lines that would form the star, but right now I had the feeling that if I did I would trigger a magical event.

Should I? I felt around inside my hip pouch and realized I had no weapons at all. I had the portal stones, a lighter, the squares of waxy tailor's chalk, and my glasses. Everything else was in the duffel bag on the second floor.

DOWNSTAIRS, there was no debate about which room to explore first. Mom's, with the hidden drawer in her desk. This one was oak, like the desk upstairs, only a smaller and simpler design. Crouching, I pulled out one drawer after the other, mimicking the lifting and unfolding movement recorded by the particles. I broke the handles off two of the drawers and managed to crack the dovetail joinery attaching the front of the thinnest drawer to both its sides.

I winced. I wasn't here to break shit, I was here to—*Oh.* The crack was a good thing. I grabbed the front of the drawer with both hands, gave it a sharp tug, then pulled it toward me and twisted the entire thing. Yet another click and the top of the desk raised, revealing a shallow space and a book. I propped the disassembled drawer against my thighs and reached for the album-sized tome with its matte brown cover.

Damn thing wouldn't budge. I left everything where it was and dashed to my duffel bag for a knife. Blood magic. My mother had keyed her grimoire to her blood and, at some point, had keyed me, Beryl, and Clementine to the book too. Because surely we were next in line to inherit her knowledge and because Moira Brodeur was smart. She would have known that something completely unexpected could happen to her and her daughters would need, would *deserve*, to have access to her knowledge.

Goddess, I was good at justifying my actions. I stood over the recalcitrant book, pressed the tip of the knife into my forefinger, and brought the swelling drop of blood to the deckled edges on the righthand side.

Nothing clicked, but something sipped and slurped, and I forced myself to not jerk my hand away. My mother's grimoire was thirsty and the more blood it drew from my finger the more the cover shifted and changed until a three-dimensional landscape appeared, with a pentagram at its center.

"Would you look at that," I whispered to no one. The book stopped pulling and let me go with a sigh. I reached to pick it up. This time it didn't resist, though it was heavy. I sat on the nearby chair, set the book on my lap, and went to open the cover. It resisted. I turned it in place, noticed one-quarter of the pages were now tipped with metallic red ink, and slid my thumbnail where those pages began.

The book opened.

For Alderose. Written in a strong, flowing script, in dark green ink with my April birthdate in numbers underneath. On the next page, a lengthy table of contents, also handwritten in green ink. Three of the entries pulsed as the ink went to black:

Elements of Unbinding

The Care and Use of Scarabs

A Map of France

Where to begin? I chuffed out a breath and went with the section on scarabs. I scanned paragraphs on their history and care and harvesting and went right to recipes. There weren't many. I only needed one, and the recipe titled *For the Scarab Eaters* had to be it.

Except I had none of the ingredients. No dirt from one of a handful of places in México. No handfuls of dried *Chrysina* beetles. No nothing, and for all I could remember, the moon was waxing not waning.

I flipped to the map of France and was rewarded with a topographical illustration rendered in bright jewel tones. In a hollow in the side of a mountain just outside of Chamonix, a blood-red fence twinkled like the ink had been made of crushed rubies. I zoomed in on that specific section with my phone, took a photo, then another of the entire map.

I decided against returning the grimoire to the desk where I'd found it. If my sisters came looking for the book, they wouldn't know how to manipulate the desk's drawers. I'd leave it on the much larger desk in the workroom, out in the open. My sisters could figure out what was required of them in exchange for its opening.

I did a quick tour through the kitchen. It was deplorably bare and depressing. Memories hadn't been made here, at least not for me. Mealtimes in the Brodeur house weren't family times. I remembered having to forage, following the example of the chickens cooped in the backyard. Shaking off the memories, I revisited the front room.

People had gathered here. I had seen the evidence in the pattern worn into the plush carpet and the faint record of movement streams. My glasses hadn't shown me anything I felt I should have a second look at. I tugged on the beaded pull of the one lamp I'd turned on and closed the door behind me.

Back again in the third-floor workroom, I set my duffel near the door and emptied it out. I munched on handfuls of the dried fruit and nut mixture while I considered what to take with me, plugged my charger into a nearby outlet, and checked my phone for messages.

Malvyn. Maritza. Malvyn again. And Leilani.

I shouldn't have done that. If I listened to their voices—especially my cousin's—there was a chance I'd waver.

But maybe I *should* listen. Maybe they had information that would benefit my mission. I tapped the phone against my thigh. I'd finish getting ready, then I'd check.

I set the phone facedown, switched out the high-fashion sweats for my second-skin leather pants and began to slide my smaller knives and daggers into the reinforced pockets. I got angry all over again that the fae who captured me and Clementine in the underground cavern had tossed a couple of my favorite blades into the water.

Crap. I'd forgotten to grab a backpack. I jogged down one flight and opened the door to my father's closet. Black gear in high-tech fabric littered the floor in the closet. I chose a nearly new backpack, unzipped all the pockets, and shook the thing upside down. Nothing fell out and when I squeezed the other packs, they felt equally as empty.

I did a quick search of what was still on hangers and found

an all-weather jacket that would keep me warm and dry. It even had a hood. Stepping into the foyer, I opened the hall closet door. The contents assaulted my senses and my memories. I had to take a step back when I noticed the shoulders and sleeves of Mom's coats, the hints of color from scarves looped around the hanger hooks, the pile of hats and basket of gloves on the shelf above the bar. And my mother's perfume—or maybe it wasn't perfume, just the lingering scent of things she handled every single day that left their residue on her skin and in her clothes. Iron, chalk, silk, and linen, and something else my unskilled nose couldn't name. I had to reach high for one of the baskets and found a pair of gloves I couldn't resist. Celery green leather lined with soft brown fur, hand-stitched and like new.

That was it. Any more and I would get sucked into the maw of Memory Lane. Upstairs, I rolled my socks and underwear tight and stacked them in the main compartment of the pack along with the corset. First time I'd ever added sexy lingerie to a go-bag. The side pockets got the refilled water bottle and the rest of the snack food. I felt for the gold torc at my throat. It was so light and comfortable I'd barely noticed it during the day.

Jamming Fen's mossy, felted cloche on my head, I shouldered the pack as I stood, snapped the jacket closed, and patted the pockets to make sure I hadn't dropped a glove. Temperatures in the Alps had to be colder than Northampton this time of year.

I was ready.

"Mom, help me out here," I whispered, swiping clammy palms over the jacket and assaying the layout of the room. The brass compass in the center had to be the portal and it was time to walk the five lines of the pentagram to see if that would activate it. I started at earth—Chamonix was located in the mountains—and continued, touching each mannequin until I returned to where I began.

Nothing. I slipped my hands into the leather gloves and

retraced the five lines, touching each mannequin with the gloves. I hoped the dormant magic in the room would notice my mother's presence and my blood connection to her.

I walked the circle outside the dress forms and placed myself directly over the compass. That last bit did it—or did...something. Magic rose from the floor, encasing my boots and my legs the same moment I heard the chirp of an incoming text.

My phone was by the door. I'd forgotten to check the messages.

And I couldn't move my legs.

The nausea-inducing pull of a portal activating had me breathing in and out through my nose, fast, like a rabbit. The pull lurched. All movement stopped until I was tossed into a cold, undulating wave that pummeled me from all sides before landing me against rough bark.

It was dark. I was facing a tree, up close and quite personal, inhaling air that didn't smell like the portal deep in Boston's Emerald Necklace Parkway, or the one at my uncle's estate. I wasn't sure what to do, until a quiet, forced cough sounded from the other side of the trunk and a naked faun appeared to my left.

I'd forgotten about the prevalence of fauns as portal guides, especially in Europe.

"Bonsoir," he said.

"Hi," I answered.

He sniffed the air and sidled closer. "American. Did you not think about the time change before you left?" The points at the tops of his ears were hidden by long, tight curls, as were most of his horns. There was nothing hidden in his gaze. Brown lasers searched me up and down, darting back and forth between my chest and my throat.

"The portal activated before I was ready," I said, folding the collar flaps closed to hide the gold torc. "I'm not sure where I am."

"You have arrived in Chamonix. *Beinvenue*. What did you do, aggravate a member of the Portal Guide's guild?" One eyebrow arched as a lascivious smile curved through the opposite side of his mouth.

"I—" This guy did not need to know my business. He agreed, waving his hand in front of his face.

"Never mind. It's late and how you got here is not my problem. Where you're going next is. The Du Blanc Academy for Druidic Training is one stop away. You'll land in the courtyard of a small castle—it looks abandoned, but it's not. Ni'eve has a contract with the fae to keep it glamoured."

"I'm not looking for any druids," I said. I stopped clutching the tree and adjusted the backpack. I hadn't had time to clip on the stabilizing waist strap. "I'm looking for a man named Lionel Vigne."

A debate played out across the faun's rugged face. He finally stepped away from the tree, planted his hooves, and crossed his arms. I had a few seconds to be distracted by his physique. "Eyes up," he snapped. "There's no portal I can give you access to that will take you to his castle."

"Then how do I get there?"

"If you were invited, you would have been provided a key." He sized me up again, this time much more slowly. "Were you invited?"

"I—" I grabbed at the other shoulder strap.

"You weren't invited," he stated. The faun lowered his voice and bent forward from his waist. "Have you lost your mind?"

"I'm looking for someone connected to Lionel Vignae," I said.

"And you think the one you are looking for is at the Imperator's *fortress*?"

A slight breeze lifted the hairs that had been pulled free of Fen's hat. I pressed my hand to the top of my head as a soft pop-

pop sounded behind the portal guide. He grabbed the tree, hissed out *Merde*, and disappeared. I mimicked him, slapping my hand against the bark and fumbling for the special portal stones.

Which were in my pouch.

Which was in the backpack.

Two figures solidified from either side. Both men were dressed in somber matching suits and superior attitudes, and both moved with equal speed. My upper arms were in their single-handed grasps before I could breathe out or get a good look their faces. They squeezed my arms and lifted until my toes scrabbled on the uneven ground. The most primal part of my brain froze. I couldn't reach my knives. I was prey.

10

I REGAINED consciousness lying on a hard surface on my right side. I'd drawn my knees into my chest and my hip was numb. Gathering the blood clogging my throat, I opened my eyes and spit out a gob.

Pain radiated across the back of my skull and throughout my body. Something had happened after I was nabbed. My elbows were locked behind me, my arms were numb, and metal circled each wrist. While my magic started to groggily assess the content of the metal touching my body, I tried to call up details about the two men who grabbed me, and whoever might have hit me.

I didn't get very far. Footsteps announced I had a visitor. Fragmented memories said this visitor had a different gait than the one who'd done a number on my head. Strong, cool fingers loosened the bite of the restraints and a chin pressed against the side of my skull. "Do whatever is asked of you," the man said. "You have one ally in here and that ally is me. I can get you out if I have access to you, and I will only have access to you if you cooperate."

I struggled to turn. I wanted to see my alleged ally's face. Though they'd loosened my restraints, they hadn't separated the wrist bands from the bar keeping my hands apart. I hesitated, then rolled over my arms to my other side and got both legs to the edge of the slab.

The squarish room was empty. A chunk of bread, an apple, and a small round of cheese sat on a cutting board on the smaller bench beside me. A toilet was hidden by a half wall, and beside it, a shower head and a metal sink. Parallel to the wall to my right was a cot with a mattress, bedding, and a pillow. The legs of the cot were bolted to the stone floor.

No windows, only more stone walls and, directly in front of me, a jailhouse door of floor-to-ceiling metal bars. I could see a narrow walkway and a continuation of the same stone beyond. If there were more cells, I couldn't see them from my vantage point. Pale light leaked in from horizontal slits a foot or so from the ceiling, where dark wooden beams and wide boards completed the medieval castle look.

Go still, Alderose, whether you are the hunter or the prey. Map your surroundings as though your life depended on it. Because one day, your life will depend on your ability to function in the midst of confronting your worst fear.

My current situation wasn't my worst fear by any stretch, and if I could get my arms in front of me I could wash the blood off my face, swish water through my mouth, and better assess the situation.

Everything around you is a potential weapon. The longer you're in, the harder it will be to escape.

I wished my father had done more good guy, bad guy role-playing with me. He could have hired one of his bounty hunter buddies to throw me in a cell and wish me luck. Sitting up straight, I scanned my body. Everything hurt. Nothing was broken. I stood, wobbled, and sat right back down. Tried it again with more concentration and made it to my feet.

My bare feet. Someone had removed my boots and socks. Twisting my arms, I squatted, wiggled my butt, and got my arms in front of me. I could work with the wrist bindings, now that I could see them. Only, trying to figure out how to escape wasn't supposed to be a priority. I was here to find the fae who killed my father and hurt my sisters.

I took care of my body's needs and waited for my ally to return. The toilet flushed automatically and the sink had a single faucet. I ran the water, ducked my face under the stream, and cleaned out my mouth. Stepping away, I shook my head to get the water out of my hair.

Fuck. That hurt. A lot. Everywhere inside my skull, especially at my temples and behind my ears, banged loud and hard. I pressed the sides of my fists against my forehead and waited for the pounding to stop. With no more light beyond the slitted windows, I laid on the cot and tried to sleep.

"WELCOME to the heart of Clan Vigne. Well, one room in her many-chambered heart." Words punctuated by a dry laugh alerted me there was someone else inside the cell. Their voice was sharper than my faceless ally's. I had my back to the visitor, with the rough wool blanket drawn up and over my shoulder. I could pretend to be asleep, or I could roll over and see who had joined me.

I stared at the individual rocks in the wall close to my face, and catalogued the sets of scratches. More than one inhabitant had marked their days, or marked some other aspect of the capture, and now it was time to play the game. I shoved the blanket down my legs and went through the same awkward rolling and pushing to get myself to sitting. My hair was in my face and I couldn't see. Before I could ask for help, leather-covered fingers brushed the stragglers behind one ear, then the other, carefully repeating the motion until no strays were left.

"Arnaud, my chair."

I recognized the auburn-haired, freckled-face man stepping into the room as one of the men from the portal tree. Arnaud held a high-backed, carved wooden chair with a padded, velvet seat in front of him. He placed it on the stone floor, facing me and the cot. The silver-haired man standing to the side tapped one chair leg, and another, and sat.

The ageless, aristocratic face appraising me had to belong to Lionel Vigne. He tested the single pearl button on each wrist of his dove gray gloves. The leather was so thin I could see the man's veins.

"Would you like to tell us what has brought you here, ma petite sorcière? Or should we play a guessing game?" He raised his arm. Arnaud slipped the top loop of my backpack onto the man's fingers and took a step back. "Indulge an old man. I shall look through your satchel and tell you what I think. Life holds fewer and fewer surprises as we age and your unexpected arrival has been quite the surprise."

I hadn't spoken. I didn't get the sense the man seated in front of me really cared to hear my voice. I finally said, "I like games."

"Oh, I do too. Correct, Arnaud?" Arnaud nodded. "But humor me. Allow me to examine your belongings, perhaps make up a story. I enjoy stories almost as much as I enjoy games."

He wiggled the water bottle out of one side pocket and the plastic bag of dried fruits and nuts from the other and set them on the stone. Other exterior pockets were explored with caution. He came up empty, until he unzipped the main compartment, pulled out my hip pouch, and set it on his lap. The backpack was left to slump against a chair leg. The man hefted the pouch and grinned. "And what do we have here?"

He palmed the plastic bag with the pieces of tailor's chalk and handed it off to Arnaud. He flicked the top of the vintage lighter off and on repeatedly before snapping it closed, and when he came to the drawstring bag with the portal stones, he grinned again, like a kid at Christmas who'd just figured out what was in the biggest box.

The man rolled one of the stones between his fingers, held it to his nose, then licked it. "Blood. Whatever this is has been keyed to a specific individual. I am guessing that individual would be you?"

I didn't say anything. He was back to pawing through the hip pouch and I was waiting to hear his assessment of the glasses. Those were the only item left. He took out the specially molded case and handed the hip pouch to Arnaud, who put the stones, the lighter, and the chalk back inside.

"Are these your reading glasses?" he asked, studying the transparent frames. "Or do they help you to see something else, something beyond what is right in front of your face?"

He held up the glasses, not allowing the material to touch his skin. "I know the sorcerer who made these. Very skilled. Very, *very* skilled. And very, *very* expensive." He carefully refolded the earpieces, placed the glasses into the case, and again handed it over to Arnaud. "It would be a shame if they broke."

Leaning to the side, not looking at what he was doing, he reached into the backpack and brought out the corset. The garment seemed to delight him, until he brought it close to his face and examined the lining. He spread the corset over his thighs, rubbed his finger over the seams, and tapped the tiny label.

"Even now, she disturbs my peace." He ironed the silk with his leather-covered palms then carefully folded the corset in half, slowly drawing the ribbons through his fingers as he spoke. "You will wear this corset to dinner at my table. We dine at seven. Arnaud will assist you with bathing and will bring other items for you to wear." He stared hard into my eyes. "Please do not speak. There is nothing I wish to hear from you until I have had a chance to consider what confluence of planets and stars has brought you and this to me at this point in time."

He stood, dropped the folded corset onto the chair, and left. Arnaud returned the hip pouch to the backpack, re-zipped everything closed, and set the bag in the narrow hallway. "I shall return with Guillaume to bathe you."

Arnaud and Guillaume. Fen had mentioned both men, saying Lionel made Guillaume do the hurting. Guillaume and Arnaud and a woman named Linette. I looked forward to the next set of steps in this dance.

I'd been around enough fae to know that the glamouring used by both Arnaud and the man I assumed to be Lionel Vigne was good. They looked...different, the kind of different that would make curious humans stop and admire the refinement in their features and an inexplicable, unnameable...something.

But to my knowledge, I had never met a vampire.

A SECOND MAN appeared in the hallway with Arnaud and waited for the fae to unlock the bars. He didn't look at me, he didn't say anything, he just closed the section of bars behind himself, unbuttoned his white shirt cuffs, and rolled up his sleeves. I rubbed my feet one at a time against the gritty surface of the stone floor and made a connection to the ground below. I used that connection to temper my magic; it was way too early to start a fight.

He looked at me from beneath a hank of dark hair and gestured for me to stand. Together, he and Arnaud worked as a team. They unzipped my leather pants, rolled them over my hips and down my legs, and had me step out. My underwear followed. Guillaume shackled my ankles and attached those rings to a rod that would keep my legs apart. Occasionally, one or the other's shoulder would bump against me. The vampire was less gentle than Arnaud, who was efficient with his movements and clearly unmoved by my request that he go more slowly when he tried to undo what was left of my tangled braid.

"How did you get the blood in your hair, witch?"

"I was going to ask you that question," I said. "I figured you two roughed me up between the portal tree and getting me onto that super comfy rock slab."

"It wasn't either one of us," Arnaud said, shaking his head.

The vampire circled his arm around my neck from behind as Arnaud freed my wrists and stripped off the all-weather jacket I'd taken from my father's closet. When the fae saw the vest Maritza made, replete with my uncle's iron filigree work, he took a step back and pointed at my chest.

Even the best glamouring couldn't protect Arnaud from iron's ability to hurt his kind. Guillaume didn't say anything, just undid the side zipper, pulled the vest over my head along with my stretchy bra, and reset the restraints. He then raised my arms and connected the bar between the wrist rings to an overhead hook. Stepping aside, the two held a muted conversation. Arnaud set the carved wooden chair nearby, placed two white towels on the seat, and set soap and shampoo on the stone tiles.

"I shall return with the clothes the Imperator requested." His departure was marked by the clank of metal on metal. Guillaume came to my side. Out the corners of my eyes I watched him disrobe with efficient movements. He draped his clothes on the end of the cot, then reached past me to press his hand against the wall. Even in the dim light, I could make out the muscles in his upper body and the smattering of fine hair under his arm.

So far, every one of their movements was manageable. I could read the back and forth of a long relationship in the silent looks and gestures Arnaud and Guillaume passed back and forth. And I was beginning to build a story about Lionel Vigne and his quirks.

The water coming from the showerhead had warmed. I let it flow down my arms and over my belly and back, drawing the heat into my body. Heat made the metal inside me more pliable and while I chaffed to provoke my captors, I was the one in chains.

Guillaume suddenly pressed his mouth against the side of my head. "You should know the walls have eyes when I am around," he murmured. "The Imperator likes to watch me interact with his guests."

The moment he spoke, I knew the vampire was my ally, the one who'd come into the cell the first time I woke up. He pushed my head forward, holding the back of my neck until my hair was soaked then pulling me back roughly.

"Ouch! Fuck, Guillaume, I think I've got cuts and bruises back there."

He didn't apologise, only softened his grip. Reaching for the shampoo, he drew me against his front. He was shorter than Arnaud, which still made him a lot taller than me, and his front was as warm and inviting as a stainless steel sculpture. The back of my head bounced off his sternum. I whimpered again. "Try not to overreact to anything I say, and please try to go along with what I must do."

"Can you at least stop pulling my hair?" Under normal circumstance, I enjoyed having someone else wash my hair and massage my scalp. Guillaume's touch was a blend of violence and eroticism, anger and desire, pain and more pain. I tried to go along with it. "How do you know me?" I asked, barely moving my lips.

"Your blood smells like your sister's."

I froze. "Which sister?"

"She has short hair. She was wearing a green gown when we met." He guided my head forward again, gently this time, and rinsed the shampoo out of my hair. When that was done, he took the soap, lathered his hands, and scrubbed my body, starting with my arms. His hands swept over my breasts and lingered on my waist. He followed that by pressing himself hard against my ass and whispering, "I am so, so sorry" into my ear. "I had to injure your sister to keep up the charade," he added. "But I made certain she would not die."

Guillaume's confession reignited the sisterly feelings that had driven me here in the first place. I went to respond with a heel to his groin. He crouched, and grabbed my ankle. His short hiss reminded me to lock it down, and when he stood and spun me to face him, I mouthed, *Fuck you*.

He circled my throat with both hands and brought me close. His voice was so low I barely caught his words under the steady hammering of the shower. "Sixty-eight days, witch. Sixty-eight days until I am free. I have served a cruel master for almost two-hundred-fifty years and if you so much as *hint* that I have put my life on the line for you and your sister, I *will* kill you, no matter how entertaining he thinks you are."

He stepped away, the hardness in his eyes echoed in the water-splattered planes of his body, and dried me off with one towel. Unhooking my arms, which were almost numb, he had me lean forward while he squeezed the water out of my hair. Once I straightened, he looked me in the eyes—his, a pale blue sheltering sky to my earthy dark brown. I answered his question with a nod. Hearing steps outside, he pressed his chest to mine and turned my back to Arnaud as he drew the metal bars open.

"Did you enjoy the Imperator's gift, Guillaume?" the fae asked.

"Very much," Guillaume said, turning on the forced charm as he lifted my chin and placed a tender kiss on my lips. "I shall be certain to thank him."

11

"We've been told to dress her in this." Arnaud let the hanger of a gown bag swing from his finger. "I'll wait in the hall until you're finished, then I'll escort the witch out while you ready yourself for dinner. You should know he's expecting a show tonight."

"Then a show is what we shall give." Guillaume's grin was tight. He let the tip of one of his upper fangs press into his full lower lip just as the persistent lock of dark brown hair swept across his forehead. "I refrained from sampling our guest so he might witness her first bite."

"If I'm a guest, does that mean I can leave? And how do you know I've never been with a vamp?" I asked, summoning a bit of bravado. Guillaume shook out his shirt, put it on without doing up the buttons, and quickly drew on his pants. More of his hair fell across his face.

"Aside from a few scars from knife wounds and a possible case of childhood chicken pox, your skin is as unblemished as Mont Blanc after a fresh snow."

Arnaud placed the dress bag onto the cot, unzipped it, and left the cell. He took up a spot in the hall just outside after locking the door and pocketing the skeleton key. I unwrapped the towel covering my torso and handed it to Guillaume. Being comfortable in my skin was one of my superpowers. The more I practiced, the better I did under duress.

"Are you going to undo my shackles?"

"Sit on the bed."

I swung one leg forward at a time and sank onto the thin mattress. The vamp crouched in front of me, undid the bar and the ankle cuffs, and set them aside. Damp curls formed at his nape, and in the hairs on the bit of his belly I could see in the shadows cast by his shirt.

"Now?" I lifted my arms. He shook his head.

"You're new here," he said, resting his elbow on his knee. "Your muscle tone and the shape of your scars tell me you not only know how to fight, you probably don't like to lose. You've been invited to dine, not to brawl."

"Is the Imperator a betting man?"

He ignored my question and helped me stand. "Turn around," he said. Facing the wall, my shins against the frame of the cot, I sucked in a breath as he stepped close once again and pressed the corset to my belly. He leaned back, drew the garment around my ribcage, and began to restring the laces. When the corset was snug, Guillaume bent me forward, allowing my breasts to fill the demi-cups. I straightened and exhaled when asked. He finished tying me in.

"Turn to face me. Lift your foot." Stretchy, cherry red silk hissed against my legs and over my butt. Guillaume adjusted the soft elastic at my hips and around my legs.

"It's cutting me a little," I said, wiggling against his hand, testing him. He gripped my inner thigh and ran one finger between the silk and my sex. The movement was almost clinical.

"Lift your foot again. And the other one." The vampire drew a floor-length skirt up my legs, had me turn again, and fastened the waistband in the back. I could see my bare legs under the sheer layers of black and red silk netting.

"Arnaud. Come here. I have something for you." I tried to twist. Guillaume wrapped his other arm around my waist and pulled me against his front. "Have you ever tasted a witch?" he asked his cohort.

"I prefer the taste of you, Guill." Arnaud moved in next to the vamp. I couldn't see what they were doing but it sounded like they were kissing.

"Are the two of you part of tonight's performance too?" I asked.

"If the Imperator wishes."

"Will I be allowed to wear shoes?"

"There's a pair of heels in the bag and a brush and something for your lips."

"Have either of you seen my torc?" Guillaume swayed as the fae moved away. This time, Arnaud didn't leave the room. Instead, he drew the chair closer and relaxed into its padded back.

"You'll see your torc later." He reached over, found the hairbrush, and handed it to Guillaume. "Do you mind if I watch?"

"Not at all."

Arnaud stared over my head at Guillaume, who was attempting to get the brush through my damp, tangled hair. "We'd get to dinner faster if you let me do that," I said.

"We are under orders to keep you in restraints and we always follow orders. N'est-ce pas vrais, mon vampire?"

"Oui," Guillaume leaned forward and whispered against the side of my exposed neck. "Oui."

Arnaud continued to watch the vampire's every move, even handing him a length of velvet ribbon to tie back my hair. He also pulled out the tube of lipstick. "May I?" he asked.

Guillaume answered for me. "It would be her pleasure."

The fae unfolded his legs, towering over me as he uncapped the jeweled tube and gripped my jaw. He tilted my head to one side, and the other, critiquing the shape of my mouth and my décolletage with his gaze. "Open up, witch."

He traced the curves of my upper and lower lips, sweeping the creamy lipstick in short strokes to fill in between the lines. Satisfied, he leaned back, pressed his thumb to the skin above my breast and lifted until my nipple peeked over the top of the corset. He brushed the lipstick around the aureole, smudged it with his fingertip, and repeated with the other nipple.

I held my breath. My lips and nipples felt like they were heating up. I'd been caught up in Arnaud's and Guillaume's flirting and hadn't thought to ask to examine the lipstick before it was applied. There had been nothing in my training about how to manage magically induced sexual arousal.

"That's enough, Arnaud. Don't overdo it. He prefers the coquette, not the slut," Guillaume cautioned.

Arnaud's grin was wicked. Suggestive. "I'm picturing her as an aperitif," he said. "An—amuse bouche. I'll help with her shoes. You, go dress."

Guillaume left without saying anything more.

"Speaking of shoes," I said to Arnaud, "Where are my boots?"

"Your boots and knives are—somewhere." Arnaud waved his hand in a vague direction that conveyed my blades were anywhere but here. He reached inside the bag again and withdrew a cloth sack. He took his time loosening the strings and teased out one red, high-heeled platform pump and another.

"Never been worn," the fae added.

"Is that your way of assuring me these weren't taken off a dead body?"

"As if." He shuddered, lowered himself to my height, and

brushed grit off the bottom of one foot, wiggled the shoe on, and cleaned off my other foot.

"Can you let me do this one? I broke these toes a few times and—"

Arnaud *tsk-tsk*d. "I will hold the shoe. Those heels could put out an eye and I like my eyes."

"It's like you read my mind." I used the blanket to wipe the sweat off my foot and carefully inserted my foot. Arnaud grabbed both of my ankles in one hand, slid his other hand behind my neck, and brought our foreheads together. And here I thought my attempts at humor were softening him up. I couldn't move as he pinioned the side of his face against mine and spoke against my jaw. He drew his words out.

"You may think this is a joke, witch, getting dressed up for the Imperator, being invited to dine with him. It is *not* a joke, not to *any* of us. You will mind your manners. You will do as you are told and answer any questions he asks. If you do not, he will distribute his displeasure amongst *all* of us—which will not endear you to *any* of us."

"How many like me are in here?" I whispered.

"That is not for me to say."

"Is everyone here a prisoner?"

Arnaud shoved my head away and glared at me, his blood-less lips pressed together. I remembered what Guillaume had said about the room having eyes when he was with me. I had no way of knowing if the same was true for Arnaud.

"Could you help me to stand?" I asked, making my voice overly loud. Once I was on both legs I could adjust the skirt and the fit of both shoes and compose myself.

"One more thing," Arnaud said. He shook out a plum, light-weight cape. "The hood will hide your face. I'll tie the ribbons at your throat and wrists. The Imperator has a newfound obses-sion with undoing his dinner guests." Arnaud drew the sides of the cape away and waited for them to float back toward my body in an artful way. Then he fluffed out the hood, positioned the front edge to obscure my face, and tied loopy, lavender satin bows at my throat and at both wrists.

He stepped back. "You're perfect."

My legs were cold underneath the sheer layers of the skirt. My head still hurt. Neither the fae nor Guillaume had said anything aloud about how I might have gotten the cut on my scalp. There was no mirror to confirm my hunch, but I felt like I was dressed as Little Purple Riding Hood with extra plump lips on her way to see the wolf. The roiling in my gut said Lionel Vigne was a much wilier wolf than any shifter I'd ever known, and that Guillaume and Arnaud were second tier at best. I pulled my magic in toward the tender places in my belly and shielded my fear.

Arnaud steered me ahead of him, locked the bars behind us, and took hold of my elbow. Most of the time we were able to walk side-by-side in the narrow hall. I didn't regularly wear heels this high and navigating the uneven stone floor took concentration.

We passed the occasional closed wooden door or empty cell. The only sounds were echoing steps and our breaths, until we arrived into a high-ceilinged rotunda. Guillaume had his back to us. I gasped as I stepped into the space. Pillars ringed the curved walls, creating a covered walkway. Carved statues of mythological creatures punctuated the inner area and the floor was covered with a layer of fine sand.

Arnaud jerked my arm, preventing me from messing up the pattern raked into the sand, and turned to face Guillaume's side. Sandwiched as snugly as I was, the current passing between them was palpable—though it wasn't balanced. Arnaud, who was stroking the front of the vampire's black dress pants, was exuding way more desire than was coming his way.

Guillaume interlaced his fingers with Arnaud's and whispered, "Later, mon coeur. We have all night." I glanced at their hands. Arnaud's skin was shimmering much the way Sidan's did when she was aroused. The vampire's didn't change color. Or temperature, as I found out when I placed my shackled hands on theirs.

"And all of tomorrow."

"And the next day," the vampire added.

"And into forever."

I offered to move aside so they could ease the tension—and so I could continue to read their body language. Arnaud laughed, stepped away from me, and noticed the purple cape needing rearranging. "Then we would *all* be late for dinner, which would displease the Imperator."

"And pleasing him is a priority," I stated.

"You learn fast, witch. Having someone new and fresh at the dinner table will ease some of the...stress that has been accumulating."

"He's not planning to eat me, is he?" I lowered my voice so it wouldn't echo around the circular room.

Guillaume's jaw twitched. "We should go."

Three sets of shoes sent echoes bouncing across the room as the two men guided me around the periphery. My shorter stride tap-tapped alongside their solid beats. Entering a wide hallway, I almost stumbled as my heels met a rug. I had to insist we slow down.

Guillaume stopped our trio. He took a turn adjusting the position of the cloak's hood, checked the bows at my throat and wrists, and saw that the lipstick on my mouth and nipples hadn't smudged. I passed muster and onward we went, once he and Arnaud had adjusted each other's cravats and waistcoats. We didn't stop until two unglamoured fae in matching dark charcoal business suits opened a set of doors to the dining room.

Plush, lush, and stuffed to the gills were my first impressions of the room. Layered carpets muffled sounds. Framed paintings were stacked two and three deep against high walls covered in artwork. The massive table, set for eight, was bare of candles and centerpieces. "We wait here," Arnaud said. "It pleases the Imperator to choose the night's seating arrangement."

"Are there others coming?"

A commotion at the doors answered my question. I turned slightly to see Lionel enter the room, followed by two women and two men. Lionel had added a tailored dinner jacket to his attire. The guest nearest to me was the faun who'd met me at the tree in Chamonix. He was adorned with gold chains, starting with one around his neck and attached to another slung low around his hips. More gold tipped his horns and pierced his pointed ears. It took me a moment to notice the slender leash linking him to the woman at his side—and the chains linking the rings around his wrists to the chain at his waist.

Adorned was the wrong word for the faun. Fettered was better. His handler was adorned. Her see-through dress was made from material similar to my skirt, her nipples were highlighted, as were her lips, and her jewelry was plentiful and delicate. She had a wide smile on her face, unlike me or the faun. Metallic bits dangling from the chains at her neck and wrists added music to her sashay.

Lionel was at the table, directing the seating. "Linette, you and the faun are over—here. Talon, I would like to see you and Sheenah" —the Imperator affected the stance of a curator, resting his weight on one leg and propping his chin in his hand — "at the far end of the table. If she changes again, there's more room for her on the floor."

The lower half of Sheenah's mouth was encased in a muzzle and her eyes... I tried not to shudder in reaction to her eyes. She looked drugged, but she dutifully shuffled behind the man named Talon and waited to the side of her designated chair.

"Arnaud. Guillaume. Bring the witch here. The three of you shall sit near me." Lionel adjusted the chair to his left, bringing it close enough it almost shared his position at the head of the table. Arnaud guided me over, then went to Lionel's right. Guillaume took the chair to my left.

"So cozy, yes, like family?" Lionel asked, taking his seat. And like a family of tumbling dominos, the seven of us sat one after the other. The faun, the female shifter, and I shared similar expressions. Or, lack of expressions. None of us looked to be a variation of our kind, one of the rarities Lionel was purported to collect. As servers approached with covered plates, I wondered if Fen had ever been invited to dine at this table. I also wondered how I was going to eat, what with my hands held eight inches apart by the metal bar and the cape's hood slowly slipping over my forehead toward my nose.

Maybe me eating wasn't the point of the dinner.

Someone came up behind me and adjusted the position of my chair until I nearly faced Lionel. The Imperator's eyes stayed cold as his mouth formed a smile. He reached for the ribbon at my neck, and gently pulled the ends until the bow slipped into nothing. He slid his fingertips across my cheeks, spread the hood, and guided it off my head. The weight of the fabric pooled down my back, exposing my shoulders, neck, and throat.

"The gods were generous with your assets," he purred, trailing his fingertips over the tops of my breasts and across my nipples before sweeping his fingertips underneath one breast.

I shivered. One of the servers paused between Lionel and Arnaud, leaned forward, and placed an oval platter in front of Lionel. The table was wide enough the covered dish could sit lengthwise without pushing anyone else's place setting away. The server made no move to lift the cover. Instead, he and the others kept their gazes on their tasks and began to remove the covers over our plates.

I didn't recognize the arrangement of foods on mine. My nose said fruit. My eyes saw succulence, juices beading along the surface of each bright piece. My fingers ached to help themselves to the bounty as my mouth watered. Lionel noticed. If I'd never understood the phrase *dark chuckle* before, I understood it now.

He lifted a piece of fruit shaped like a section of citrus and brought it to my lips. He squeezed as I opened my mouth. The fruit's tang hit my tongue as juice drizzled down my chin and onto my chest. Lionel slipped one end of the fruit into my mouth, along with his finger, then withdrew slowly and wiped the piece over my skin.

My nipples pebbled and my lips began to turn fiery as they had when Arnaud applied the lipstick. I couldn't stop my body's reaction. Though the fruit was cold, the Imperator's fingers were colder, and his eyes were frozen. I stayed still. Quiet conversation started up. Guillaume asked something of Talon, perhaps something about the woman with the cage across her mouth.

Their words didn't register with Lionel. He leaned over me and licked the juice from the upper curve of my breasts. His tongue was warm, he groaned, and within that rumble rising through his chest, whatever glamour he'd walked in with dropped away.

Not even Sidan had let me see her in the full glory of what, of who, she was born to be. Lionel's transformation gave the three other fae at the table permission to drop their glamour as well. Juice dried on my skin as I watched Arnaud, Talon, and Linette grow taller, more filled out, more imposing. The tops of their ears elongated, following the curves of their heads. Their hair grew lusher, the colors shifted into more otherworldly hues of what they wore behind their human masks.

Lionel pressed his hands against the arms of his chair and closed his eyes. Guillaume brushed the back of his fingertips across the side of my thigh and stared at Arnaud—whose heavy-lidded gaze was reserved for the vampire.

Sheenah stared straight ahead.

The faun batted his eyelids at his handler. Linette tugged on the chains attaching him to her. There was definitely something going on underneath the table.

"Now, we eat."

12

LIONEL MOTIONED for Arnaud to undo my bindings. Though my appetite had fled the room, I made myself try everything on my plate. The fruit—or whatever it was—brought a pleasure to my tongue I'd never experienced with food. Food sated hunger. Though on occasion, eating had become an erotic experience, one that usually ended with me and my date asking for the bill and a to-go container. This was not like that. This food nourished an unmet longing in my soul. Tears mixed with the sticky juice. My face and throat were a mess.

Guillaume moved a piece of something on his plate to mine and mimed me eating, when Lionel turned his attention to Arnaud. I popped the slice into my mouth. My emotions calmed. The starved poet inside of me shut up about the soul's deepest desires and instead asked for more of whatever it was the vampire had shared. He shook his head once.

Lionel made a show of decanting a waiting bottle of red wine with a faded label and dust on its shoulders. He poured the wine into his glass, approved it, and gestured for the closest server to take the decanter around the table.

When he lifted his glass, everyone quieted. "Tonight, we

celebrate. The guest seated beside me was not originally invited to this dinner. However, she has brought a collection of personal objects with her and it has put me in the mood for a *game*. Each of you shall choose one of her belongings and whomever tells us the most intriguing story about the object, wins." He sipped from his glass and set it on the table. "I imagine you're all wondering what the prize is?"

He slipped his metal-tipped fingers underneath mine, brought me to standing, and had me turn in a circle. "The witch shall be yours for the night. Or mine, if I decide my story is the best." Polite laughter followed, along with tapping on the wine glasses.

I followed him down as he sat. He waved over two servers and had them remove the lid from the platter. Arrayed across the polished silver were some of my belongings. The pouch of portal stones, the pieces of tailor's chalk, Fen's little hat, the lighter, my mother's pale green gloves, the gold torc, and the special glasses. Their case was missing.

One server picked up the platter, waited for Lionel to signal who would choose first, then walked around the table and presented the tray to Linette. She extended one blade-tipped finger and hooked the brim of Fen's hat. The faun chose the pouch and Guillaume went right for the gold torc.

"I knew you would pick that piece," Lionel said, leaning forward. "Given your fascination with precious metals and pretty necks." Guillaume batted his eyelashes at our host, who refused to take anything off the tray until everyone else had chosen theirs.

The server bypassed me and stopped at Arnaud's chair. He chose the eyeglasses, picking them up with a delicate touch. Talon had to coach Sheenah into making her choice. She finally placed one hand on the gloves and nodded. Talon set them bedside her plate then examined both the lighter and the tailor's chalk and chose the lighter.

The server presented the lone remaining item to Lionel, who picked up the small, square plastic bag with two fingers and blatant disdain and deposited it near his water glass. "Who would like to begin?" he asked, settling back into his chair and swirling the wine in the crystal goblet.

"I shall," Linette said. She slipped her hands inside the felted hat and rested her elbows on the table, sending her myriad bracelets tumbling down her forearms. Flicking her wrists, she rotated the hat a few times, flared her nostrils, and took a long inhale. "This hat smells of marsh water, willow, horsetail, and dead snails. I would venture to guess it belongs to a will-o'-wisp who has most recently spent time in" —Linette leaned in again and sniffed— "the west coast of Canada."

Dread tickled my back. I hadn't been with Sidan long enough to know a lot about the fae and I was wishing I had paid less attention to her body and more attention to the info drops she sprinkled throughout our conversations. Seeing the earlier transformation right here at the table affirmed fae wore glamour amongst themselves, and that every single one I encountered, from Sidan to One-Becomes-Three, to the four at this table, had a built-in weapons system at their literal fingertips.

Linette directed her gaze toward the opposite end of the table, staring at me for a beat before settling on Lionel. "Now, why this *witch* had it on her head, brother, I do not know. Nothing else carries this particular scent and now that I think about it, this same hat has made an appearance at our table before. Weren't we in possession of a marsh creature and her offspring until five, ten years ago?" Linette stopped twirling the hat, wrinkled her nose as she took one last sniff, and set it on the table.

Talon took his cue, dipped his napkin into his finger bowl,

and rubbed the cloth over both sides of the lighter. Linette set a candlestick closer to his plate. They examined the surface together. Talon flicked the lighter's cap and hit the flint. A steady flame glowed as the scent of lighter fluid wafted the length of the table. I had known that smell since childhood. "The original owner is—or was—left-handed," he began. "And as we can now see, engraved on one side is a set of initials and on the other side, we have a beetle. Its wings are semi-open."

Talon flicked the cap closed and used his napkin to polish the entire surface of the lighter. "The beetle is a symbol of those who inhabit both the earth and the sky. One could say it is a symbol of transition, of moving from life to death. It is a worthy icon for one who is equally comfortable travelling those two realms." He brought the lighter closer to his face. "The work is quite detailed."

"And the initials?" Lionel asked. I knew the answer, though the lighter had been so tarnished I'd had no idea it was personalized with my father's insignias.

Talon flipped the lighter. "Capital H. Lower case d. Capital V."

"I hired a man with those initials. Once. He was not able to complete the job." Lionel sipped his wine and directed his comments to Talon. "He insisted on refunding me the deposit. Though I was willing to let him keep it given the expenses he incurred." He leaned sideways, toward me. "Perhaps our guest is related to the Scarab Eater?"

I declined to answer. I was trying to stay alert to the nuances of the game the fae were playing and what the possible outcome might be. Plus, it didn't seem like Lionel expected me to say anything because he'd already moved on to the next player by the time I lifted my gaze off my hands.

"Sheenah is very new to us. Less than a full day. She is a

jaguar shifter and we are just beginning to learn of her talents. Tell us, mon petit chaton, about the object you chose."

Sheenah took her time sliding one glove then the other onto her hands. Her movements were protracted, slumberous. Whether that was her nature or because she was drugged, I couldn't tell. Though I decided she was under the influence of something as soon as she began to speak. "The bonds between mothers and daughters are being tested," she said, slurring her words. "As when someone tries to fit their big paws inside a glove made for a much more delicate hand." The seams of one glove burst as Sheenah's fingers developed polished black claws and the skin on that arm darkened to a mottled black. "The leather absorbed the scent of the witch who made these gloves. I recognize her smell." Her head rolled to one side of her high-backed chair and she waved the hand with the busted glove in Talon's direction. He helped remove it, setting it on the table when Sheenah shook her head, and leaned in to hear what she was saying.

"Sheenah would like the Imperator to know she is sorry she ruined the glove."

Lionel stroked the plastic bag with the pieces of tailor's chalk. "Does she know the identity of whoever made the gloves?" he asked.

The shifter shook her head and spoke. Talon again repeated her words. "She says no, though she adds we have recently come in contact with two witches who are related to the maker, Imperator."

Silence floated above the table and through the room. Lionel and Linette conversed in a wordless back and forth. I sensed they were discussing my mother. Or my sisters. And possibly another missing piece or two I couldn't grasp. I re-grounded in my magic, coaxing the metal floating through me to stay alert.

The faun opened the pouch and pour out the stones. He

slowly rolled them between his fingers, examining their surfaces, and began to theorize about their origin once Linette and Lionel turned their attention outward. "These are magic-made, not naturally occurring. I believe they are portal stones." He spread his thighs and invited Linette to make herself comfortable in his lap. She did, and he smiled his pleasure, wrapped his free arm around her and brought her mouth to his. Their kissing was sexual and loud and impossible to look away from.

His performance—because it dawned on me that's what it was, a performance—entranced the rest of the table as his arousal made itself obvious. One strap of Linette's gown slipped over her shoulder, exposing flesh plumped and coddled by intricate undergarments. The faun, still rolling the three balls in his fingers, bounced his leg, making Linette's breasts jiggle. He continued to act the lascivious buffoon, right up until the moment he spun to face me, begged my forgiveness, and slammed all three stones against his chest. He disappeared, swallowed by the chair. Linette disappeared with him.

Instead of becoming enraged, Lionel laughed. Just...laughed. Hard enough he had to withdraw a handkerchief from his pocket and wipe his eyes. A wide-eyed Sheenah barely moved. Talon, Arnaud, and Guillaume followed Lionel's lead, though with less exuberance.

"How is it that faun *always* manages to find a way to escape?" Arnaud asked, slapping his hand against the table. "This time he's gone *pouf!* and he's even taken my mother. It'll be days before we hear from her."

"Let them enjoy their little adventure," Lionel said. He settled back into his chair and re-crossed his legs. "She deserves a few days in bed, or in his tree, or wherever they've gone off to." He turned to me. "Do you know which location those the portal stones were keyed to?"

"No, I don't."

"Where did you get them?"

"I...picked them up on one of my trips. I really don't remember where."

Lionel lifted a single eyebrow. He didn't believe my story. I wouldn't either, given how I squirmed in the chair. He returned his attention to Arnaud and Guillaume. "That leaves the three of us. Would either of you care to go next?" He almost sounded bored.

Arnaud spoke. "You should go, Imperator. There are times when the most mundane objects hold the most interesting stories."

"Yes, well," he said, picking at the small, clear plastic bag, "the only discernible markings on this piece of tailor's chalk were made by the witch to my left. Do you sew?"

"I can. Though I am more adept with knives than with needles."

Lionel laughed, a full, throaty response to my confession, and tossed the bag onto the table. "This time you speak the truth, witch. Arnaud, tell us about the glasses."

"These," he said, resting them on his uplifted palm, "are a thing of beauty and exquisite craftsmanship. Spectacles were designed to help us to see more clearly. At least, that is their *assumed* function. One could surmise the witch has less than perfect eyesight—or wields magic that is enhanced when she wears these." He opened the opalescent earpieces, slid the glasses onto his face, and looked up and down the table and around the room. He seemed on the verge of removing them when he stopped and stared at Guillaume, then at me. The lenses enlarged his pupils, eyelids, and lashes, giving him an almost comical appearance.

The fae pressed his fingertips to the earpieces, drew the glass forward, and folded them. "Ley lines. Desire lines. These glasses were likely created for the purpose of reading the past and then tuned to fit the witch's specific gift."

"Did you see anything...interesting, Arnaud?"

His gave a half-smile and shook his head. "Nothing I wasn't expecting," he said. "But when you add all of these objects together, along with the knives we removed from her clothing, I think we can only assume one thing."

"And what is that, my friend?"

"She is a spy."

Lionel turned to me. "Have you come here to spy on me, witch?"

Pressing my lips together, I shook my head. I had been piecing together my back story as the evening unfolded. "I came to Chamonix to visit The Du Blanc Academy for Druidic Training. I have no idea how I ended up here."

Arnaud hissed and turned to Lionel. "We were summoned, Guillaume and I, to the portal tree. The faun said—" He smacked the table with the side of his fist. "That *asshole*."

"You've come here to train with Ni'eve du Blanc?" When I nodded, Lionel asked, "Why?"

"I'm bored," I said, shrugging. I had to come up with a more plausible explanation. "There's been some recent changes within my family's business and I've been unable to find a place within the structure for my particular skill set."

"And what would those skills be?"

"Crowd control. Tracking large groups of people."

"Humor me." He ran the tip of his finger around the rim of his wineglass. "Explain to me how a twelve-year training with the world's most renowned druidess complements your expertise in crowd control?"

Fuck, this was challenging. Especially because I was loopy from the lingering effects of whatever was in the lipstick and the strange food. "Well, actually, Ni'eve approached *me*." Yeah, that sounded good. I could riff on this. "My magic—which is enhanced by the eyeglasses—allows me to track Magicals all over the human world. Ni'eve has a project she's been considering implementing. She contacted me, and here I am." I slouched in my chair and snugged the sides of the cape over my legs. The fortress or castle or whatever this place was, was drafty and even with the layers of rugs the floor was cold. "I always carry extra portal stones with me, the gloves and the hat I picked up at a thrift store, and the lighter was given to me by a warlock who liked cigars.

"The glasses are one of a kind and as you deduced, they were created for me by a skilled sorcerer. And you were right. They were *very* expensive."

"I collect one of a kind...objects. It's too bad the glasses work only for you." Lionel stopped trying to get his goblet to make sound. "What is your full name?"

I dipped back one generation of my mother's side of the family, before my mother and her two siblings moved to Canada and the US and changed the spelling of their last name. "Alderose Bordador, at your service."

"Well, Alderose Bordador, until I confirm your story with my friend Ni'eve, you shall remain in your room." He planted his hands on the arms of his chair and stood in one fluid motion. "And your things shall remain with me. Though I had hoped for something more entertaining tonight, Guillaume. A chance for you to sample another witch's blood, perhaps enjoy the opportunity to compare?" He turned on his heel and clasped his hands together. "That's what we shall do, a blood tasting!"

"When?" the vampire asked.

"Now! Come, let us convene in the smaller drawing room. Arnaud, have them set a fire. Talon, bring your cat. Keep her on the leash. And you, witch, let us see what your blood has to say."

.　.　.

AT ONE POINT, after first entering the dining room, I'd worried Lionel would order me splayed out on the enormous table. I'd allowed a sense of relief to filter into my body when my story about the school for druids gave him a moment's pause. It helped my case that the portal-keeping faun had misbehaved in the past.

Stepping into the smaller room drained any confidence I was going to get through the next part of the evening unscathed. Plush velvet divans and wide, overstuffed armchairs were arranged in a rough circle in the center of the room. One end opened to a massive fireplace, now set with crackling logs. The other wall made me suck in my breath. "You like to play, Alderose?" Arnaud asked, pointing to the display of restraints. "We are able to accommodate many desires."

"Not so much," I said. "I bruise easily."

At a wave of Lionel's hand, Arnaud removed my purple cape and guided me to a low, armless lounge near the fire. I welcomed the warmth. Guillaume came around behind me and gestured for me to raise my arms.

"I'm going to switch your restraints," he said, "for something more comfortable." He unlocked the metal bar and shackles, drew sheepskin-lined straps from behind the back of the lounge, and snugged one around each wrist before moving toward my legs. He had me place one foot on the floor and secured that ankle to the chaise. My other leg was left free.

Walking behind me again, he withdrew the small pillow from behind my head. I adjusted my position, which caused my spine to arch, lifting my breasts. Guillaume slid his hands behind my head and gently drew my hair to one side, twisted it, and tucked it behind my arm. Taking my head once more, he turned my face to the fire and called for Lionel.

"She's ready, sire," he said, stroking the exposed side of my throat.

13

TAKE AWAY the restraints and I could have been a model posing for a painter, or a slightly tipsy dinner guest feeling the effects of one too many glasses of wine. But the straps were going nowhere and neither was I. And that intrigued and challenged me.

Arnaud finished lighting the candles in the room, turned off the table lamps, and closed the double doors. Guillaume passed by and returned with a fringed blanket. He draped it over me before turning to the side and unbuttoning his dinner jacket and the cuffs of his shirtsleeves.

Talon guided Sheenah close to one of the chairs, where a sumptuous, tufted pillow rested on the floor. She arranged herself on top; her handler removed her muzzle and left the collar and chest piece buckled on. Admonishing the shifter to be good, Talon settled behind her, one end of the leather leash securely wrapped around his hand. Sheenah stared from the shadows, past me and into the fire.

The stage appeared to be set for Lionel's show. Guillaume moved toward my couch. I tensed when he first touched my bare skin. He lingered at my cheek, stroking his knuckles in little circles. His fingertips grazed my opposite arm. My exposed knee. I fought to not feel anything, and worried that some twisted aspect of my family's curse was playing with my touch receptors. How could a part of me...*like* this?

"Guill. Let us see you," Lionel said.

"Yes, sire." Guillaume shifted the position of the couch, exposing more of me to the fire and showing his front to the audience in the room. He loosened his wide cravat, pulled it away from his collar, and undid the top two buttons of his formal shirt. His languid movements were at odds with the steely expression in his eyes.

I had to continue to play along. I drew the warmth coming off the burning logs into my body. I let my head drop back to where I could see Lionel and the others upside down, leaving my throat exposed. My pulse beat a rhythm and directed it to the vampire.

Guillaume took a lengthy pause, then swooped in, pressing his hands to my wrists and opening his mouth against the side of my neck. His lips were firm and absolutely confident. He bared his teeth, rubbing them across my skin and tendons. I made myself relax, focusing on the solid upholstery underneath my back, only reacting when the vampire nicked my collar bone with his tooth.

Lionel gave a contented sigh. "So direct."

Guillaume moved down the length of the lounge, pressing against the side of my thigh, tracing his hands along my arms to rest to either side of my chest. He held me there, scraped his mouth over my breasts, and hovered above one. His breath on my skin had the same effect as a waft of cool air. "Here, sire?" he asked.

"Lower."

The vampire took his hands to my hips, rose above me, and parted the flimsy layers of skirt. I lifted my head to watch. His eyes were heavy-lidded and his hair obscured most of his forehead. Behind me, Lionel clapped. A heavy body landed on the rug and padded toward the lounge. Sheenah nuzzled my leg before licking my raised arm. It took a moment for me to register that she was in her cat form and that I had just been licked by a jaguar.

Guillaume stroked her fur. "Shh," he murmured, when she rested her head next to my hip and whimpered. "Shh. She'll be fine."

Pressing his hands against my inner thighs and pushing my knees farther apart, he struck fast, sinking his fangs into the soft flesh. Only, the teeth didn't sink so much as land and meet the layer of resistance my magic had created. The vampire added more pressure, sending in one fang after the other with four soft punctures until fire burned through my inner leg and I couldn't move. I didn't want to move. I wanted to keep watching, assessing, playing with this wholly new combination of danger and desire.

Rolling my head to the side, I caught sight of the big cat rising onto her back legs, one paw on the lounge, the other on its way to my corseted chest. She slashed downward, whimpering, ripping the fabric, catching my skin, and nicking Guillaume's shoulder. Someone jerked her leash. The vampire stopped, pushed me further into the cushion, and slowly withdrew his fangs. Leaving his mouth pressed against my skin, he licked once, twice, across the punctures and settled back on his heels. Deep inside my upper legs, where tendons met my pelvic bones, I started to shake. The most private part of my body wanted to run from the room.

"She is tasty," Guillaume said, more for Lionel's benefit than for mine. "Thank you for gifting me the privilege of first bite, sire."

The Imperator had come up behind Guillaume and was stroking the vampire's hair. "It is my dearest hope that you will stay past the end of your indenture, Guill. You have been like a son to me and a witch's plump thigh is the least I could offer you this night."

Guillaume tilted his head back, exposing his own pale throat. "And what is the most you could offer me?"

That seemed to delight Lionel more than anything. He cupped the vampire's jaw and said, "Spend the night with whomever you wish. Take two guests. Or three. Though if you choose the witch, I must insist she remains confined to her room. And chained."

"I choose the witch. And thank you, sire." Guillaume rested his cheek against Lionel's hand.

"My own son could learn a thing or two about fealty from you. Perhaps it is time for me to rethink Odilon's ascension to Scion and see how he feels about sharing the responsibility of leading Clan Vigne into the future."

"I am simply honored to be here with you in the present."

I watched these two, listening for what was left unsaid in their back and forth. My leg was throbbing, I'd just been bitten by a vampire, and I was far more drawn to the unfolding drama than into feelings of being forced to participate against my will.

LIONEL INSISTED a different set of fae lead me back to my room. These two took their assignment seriously. They didn't speak, they walked even faster than Arnaud and Guillaume, and they didn't appear to care that their fingers bruised my arms and their blade-like nails nicked my skin.

They locked the bars and left me on my own. I soaked the

corner of a towel, washed my leg, and looked for warmer clothes. The vest with the iron embellishments had been stuffed into the underside of the pillowcase. The backpack I'd nabbed from my father's closet hadn't been returned. My leather pants and zippered jacket were draped over the back of the padded chair. I patted the pockets, already sure they'd been emptied of weapons. Aside from those two items I had the underwear I walked in with and the silk pair I had on, the damaged corset, and a useless bit of froth masquerading as a skirt. Not even an elastic to keep my hair out of my face.

I sat on the bed and removed the shoes. Lionel had reacted to the stitching on the inside of the corset. What was it he said...? *Even now she disturbs my peace.* Tucking the blanket around my legs, I reached behind me, undid the knot and loosened the ribbons, and tugged on the corset until the back was in the front. I finished undoing the ties, pulled it off, and rested the thing on my lap while braiding my hair.

One problem solved. Two, actually, because now I could breathe freely. The corset no longer held my ribs hostage. I couldn't read anything in the same seams and threads that offended Lionel. I held the garment closer to my face. The dim light didn't make anything clearer. To my eyes the stitches looked like most every other set of stitches made by a competent seamstress. Still, I folded it with reverence and set it on my bed.

Shivering, I slid my arms into the jacket and zipped it up, used the toilet, and stripped off the skirt. Placing one foot on the chair, I examined the inside of my thigh where Guillaume had bit me. Four punctures, sealed, with only the barest hint of bruising. I had been able to feel him pull on my blood—and that sensation was not unpleasant.

I wanted Guillaume to return. I had questions. Could he taste the magic in my blood? And could my magic travel into him? Or did some...power, or substance inherent to vampires neutralize any magic in the blood they consumed?

I finished inspecting my skin and was on my way to getting a leg into the leather pants when the vampire returned. He'd changed into a pair of dark jeans, a rumpled V-neck sweater, and slip-on shoes. A large skeleton key dangled from his finger and he'd draped the purple cloak over his arm.

"I thought you could use this to stay warm," he said. He inserted the key, opened the bars, and tucked the key into his pocket. "And you're not going to need those." He tossed the cape onto the cot and pointed to my pants.

"So I *am* your gift for the rest of the night?" He nodded, stepped closer, and lowered the zipper on my jacket. I circled his wrist and held fast. I remembered he'd said the room had eyes that liked to watch him, but I needed to know more about the script he was using for the rest of the night's performance. "What's that mean, I'm your gift? And you owe me an explanation."

"I'm going to give you that explanation," he said, then added in the barest whisper, "And hopefully get you out of here."

I held on to his wrist while he used his other hand to separate the end of the zipper and spread the sides of the jacket. He barely brushed his fingertips over my breasts before sliding his hand behind my back and drawing me closer. I shifted my grip on his wrist and jerked that arm behind him, a move I used enough I could have added a knee to the groin if I wanted. Guillaume was too tall for me to head butt.

He winced, lifted me onto my toes, and brought his forehead to mine. "Believe me when I say I do not want to get into your pants, Alderose. I have your sister's wand, and I have a map for you. I want you to go home, gather the best people you know and bring them here to save me and the rest of Lionel's prisoners. Am I clear?"

"Very clear."

He lowered me enough my feet were on the floor, slid his hand between my underwear and my butt, and muscled his other arm out of my grasp. "Vixen," he said, much louder.

"Asshole."

Guillaume grabbed my jaw. "Just living up to your highest expectations."

Something happened between his confession, and him taking hold of my jaw. Guillaume's hold on my backside softened. His whole body relaxed, starting with his legs and travelling up his spine. He played with his lower lip with one of his upper canines and in slow motion, his knees folded. He landed on the cot, drew me on top of him, and crashed his mouth onto mine. His touch, centered on his hold on my ass and extended to his lips, exuded desperation and throttled desire, and he smelled like the world's finest cologne.

I pulled the front halves of my jacket apart and kissed him back. I let longing and guilt and fear and frustration take the reins and drive me wherever they wanted. And what they wanted was more of the vampire. I searched the front of his jeans for a zipper. The damn things were button-up.

"No," he said. "That's taking this much further than I had planned."

"Yeah, this is a leap even for me."

He started to move, groaning low as he did so. "This is all I want, witch."

I stayed in character as I looped my arms around his neck to give myself better access to his ear. "Does Lionel expect you to bite me?"

He nodded. "He's watching me. Us."

"Then we better make this believable," I said, pressing against his chest

"I—I should probably bite you soon."

"Can you bite my neck this time? I know it's kind of clichéd, but—" I was going to say one more thing when I heard the snap of his fangs and felt the four tips enter the side of my neck in one smooth, practiced bite.

Time did one of those stopping things before the vampire wrapped his arms around me, flipped me over, and dumped me onto the bed. He drew up onto all fours, trapping me on the narrow mattress.

Trembling, I relaxed my arms. Guillaume swiped a fingertip through the blood on my neck and began to draw lines on the bared skin of my chest and belly. He bit me again, gently this time, and continued to mark my torso. I thought it was vampire thing, or one of his kinks. I lifted my head to see he was using my blood to draw me a map.

He gazed down from the dark and spoke. "Pretend to faint. I'll close the wound to your neck and you'll be fine. You'll want to have the cat's scratches on your ribs looked at."

I let my head loll to the side. Guillaume finished drawing on me and when he licked my neck he whispered one more thing while he closed the front of my jacket and slipped something behind my head. "Please don't forget me."

The vampire said something else, only I couldn't make out what it was as he stepped away from the cot, adjusted his clothes, and left my cell. I stayed still, listening to his footsteps disappearing down the winding hall, and waited. The blood had to dry fully and I had to wrap my head around what just happened. I reached behind me to see what he'd tucked under my head.

The vampire had returned my torc. And if the torc hadn't been emptied, I might have a way out. Guillaume had said Lionel liked to spy on him when the vampire was with the guests. He hadn't said anything about Lionel wanting to spy on me. I imagined he did and gave him my best drunk witch act.

I rolled onto my elbows and knees to keep from smudging the map. I couldn't see much of anything until I scrabbled off the cot and stood closer to the bars and the weak light coming from the far end.

Guillaume had marked the location of a portal tree, placing it outside the door at the opposite end of the hall, to the right. On the other side of my chest he'd drawn a cage, a tower, an F, and an X.

I felt for the torc and emptied it into my palm. Six beetles and six stones. I palmed two bugs and three stones, and set two of the portal stones under the cot where the floor and wall met. Leaving them here meant I had the option of returning to the cell.

The beetles went into my mouth. I didn't overthink it, I just chewed, swallowed, and paused again, listening for anything in the hall or on the other side of the wall.

Nothing.

I snapped the torc around my neck. Beryl's wand was right where Guillaume said he'd put it. I slid the familiar piece of polished and embellished wood down my front and stood near the bars. A slight power surge went from the underside of my tongue to my fingertips. I curled my fingers around the cold, fae-cast metal tight in my hands, intending to whisper, "Open," when the bars swung outward.

Guillaume hadn't locked me in. Either that or one tiny beetle packed a lot of magical punch. I kept with the drunk act and stumbled down the hall to the outer door. It too opened without resistance and, right there, like it was planted near the high walls of the castle out of sheer laziness, was a single tree with sturdy branches looming up into the night sky.

Ten steps brought me to its base. I held the third compact gold portal stone in my fingertips and paused. Where was I going? Should I go home, to New York, where I had weapons and access to databases? Should I go back to the island, to my uncle's house, where I had access to family and their accumulated knowledge and connections? Or should I choose Northampton?

Indecision will be your downfall, Alderose.

Not tonight, Dad.

14

I LANDED on my ass in the middle of a circle of mannequins. Sunlight streamed in through the third-floor windows, providing at least one of the mannequins with a wicked, head-less shadow. I'd lost track of how many time changes I'd gone through over the past I-didn't-know-how-many days and I was confused. The duffel bag I'd left near the door was missing. So was my phone and the charger. Which meant someone had been here.

It also meant I had no weapons, no immediate means of communicating anything to anyone, and no clean underwear.

Also, I had no cash. No credit cards, no debit card, no...nothing.

Think, Rosey. Think.

I rolled to my back and raised my arm. The jacket sleeve fell to my elbow. Dust motes slow danced around my spread fingers.

Embrace your gift.

Embracing my gift hurt. A recent conversation with my aunt, held on this very rug with my sisters in attendance, echoed through my head.

Your mother was one of the most powerful witches I have ever met. She was a born Triple Binder, one who carries the gifts and burdens of the Cult of Three. After she birthed her third daughter, her powers coalesced. Had she lived, I think she would have inducted you into her business, so she could share the joys and the burdens of her work.

Centuries ago, our early mothers dedicated themselves to the Fates, the Morai—Clotho, Lachesis, and Atropos. Clotho spun the thread that marked the beginning of a being's life. Lachesis measured the length of the thread—a length that could not be altered no matter how powerful the being. And Atropos cut the thread created by her sister, marking the end of each being's life.

Moira embodied the work of all three Fates. Because she was a brilliant witch, a savvy businesswoman, and wanted to focus on life rather than death, she turned her talents to love. To beginnings, rather than endings. She did not wish to carry the weight of making the final cut. As each of you began to show magical promise, your mother understood her gift had divided itself between her offspring. Alderose, you wield the sword, am I correct?

Yes, Tía, I wield the sword. And the knife and sharp objects in general. And though I knew a well-tended blade cut best, no matter if it was cutting through silk or skin or bone, I'd recently felt the sting of a vampire's sharpened fangs and had the realization that going after bad guys wasn't always a clear cut proposition. Games had to be played. Magic could also be played. There had been no need for me to reveal my entire hand my first visit to Chamonix.

Chamonix and Lionel Vigne.

Chamonix and Guillaume.

Revealing my entire hand would mean calling up my magic, and calling up my magic hurt. The weightless motes floating in the air left no impressions on my skin, but to fully embrace and accept the metal in my cells would be akin to turning those dust motes into the thinnest razor blades. Every pass over my skin would leave a burning mark and a drop of blood if I chose to complete the series of rituals that began when I turned fourteen. Was I too old at thirty-four to step into the skin that waited for me? Because continuing to work crowd control at conventions would be the far more secure, far safer, far less bloody route.

I lowered my arm, ran my fingers over where Guillaume had first bitten me on the inner thigh, then touched my neck. Two bites, both of which started out as performance punctures. One ended with clapping hands from a pleased, live audience. The second, in front of a hidden audience of one, ended with me understanding that a combination of sexual pleasure and physical pain was tolerable. I could imagine exploring that combination regularly.

If I chose it. Working with my magic would mean I would live with pain on a daily basis, at least for the duration of the rituals, because there was no cure for the Goddess-blessed gift of Unbinding once it was fully embraced by the receiver.

Which led me to think of my father. He never spoke of his gift in terms of how much pain he bore. Perhaps there was something in the Scarab Eater's mixture my mother developed that soothed my father's constant pain.

I watched the motes some more and waved my arm, bringing turbulence to the tiny particles and sending them eddying and swirling through the air. I would likely live longer than either of my parents because I could live out in the open amongst supportive kin and friends. I wouldn't have to exist within the shadows like my father or hide behind the façade of a retail establishment like my mother in order to carry on my work.

Decision made, I lowered my arm to the floor and closed my eyes.

"ALDEROSE. *ALDEROSE.*"

Sidan's face hovered over mine. She was looking impossibly beautiful in her sheer cloak of dust motes and sunshine and my overactive imagination. "Is that really the real you?" I asked, waving my hand in the air. Her very solid cheek bone answered my question.

"What is it with you and falling over and not responding to my messages?"

"I was in France. What day is it?"

"Friday, October twenty-fifth."

"It's my sister's birthday. She's twenty-eight."

"And what, you went to France to get her croissants?"

I laughed. "Sid, you have no idea."

"I have some ideas, Rós." She lowered her head and sniffed my neck. "You've been with a vampire and your metal levels are very high."

"My metal levels?" I rolled to my side and let her help me stand. My legs were wobbly.

Sidan released the blades within her fingertips and waved her hands over the front of my body. "Metal recognizes metal." She tapped the side of her nose. "You've showered recently using soap made from goat's milk and infused with lavender, both of which came from France. And your jacket—" She shook her head like she was disappointed in me.

"What about my jacket?"

"The inside of the collar has your blood on it and the evenly spaced bruises on your neck tell me the vampire who feasted on you got sloppy. What were you doing while they drank?"

"I was making out with him in order to save our lives." I looked down, then looked right back up. I wasn't going to feel ashamed about my choices. "Let me rephrase that. While attempting to make what he was doing look very real, my body has some very real responses—as did his."

"I did." Sidan swiped her empty bowl with another hunk of bread. "Which is where things began to get really interesting." She finished chewing and leaned back into the corner of the couch, one hand on her belly. "One-Become-Three is an assassin clan. There can be no more than one bearing that title at any given time, and there has been a succession of them throughout our history. I guess we could say she—they—are mythological figures come to life."

"So splitting yourself into two or three or more physical bodies isn't something every fae can do?"

"No. I mean, *I* can't and I don't know anyone else who can. There are fae who become really adept at using glamour, who can become invisible and maintain that state...indefinitely. I'm one. We're like elite athletes of invisibility, of—of blending in. But holding two or more selves within your One Self and being able to separate those selves so they move independently?" She swept her hand down her body, appraised one leg then the other. "One's enough for me. I have no idea how the splitting is done."

"Who would know?"

"That's next on my agenda. Unless you need me to do something else?" Sid nudged my foot with hers. "Do I need to be jealous of this vampire dude?"

"No." I swallowed hard. "But maybe you can help me process what happened. Because I need to know if you're okay with it, or—"

"Let's start with you telling me if *you're* okay with it."

I launched into telling Sidan everything I could remember, starting with standing in the kitchen in my uncle's house and overhearing his two employees talking and ending with my decision to come to Northampton rather than any other destination.

"I'm glad you decided to come here," Sid said. "I mean, I

would have looked for you at your place in New York, but I have no contact info for any of your family. It's been two days since I messaged you. I was getting worried."

"My stuff's gone and so is my phone," I said. "I have no idea who took it. And I'm sorry."

"You're forgiven." Sidan extended her hand to me and curled her fingers around mine. "So answer me. Are you okay with what happened between you and Guillaume?"

I squirmed.

Honesty, Alderose. Remember?

"I am," I said.

"Then that's settled." Sid dragged me across the couch and wrapped me in her arms and legs. "You've been through some shit, Rós. And I have a plan. You're going back to France and you're taking me with you."

"But—"

"Lionel Vigne is a fucking bad guy. Very. Fucking. Bad. Like, you have no idea how bad. You've seen *one side* of him, the side that wants to be amused and surprised. And now you've gotten involved with a two-hundred-fifty-year-old vamp who's been at Lionel's side since he was a kid. Guillaume wants to be free— and if you think he's the real deal, I'm willing to help. But I want to be absolutely clear here. My involvement is because of you" —she kissed the top of my head— "and whomever Lionel has caged up there in the French Alps. Those poor souls need us and anyone else willing to go up against him."

"So do we gather the troops now and storm the gates?"

She shook her head, threaded her fingers through the rat's nest in my hair, and held me closer. "Better it's just the two of us to start and the sooner we portal out of here the better. I have everything I need to stay invisible. And you should let your family know you're okay."

"Can't do that," I said. "They'll rush out here and I don't

know enough yet to fill them in on what's going on, let alone form a plan. Plus, they'll argue with me about going back to France."

I took a deep breath and let it out. "They're probably upset with me. My uncle and my aunt left voicemail. So did my cousin. I'm surprised they didn't try to get my dead parents to leave messages. And I meant to listen to the messages, but I got sucked into the portal. I didn't even have time to do a gear check." Even if my uncle and my aunt tried to talk me into waiting, I couldn't. Sid was right, the faster we got back to my cell, the better. I pushed myself to sitting.

"Then we should grab you some gear and get a move on."

"Do you think you could buy me some underwear? I've been wearing this pair for three days." I tugged the elastic waistband up my belly and pouted. I wasn't above flirting as a means to an end.

Sidan snorted. "The things I do for you."

I washed dishes and gathered a short paring knife from the kitchen and a couple pairs of scissors from my mother's workroom while Sidan was out. When she joined me on the third floor and handed me a three-pack of underwear, I was ready.

"How do we do this?" she asked, once I had changed back into the clothes I arrived in and zipped up the same jacket. Sid was bouncing on the balls of her feet and ready. So was I.

"Hold my hand," I said. "We're going to circle the room, then walk the lines of the pentacle. Twice. And hopefully we'll end up at that same tree in Chamonix."

"What if the faun's there?"

"Punch him," I said.

15

THE FAUN WAS THERE and Sidan punched him. Right in the nose. The faun didn't see her fist coming because she was already invisible when we arrived. He crumpled into a pile of horns and hooves and general hairiness at the base of the tree, and I reminded Sid that talking was a no-go.

We used one of the gold balls to return to my cell. The hallway was silent and the bars were closed. I dropped onto the bed and rolled to my side, my back to the center of the room, and pulled the blanket up and over my legs and shoulders. The reassuring weight of Sid's hand landed on my ankle steadied me as I slipped Beryl's wand, the paring knife, and the small scissors between the thin mattress and the metal bedframe.

This was a new experience, working with a partner who wasn't my father or one of my sisters. I had to treat this as an official case, as a mission, and though neither of us was in charge, I would defer to Sidan's knowledge in all things fae-related.

Also, as I had to remind myself more than once, we were here to gather information we could take back to my uncle, not run in, weapons held high.

It's mostly about the waiting, Rosey.

Got it, Dad. I had gotten adept at waiting. I wedged the pillow under the side of my head and concentrated on quieting my breath, slowing my heart rate, and listening for footsteps in the hall. I reviewed my weapons and where I'd placed them and touched each one in order. Ideally, I would have brought more. A lot more. And ideally, I would have kept them on me, within easy reach.

My gut tightened. I'd left the shredded corset in Northampton. I slid my hand over the sheet and felt for the long skirt I'd been forced to wear to dinner. I found it near the pillow. I'd have to make up something about the corset if anyone bothered to ask.

Sidan and I had left Northampton in the evening, maybe two hours max after I'd landed. Local time had to be around two or three in the morning. The deep silence in this part of the castle made it seem that everyone was asleep—until I heard dampened footfalls in the hallway.

Someone inserted a metal key in the lock and turned. I kept breathing. The bars were opened and closed. The lock clicked. Something landed with a soft thud against one of the cot's legs, a knee sank on the mattress, and a body larger and heavier than mine molded to my backside.

Sidan squeezed my ankle and stayed connected. Guillaume swiped my hair off my face and brought his mouth to my ear. "It is time to set things into motion, witch. And I have a confession to make in case I do not make it through to see myself on the other side of this prison."

I slid my hand atop his.

"I told you I hurt your sister, the one named for a stone."

"Her name is Beryl," I said.

"Beryl," he repeated. "Days ago, I accompanied Lionel to the demon realm. The queen was holding a ball. My master had heard rumor of curiosities living in her palace. He wanted to see them for himself." The vampire rested his forehead on our stacked hands. "He saw a child, the product of a demon and shifter. He also saw the child's mother, Sheenah, the shifter you met at dinner."

I nodded my understanding.

"The Imperator was making his decision as to which one he would bring with him—the child was unique but the mother could be bred—when your sister interrupted. This was your other sister, the one who is mated to the demon."

Clementine. And Laszlo. "How do you know it was my sister?"

"The connection is there in the smell of your skin and the look in your eyes. The three of you are unmistakably related. Though I have not tasted her, this sister said something to Lionel that diverted his attention off the child. Beryl arrived as they were speaking. Lionel ordered Arnaud to put her into a trance alongside the shifter. But we had to get out of the palace. Your sister conjured a bird from her skirt who flew her and the child to safety. We fled the palace under a group glamour. As we neared the vampire's temple and our portal, Lionel said another choice had to be made.

"He ordered me to drain Beryl and leave her to die. Sheenah shifted and tried to stop me, which is why Beryl was marked by both my fangs and the shifter's claws. That is also why the cat became anxious when I first drank from you."

I rolled onto my back and made Guillaume straddle me and duck his head in close to mine. "I have portal stones," I began. "We can escape together. I used one to leave after you drew the map."

"You left and came *back*?" he asked, astounded, capturing my head between his hands.

"Yes."

"But you didn't bring anyone to fight with you?"

"I brought my girlfriend. She's sitting on the floor at the end of the bed. Her hand is on my ankle."

Guillaume froze, then sank his weight onto me. "You confuse me, witch."

"You're not the first one who's said that. My friend is fae. You can't see her because she's made herself invisible. Tell me more about Arnaud."

"He has had my body. At one time, he might have had my heart. We are friends, more out of necessity than true kinship. He is not an unkind fae. But Linette is his mother. I believe he will always feel pulled to side with the Imperator. Though I could be wrong." Guillaume adjusted his position. "You brought weapons with you."

"How can you tell?"

"I smell the differing metals."

"Can you smell my friend?" He shook his head, now lodged against the side of my neck. His hair tickled my face and caught on my lips. "Tell me what you meant when you said it was time to set things in motion," I whispered.

"You need to see the cages for yourself."

"You know I believe you."

"Yes. But when you see what I have been witness to for decades, you will understand my urgency. Lionel's scientists are ready. You will never be able to erase the faces of those they have captured from your memory and because of that, it will drive you to help them no matter what happens." Sidan let go of my ankle. A moment later her hand rested on my forehead. She must have touched Guillaume as well. His body jerked.

"She is right here," he whispered.

"Yes, she is. Her name is Sidan and she has to stay invisible. Now, tell us your plan."

. . .

GUILLAUME WAS succinct and once he laid out his ideas, he left. Sidan rested her head on the pillow and stroked my hair. "My heart weeps for these creatures," she said. It was strange to hear and feel her without seeing her. "And I haven't even seen them yet."

"I'm worried for Guillaume. He's desperate for freedom. And he's right, we need to see the cages and the facilities for ourselves."

"It is no small thing to put yourself in danger, Rós. As it is no small thing to play the long game, as the vampire is doing. You have a role, one which may force you to offer your body or information or your skills with the knife in exchange for seeing the cages. Old fae like Lionel Vigne get tricky with age. His boredom makes him even more dangerous and difficult to please."

"Are you going to be okay staying here?" I asked. Guillaume expressed concerned that with so many fae in the castle, Sidan's presence would be felt, no matter how good she was at staying invisible. Sid agreed to remain behind inside the cell, though she suggested she might explore the halls. She promised to exercise extreme caution.

"I will be fine," she said.

"I'm going to try to sleep."

"I'm right here."

MY FATHER COULD MAKE himself fall asleep anywhere, anytime, in any position. He trained me to do the same. The next visitor to my luxurious accommodations made a lot more noise than Guillaume. I was awakened by wood striking metal, a voice announcing my presence was requested at the breakfast table, and the sight of a fae dressed as a nurse from my grandmothers' era, complete with a starched white cap and a short, navy blue cape.

"I've brought you clothes for the day," she said. She slid another dress bag between the bars, followed by a pair of white, practical shoes. "Call when you have showered and dressed. I shall be nearby."

"How much time do I have?" I asked. "And what's your name?"

"I am Nadège. The Imperator's mood is mercurial. I suggest you hurry."

"Let's see what's in dress bag number two," I mumbled, shoving the blankets to the end of the cot and planting my feet on the cold stone. Today's themed dress code was— "Naughty nurse?" A soft snort came from the direction of the bed. I shrugged out of my zippered jacket and the filigreed vest and peeled off my pants. The vest went back inside the pillowcase. Lionel or whomever was in charge of his guests' wardrobe had kindly added white pantyhose, high-waisted cotton underwear, and a vintage long-waisted brassiere in pale pink quilted cotton. I had to go with it. I braided my hair, started the shower running, and as soon as it had warmed, I scrubbed every inch of my body. I did that part for me and the others caught inside these walls, not for Lionel.

Dressing was interesting. I couldn't ask Sidan for help, and though I was sure she would have given me a running commentary if we were anywhere but here, she managed to stay quiet. I sat on the bed to roll the pantyhose and get my roughened feet into them without snagging the material. Lionel was definitely the type to frown on his nurse showing up with a run in her stockings.

Dirt. Stocking material and thick soles would create a barrier between me and the ground, but my magic required that connection. Leaning forward, I gathered a pile of grit from underneath the cot with the side of my hand. I pressed my foot onto it, curled my toes to gather more, and then got those stockings on.

Standing, I adjusted my ensemble, found a brush in the bag and a packet of hair elastics, and finished getting into the *required* character. Personalizing came next. I removed the end of the torc, dropped a couple of scarabs into my palm, and tucked them in one pocket. I palmed the embroidery scissors I'd stashed under the mattress and slid them into the other pocket. My mother's magic whispered along the edges of the blades to the pointed tips. I smiled at the gift of her presence.

Tapping on the cell's bars, I smoothed the front of the uniform and called for Nadège. She arrived in under a minute, looked me up and down and up again, and gestured for me to unbutton the front of the dress. I did. She reached through the bars to adjust the bra, had me re-button the dress, and declared me suitable for breakfast.

"Lift your arms," she said. She made the set of wrist restraints hanging from her belt visible and locked me into them before opening the door. "After you."

We followed the same route to the big room. This time, I paid more attention. I had to be able to navigate this section of the castle on my own, especially with one escape route situated through the door at the end of my hall and the portal tree outside.

Steps from the big round room, sunlight streamed in through paned windows in the domed ceiling. The light was sharpest at the top, with an optimistic blue sky above. I rubbed my upper arms. Cold air seeped up through the ground and in through the outer walls. My sensible nurse's shoes cushioned my feet; the hosiery provided little warmth.

Nadège led me to yet another room off the rotunda, a castle designer's interpretation of a breakfast nook. Only this one had another long table punctuated with vases of hothouse flowers and a view to the Alps outside diamond-paned windows.

"You sit here." She tapped one of the chair's finials. "Please remain silent. When the Imperator has declared his intention to dine with his associates, he requests there be no conversation until he has arrived."

On the back of the chair, between two carved acorns, was a folded cape in regulation navy blue serge. Set in front of my plate was a nurse's cap. I took the offered seat and waited for help to arrive. With my hands shackled in my lap, I'd have to spread my thighs, grab the front of the chair, lift my ass and pull to get closer to my plate. I doubted the move would have won me points for grace or style. I used the wait instead to assess the weapon-worthiness of the table settings and get the lay of the room.

Dull-edged butter knives and demitasse spoons weren't going to get me out of a castle built to withstand a siege. Still, I surveyed the room and its furnishings and used the angle of the sun to determine where in the castle we were located. As other diners began to arrive and take their seats, I sensed there was a theme to the day—and it wasn't escape.

Arnaud pulled out the chair beside me. Guillaume cleared his throat and helped move my chair so I could face the table. He was catching on that, as a six-feet-tall vampire compared to my five-feet-two-inches of witch, he didn't have to lift very much in order to get me moving in the right direction. He settled the chair gently and walked around the head of the table, placing himself directly across from me. His face was the epitome of neutrality. Both he and Arnaud were dressed in white lab coats, complete with crisp white button-down shirts, conservative ties, and name badges.

This was getting stranger by the moment. Nadège touched my elbow, released my wrists, and attached the left cuff to the chair leg. Her seat was farther down the table, alongside other similarly dressed fae with unfamiliar faces. A general straightening of spines and ceasing of fidgeting announced Lionel's arrival.

A wall of baby blue seated itself to my left. A folded stethoscope peeked from a breast pocket and a white T-shirt showed underneath the V-neck of the medical scrub suit. The wrinkle-free costume smelled of laundry detergent and a hot iron. A server stepped in to place the Imperator's napkin his lap. Other servers followed with bowls holding something that resembled a pink grapefruit. A spoon with teeth was placed to my right.

"Good morning. Please, eat." Lionel lifted his spoon, secured the fruit with his other hand, and performed a deft maneuver that separated a section. "Someone help her," he said, swinging his spoon at me before returning to methodically attacking his fruit.

Arnaud took my bowl and spoon and had the fruit in pieces in moments. "Do you need me to feed you?" he asked.

"I think I can manage." I glanced at Guillaume. Something I'd tasted the night before had given me a loopy, slightly drugged feeling, and I wondered if I needed to be wary of breakfast. He blinked. Trusting him, I ate, and when the fruit course was followed by a selection of pastries I chose two filled with something that resembled cheese and attempted to keep the crumbs on my plate, not my lap. Aside from the sounds of food and drinks being consumed, no one spoke.

Until Lionel ordered refills of everyone's coffee and tea and waved the staff over to remove our plates. "Today, we tour the facilities," he began, leaning back in his chair. "The new shifter is ready for her initial round of tests."

"Are we initiating the standard series on her," Arnaud asked, "or...?"

Lionel hesitated, more for effect than for any real hesitation.

"Yes. My enthusiasm for the feline's potential should not get in the way of proper procedures. The laboratory staff is prepared to take her through the entire sequence, serving to inaugurate the new facilities and show us where we might have need of improvement."

"And the witch?" a fae at the other end of the table asked.

Lionel set down his cup and saucer and enclosed my shackled wrist in his hand. "Do you mean this witch?" At the fae's nod, he continued, "I think we shall keep this witch's status as *guest* of the castle. I am very much looking forward to showing her our methods and seeing what she might contribute to our efforts."

He turned his full attention to me. "Your skill lies in Unbinding, correct? Or have I misread your dossier?"

Lionel Vigne had a dossier on me. I was not flattered. "That is correct."

"And do you require any special implements or weapons to perform an Unbinding?"

"What do you mean?"

"I intend to see you have everything you need in order to do a little something for us today."

16

I ICED my expression into place. Lionel's hand on my wrist meant he was sure to feel the rise in my heart rate. Even with all of my training, I captured the agitated beat a fraction too late. The Imperator flashed a sly grin and tightened his grip before letting me go. "Your scissors and knives will be made available for your use once we are inside the facilities."

He stood, effectively silencing any follow-up question I might have. Which I didn't. All I had was the sick feeling in my gut and the knowledge it wasn't because of the food.

The wrist shackle didn't allow me to stand. Rather than point that out to anyone, I swiped my fingers across the napkin in my lap and waited. As Lionel made ready to leave the room, some fae went to him more quickly than others. Guillaume waved to Nadège and pointed to me. "I'm coming," she said. "Please get her into her cape and hat."

The nurse worked my restraints. When she finished the vampire shook out the garment, set it on my shoulders, and asked me to lift my chin. He slipped bobby pins off the white cap before he set it on my head. As he worked, he maneuvered us so his back was to the crowd gathering by the door. He exaggerated his movements as he admired his efforts and whispered, "The coming hours will test you."

Guillaume turned on his heel, smoothed the front of his thigh-length coat, and adjusted his tie. "The witch is ready."

Nadège was my designated handler for the day. She gave my completed ensemble another look down and up before following the line of fae out the door. Guillaume left the room last. Conversation amongst those in front of me was subdued. Serious. They seemed to be comparing the merits of one system of testing over another and though my French was almost non-existent and I couldn't catch the specifics, I did paid attention to our route through the castle.

We passed through a set of high, carved wood doors at the end of a long hall and entered an echoing, cavernous space. The far end was completely open to the elements and a range of snowy mountain peaks. Thick cables attached to a massive pulley system swooped down and out into...air. We were going to descend into a valley via glass-bottomed cable cars held up by tiny metal lines. Lionel and two others stepped into the first one. Guillaume, Arnaud, Nadège, and I took the second once it slotted into place and made its way to where we waited.

I ground my heels and toes into the dirt inside my shoes and held on to the metal rail circling the interior of the gondola. "Keep your eyes on the horizon," Arnaud said. "Once you've ridden in these a few times you get used to it."

I refrained from asking how long it took to get used to seeing other Magicals in cages.

We landed in a similar, smaller terminal inside a building designed to look as though it belonged to the castle. I'd ridden alongside overdosing partiers in ambulances as part of my job in New York, and arriving inside the antiseptic building was a lot like that, minus the sirens and the distinctive smell of the city. Once we were through a heavy metal and reinforced glass door, the feel of being in a hospital continued.

We rode an elevator to the top floor, which was mostly one large room. Lionel's excitement was palpable as he waved his arm through the air and pointed out the obvious. "This is the play room. It is here that we will observe the offspring play and interact. There is an aviary for those with wings, and both salt-water and fresh water pools for those who are more aquatic by nature."

"You were able to move the tree, sire." Nadège's voice was awe-filled and hushed. "Does this mean—"

"It does. We have one of the druidess's tree witches in our possession. She practically *begged* us to take her in. We have verified she is of child-bearing age and that she is fertile. All that is left is to find a suitable match, a Magical with traits that will enhance her extraordinary gift. I am tempted to offer myself to the geneticists."

I wanted to know more. I knew of witches who had deep affinities to trees, but I had never heard of tree witches. And I shuddered at the thought of all the ways Lionel could further insert himself into the breeding program.

"Come, let us walk this floor, then we shall view the maternity ward and the neo-natal unit, followed by the laboratories." Lionel clasped his hands behind his back and led the way. The fae attending him seemed more concerned with watching their leader and anticipating his reactions than in listening to him practice his tour-guide persona.

On one hand, the massive room really did look like it had been created with the safety and happiness of small children in mind, while also providing them endless entertainment and opportunities to work with all the energy coursing through their little bodies.

On the other hand, the metal rings set into the walls at regular intervals and the occasional cage spoke to the room's true purpose. Any future inhabitant of this room would be the offspring of at least one unwilling genitor. And they would be a prisoner. Perhaps for the entirety of their life.

I circled the tree housed in a ceramic planter, with a thick metal hoop circling the base of its trunk. Symbols were inscribed into the metal, and the hoop itself was linked to a chain that went to a large ring embedded in the wall. No one objected when I pressed my palm to the tree's mottled bark. It wasn't all that big, and I ventured a guess it was a fruit-bearing variety.

"Apples," Lionel said. "All the druidic trees are apples of an ancient variety so old no one remembers their name. I may be forced to step in and add Vigne to the Latin nomenclature. Or perhaps simply call them...*Malus imperatorii*. What do you think, Guillaume? Arnaud?"

"A fitting way to mark a new beginning, sire." Guillaume sounded sincere.

"I agree," Arnaud chimed in from behind me as he mimicked my gesture and stroked his hand across the surface of the bark. "Not too rough, not too smooth. I have heard the druids who can shift their forms between humans and trees are particularly adept at serving unique sexual experiences to their lovers."

"Are you thinking of offering yourself as a candidate for procreation, nephew?" The chill creeping up my back at Lionel's words must have been felt by Arnaud. He jerked his arm away.

"Only if it would please you, uncle. And then, only after subjecting myself to the most rigorous testing offered by our technicians. I should not be given preference simply because of my relationship to you, sire."

"I shall bring the idea up with your mother when she

returns. You shan't be given a head start by virtue of genetics alone, Arnaud."

"Thank you."

The two walked away, leaving me to continue to explore the tree's surface and wonder if it heard their conversation. How did it feel about being potted in here, with its roots so far from the earth and its purpose in life now controlled by a fae with unnatural intentions and twisted plans? Call me old fashioned, but I preferred to see those involved in the act of procreation doing so with clear consent all around. Consent and, hopefully, joy. The lack of sensation under my hands worried me. But I had never been a sensate witch, and perhaps there was more going on within the solid trunk and sinuous branches than my hands would ever know.

"Come, witch. Time to inspect where the births will take place."

Nadège broke away from the cluster around Lionel and tugged my elbow. "Please stay close to the group," she said. "There will be less chance of you getting into trouble and if *you* get into trouble, *I* get into trouble. Understood?"

"Understood."

The stairwell connecting all the floors had a glass wall with views to the mountains. It was all so clean and sparkly and wholesome, with sunlight bouncing off other walls covered in white tiles and mosaics of mythical Magicals. A group of fae in pristine white lab coats and blue scrubs passed us, smiling, their footsteps echoing and bouncing off the white-and-blue tiled walls. "We're just going to retrieve more data from the tree, sire," one said, lighting up at the sight of Lionel.

My nurse escort stayed with me as we entered the second floor. Soft music and softer colors on every surface greeted us. At first glance, the ward seemed normal, exactly what you'd find in most any modern hospital's labor and delivery area. The differences began to sink in as we walked the halls, which were wide enough for three Fae to walk shoulder-to-shoulder—or two Fae to walk a shifter on a leash and four paws.

Bars that could drop down from the ceiling and close off sections of the hallway were spaced every ten feet or so. Four rooms—windowless but for the one in the door—each held a single, massive aquarium. Another set of rooms each featured an enormous tree branch across their width, as well as long, horizontal windows. Others had large hospital beds, the kinds that adjusted to the patient's needs. All the rooms had rocking chairs.

The magic throughout was palpable. Invasive. Flavorful. An invisible substance was filling my nostrils and coating my tongue. I stopped following Nadège and closed my eyes. I wanted to savor the wakening of my sexual desire and experience my body ripening, growing—

Guillaume shoved a medical mask over my nose and mouth and ordered me to keep walking. "Resist the magic, witch, or Lionel will insist you get tested, too," he said, hurrying me along with one hand at my back and the other keeping the mask in place.

"Tested for what?" I asked.

"Fertility." That was enough to smack sense into me in time for us to arrive back at the stairwell.

"Now, for the pièce de résistance." Lionel pushed the door open and led the way down the stairs. His voice boomed in the contained space. "We will not enter the actual laboratory. A corridor was installed for observational purposes, as I believe that once our work has been established and our successes are out in the world, Magicals will flock to the Facility in order to witness our methods."

Where the floor above was magically inviting, this floor was sterile, clinical, void of any attempt at warmth. Everything was done in shades of pale blue that matched the underlying tone of the fae's skin. Goosebumps pebbled my entire body. Guillaume stepped closer to my back. Though his vampire-ness didn't have much warmth to offer, I welcomed the show of support.

Our group walked the entire ambit, arrived back at the central stairwell, then paused. Lionel clasped his hands against his chest and tucked his chin. The fae around me stopped breathing. "I wasn't going to show you this today," he began. "The underground rooms are not finished and a few of the inhabitants have not yet acclimated to their new surroundings."

He lifted his head and spread his arms. "But the sun is shining and I am feeling magnanimous, so down we go." He spun on his heel and pressed his hand to an inset panel beside yet another single door. A silent mechanism slid the door into the wall, revealing a separate stairwell. This one had barred windows set high above our heads. By the time the filtered sun reached where we stood, the light was pale, mottled. The smell changed from sterile and chemical to raw, animal, and earthy as the sliding door closed behind us. Lionel gripped my elbow and insisted the two of us lead his hand-picked procession down the stairs.

Twenty-four stairs later, Lionel's palm print was again required to grant entry. The door slid open only enough to allow one body to pass at a time. Lionel entered first, then pulled me through and next to him. My vision adjusted to the low light coming from bulbs set into the walls at ankle height as the rest followed.

We had walked into a veritable zoo exhibit. Or maybe a museum of natural history's wing dedicated to realistic depictions of our animal and human ancestors' natural habitats.

Living beings sprawled atop large, flat rocks, curled on hefty branches, or slept in wide, spacious nests.

"There are no bars or cages in here," Lionel said. "An innovation that fills me with such...pride." He surveyed the scene, one hand to his heart, and accepted a murmur of congratulations. What he said was true. There were no visible walls sectioning off the inhabitants, aside from the one at our backs, which extended to the left and to the right only to be swallowed in the dim lighting. My guess was the fae were using glamour to hide magical barriers and feed the illusion of freedom.

"Let us first visit the cat. Follow me single file."

Arnaud stepped in line after Lionel. Then Nadège, me, Guillaume, and the other fae. I kept my gaze on the tight bun caught in a hairnet positioned at the base of Nadège's skull and the white nurse's cap perched above. Sharply tailored shoulders warned she was not to be messed with.

I had no intentions of messing with anyone on this field trip. I was gathering info, intel, and sensory input. And trying to not irritate Lionel into demonstrating his power over the Magicals all around us—or asking me to demonstrate my skill with blades.

As if in response to that thought, the metal in me warmed. The grit in my shoes acted like a flint to stone, striking sharp sparks that lit up the underside of my skin everywhere and evenly over my entire body. I glanced down, afraid the sensation might cause me to glow in the space's special light.

I wasn't glowing. But I noticed a curious response in the metal circling my wrists. It had become almost...pliable. I pressed my thumb under the opposite band and pushed, denting the metal band a hair's width. I pushed again, over and over, thumb against the metal, quick movements until it puckered enough I could have wiggled my wrist out, wrapped the connecting chain around Nadège's throat, and threatened to kill her if—

If nothing. There was no way I would have gotten out of that scenario alive. Not with Sidan back in my cell and nothing but a tiny pair of scissors in one pocket and a couple of scarab beetles in the other. I held my tongue, wrapped my hand around the deformed metal, and inadvertently bumped against the nurse. We'd come to a stop in front of a jungle set up and there, draped across a log half hidden by a giant fern, was Sheenah. I recognized her because of the muzzle buckled to her face.

"Our first stop and, perhaps, the candidate for our first implantation. Who has her chart?"

One of the nameless fae stepped forward and lit up her device. "Would you like to see the data we have collected thus far, sire?" she asked.

Lionel shook his head, his rapt gaze on the jaguar with the black rosettes on her side and the twitchy tail. "Why don't you present us the salient details. This one has caused me trouble and yet...and yet I am drawn to her."

"Sheenah. Female. Age thirty-one. Black jaguar shifter, a species also referred to as panther. Frequency, rare. Born in the wild in Belize. Impregnated at age twenty-six by a demon male, now deceased. Delivered a healthy female child. The girl is now four and shows definitive signs of genetic compatibility between both lineages in the form of first-set demon horns, accompanied by panther ears and tail."

"We have proof she can produce a viable child. The question now is, who or what to mate her with?" Lionel cupped his elbow with his other hand and tapped his chin. "And yes, Arnaud, I am actively considering a fae male. Should she produce a child that wields both claws and blades...that would be something to see."

Lionel continued to stare at Sheenah, then abruptly

resumed walking. "While we continue to consider her future, there is another curiosity I would have us take a look at."

The air grew more humid the farther we walked from Sheenah. Water dripped off vegetation and as we passed deeper into darkness, grow lights came on, their purple hue illuminating a scene straight off the cover of one of the paranormal romance books my mother used to carry at her shop.

A muscle-bound human crouched beside a small pool of water. One of his ankles was chained to the flat-topped boulders stacked at his back. The metal ring was thick and the chain was chunky, cumbersome—sized to keep boats attached to piers, not men attached to rocks. Unless the man possessed a mythic kind of strength.

"This is our swamp beast. We do not know his name. He was captured in his dragon form, which he has not returned to in the time he has been here." The man was naked, covered with mud. He lifted his gaze to our group, scooped muck from the edge of the water, and spread it over one arm. He repeated the movement, swiping black muck over his arms and torso and hair.

"Nadège, bring me the witch. I would like to see if our beast reacts to her. He was entirely uninterested in the cat."

The nurse drew the cape off my shoulders as she nudged me forward, pushing until the front of my chest and shoulders were pressed against an invisible shield keeping the beast and the other inhabitants in their separate biomes. My hunch was right. *So much for no cages.* Lionel undid my wrist restraints and without giving any notice at all of his intent, created an opening in the shield and pushed me through.

I huffed out a surprised breath as I slipped on the muddied floor and landed hard on my butt. The beast had a view right up my once-pristinely white uniform to my tights and underwear. I suspected Lionel and the others were having a laugh at my expense, though from this side the shield muffled sound so effectively I couldn't hear what they were saying. And I couldn't look behind me to gauge Guillaume's reaction to the Imperator's stunt...because in front of me, the beast's eyes were trained on mine and his eyes were changing color. He rocked his weight forward onto his hands, slid his free leg, then the shackled leg, into the swamp, and backed away until he was completely submerged.

17

I LOOKED OVER MY SHOULDER. The view from this side wasn't getting any clearer. I couldn't see my reflection and if I squinted, I could see the hazy outlines of the bodies I knew were watching.

Creepy. Then again, what about this wasn't creepy?

I took the unexpected opportunity offered by the unfamiliar mud and sank my fingers in deep enough to feed my magic. I didn't recognize the flavor, but dirt was dirt was dirt and whatever type of Magical this man was, his potent, unfamiliar magic infiltrated every clump.

Curling up, I swiped my palms along the side of the uniform and felt inside the pocket for the scissors and the scarab beetles. I tucked the scissors point-down in the front of the brassiere, chewed on the bugs, and returned my fingers to the muck. I liked its spicy, heated, primal taste and how it went right into my undernourished cells like a supplement I'd been forgetting to take.

Which was a helpful thing when the top of the man's head began to surface. Only he was no longer a man—he was in full-on beast mode. And he had three heads, not one. But when the wingless, dinosaur-like creature came for me, belly low to the ground, I was ready. I rolled to my side, threw one leg over its back and grabbed around the two outer necks. Ridged scales covered his back, digging into my stomach and battering my hip bones and ribs. He planted his clawed front paws, reptilian elbows out to the sides, and twisted, straining against the chain and trying to dislodge me.

I had no time to wonder why none of the fae were helping, why Lionel hadn't ordered the beast subdued and his guest rescued, why my vampire ally hadn't yet leapt in to vanquish the beast and save the maiden. But I was no maiden, and the beast's movements called to mind a particularly large, mean wrestling teacher I'd had and how unbeatable I'd felt when I finally got him off my back and pinned to the mat. I'd had one beefy neck to contend with back then, not three.

The beast stopped lunging and reversed direction. I pressed my heels into where his back legs bent away from his torso and rode him into the muck. Backward. All the way. Thick sludge rolled up my legs. I got hold of the tiny scissors and pressed the tips into a soft spot on the side of the beast's throat as the muck filled the underside of my uniform. I managed to hiss out, "Stop," and "I can help you," as the muck reached my chin and my mouth and covered my head.

This was far worse than being submerged in the underground cavern with Clementine, my arms tied behind my back and a weight attached to my ankles. Here, I couldn't see or breathe and I couldn't let go. The beast flipped, pressing me against the sloping wall of the pool and exposing his front. I took the chance offered. I locked my legs around its midsection and I fed my magic into my muscles, into the small bits of shiny metal in my hand and stabbed him with my scissors, drawing the razor sharp tip up the side of his belly.

A burning sensation spread across my leg. I kept my lips and eyes closed tight and let go. The beast flipped again, roared forward, and shifted back into a man as I scrabbled, face up, up the slope. My head and shoulders cleared the swampy mess. The beast man straddled my chest with his knees, hands circling my neck, and hauled me between his thighs and up to sitting. He slid backward, scooped up two handfuls of the muck, and pressed the stuff to my leg, shaking his head and muttering in a language I didn't recognize.

That combination eased the pain enough for me to realize I was gagging on mud. I corked my torso to the side so I wouldn't choke. The shifter slammed his hand onto the middle of my back, grabbed my clothes, and hauled me onto my feet. Muck squicked inside my shoes. Over the heavy, agitated breathing sawing the air, on the other side of the wavering barrier, I heard clapping.

"Brava! Bravo!" Lionel shouted. "Leave the witch in there. Forget about the Unbinding predicament. We'll find someone else to do it. Start her testing. We might have found a mate for the dragon."

I spun around and threw myself at the flexible barrier that separated me from the group of onlookers. I was *not* here to be considered for anyone's mate. I was here to rescue captured Magicals, *not* spend time on *this* side of the wards. Anywhere any part of my body met the wall of reinforced magic felt like I was punching an impenetrable membrane. The magic was strong, and I was trapped on the wrong side.

One of the fae shot their arm through an opening they made and pushed me back against the dragon shifter. I stumbled as he released me, leapt onto the rock, and resumed his crouch. His ankle was free of restraints. He must have broken out when he shifted. Someone on Lionel's staff was likely making a note at the very moment about creating shackles for shifters that expanded and contracted as the Magical beings moved from one form to the other.

Being completely caked in rapidly cooling swamp mud was not my happy place, nor was being burned by corrosive dragon blood. I collapsed to my hands and knees, then further, lowering my forehead to my arms and settling back on my heels. I needed to catch my breath. I needed to assess my current predicament and figure out the fuck what was next.

And for the first time since my father's death, I wished I had his voice in my head offering me something, anything, I didn't care what. It could have been a platitude, it could have been something so wise and timely that lightbulbs would explode in my head and the way forward would light up like a runway at night.

I'd come here with Sidan to gather information. Now that I'd seen the Facility, met two of its prisoners, and witnessed Lionel's fervor, I didn't want a single captive to have anything done to them on my watch and against their will.

That was a *very* big wish. But I was the Scarab Eater's Daughter, and I had expectations to fulfill.

I wanted my glasses. They'd allow me to see through the wards and pick up movement patterns on the other side. It irritated me to think the fae were watching, observing, taking notes. Closing my eyes, hands and knees in the muck, I multiplied the flakes of metal inside me, bit down hard on my urge to scream, and forged a flexible, protective shield all through my body like another layer of fascia. And like fascial cells, every flake of metal inside of me could communicate with every other bit.

Protect. Deflect. Kill.

That was *my* voice, not my father's. Standing, I bent over and picked at the mud-caked laces. The shoes came off easily. Next, I peeled off the ruined tights. There was muck between the uniform and the brassiere, and the brassiere and my skin, and the underwear and—*uff*.

"Water." The rumbly voice came from over and behind my shoulder. "Behind the rock."

I unbuttoned the uniform and turned my back to the fae and the lone vampire watching from the other side of the wards. In front of me, stacked, flat rocks rose ten feet or so. Dragon man was perched on top, covered by a lot less mud. He rose, leaving little to my imagination, and pointed to the jagged red line on his side. "My blood contains poisons. Do not cut me again."

He watched me step around his rock. I picked my way carefully—the lighting was dim and my feet were bare. The rocks curved around another pool and inset into the wall was a shower head. Beside that were towels on hooks and a slatted bench. I disrobed, dropping chunks of mud I pushed away with my toes. The shower went off before I finished rinsing. Turning, I was met by dragon man hanging by his arms from an overhanging ledge.

"Timer," he said. "Everything is on a timer. Water. Lights. Food. Tests."

"Is the pool warm or cold?" I asked. I made no attempt at covering any part of me. Lucky for him, dragon man's gaze never left mine.

"Warm. Go. Soak."

I ducked around his side and lowered myself into the clear water up to my chin. "I'm Alderose," I said. "Who are you?" Strong feet and tapered ankles walked into my peripheral vision and stopped. My host lowered himself into the water and stretched his arms along the rocks lining the pool's rim. Holding on, he ducked his entire head under, came up, and shook the water out of his short, curly hair. His skin was mostly unblemished, but for a pattern of scars across his pectorals that appeared deliberate.

He extended his arm across the pool and cooled the fire in his eyes to an unthreatening brown. "My full name is Jonathan Jackson Winslow. You can call me Jake. New York City's my usual habitat."

"How'd you end up here?"

"Have you met Linette?" When I nodded, he continued. "Seems like she has a thing for younger men. I was in Europe, came to Chamonix to check out skiing possibilities, and she walked into the resort and came right over to me." He rested the back of his head against the rocky ledge.

"And then?"

"And the next thing I knew, she was in my bed at the hotel. And the next thing I knew after that, I was here."

"So she lured you with sex?"

Jake lifted his head and stared at me. "I don't know the answer to that, Alderose. I honestly do not."

"What kind of shifter are you?"

"Why don't you tell me something about you first?"

I went with my druid academy story, in case we were being observed or recorded, ending with, "I'm a witch."

In true shifter style, Jake had listened with more than his ears. "I'm a dragon. My parents took a trip to Russia, came across me in an orphanage, and adopted me. I don't remember anything about my life before New York. Mom and Dad have inherited wealth, they own the top floor of one of the old buildings on Park Avenue, and they're both dragons. Normal dragons, the kind everyone thinks of when you say 'dragons.'"

"As in, they have wings and hoard gold treasure?"

He smiled. "You got it, Rosey."

"How'd you know my nickname was Rosey?"

He shrugged. "I didn't, until a moment ago. One of my gifts is prescience. Although in here, surrounded by all that" —he waved his hand in the direction of the wards— "my ability to read what's coming is severely limited."

"You work in the financial sector?"

"Good guess."

"A dragon who lives in New York, takes holidays in Chamonix, and reads the future? It was an easy guess."

He leaned forward, close enough to send his whisper rippling across the surface of the water. "Thing is, you're wrong."

I brought my face closer to his. "Tell me what you do, Jake."

"I hunt humans and Magicals who do bad things, and when I catch them, I get to...respond in kind." He moved closer. "You weren't the only one who pegged me for a money man."

"You thought Linette wanted your money?"

"Honestly? Yeah, at first. But after being in here for three days, I'm not sure what to think."

"Do you have family or business associates who'll notice you're gone?"

"My parents are used to me travelling. My mother knows I've been planning to look for the orphanage where they adopted me. I was making my way toward Russia when I ran into Linette. Or, she ran into me," He sank below the water and when he resurfaced, he waited. I could see only his eyes and the top of his head until he stood.

"You seem pretty chill for a guy who's locked up in a castle in the Alps."

"My driver's license, passport, and credit cards are embedded with custom chips. My business partner is also a software designer, and if my name or any of the number sequences get typed in, they'll get flagged. And they'll start tracking me down. Especially since I haven't been answering my phone."

"You think a rescue is imminent?"

"I'm too much of a realist for magical thinking, Rosey. This place gives me the creeps, and the way they just shoved you in here like they were hoping it would provoke some kind of—response from me?" Instead of addressing his own question, he ducked under the water again. When he surfaced, he said, "I wasn't expecting to turn into a dragon at the sight of you in that nurse's uniform. Under normal circumstance, I could have stopped."

I turned, intending to exit the pool, dry off, and figure out how to deal with what was coming next. Jake moved right up behind me. I elbowed him.

"There's nothing normal about our circumstances," I said, "and you've got to give me space. I'm getting real tired of Magicals thinking just because I'm short means it's an open invitation to try to intimidate me."

"I'm sorry, Alderose. If those damn invisible walls weren't meddling with my—my magic, I would have known that. I meant it as more of a protective thing. There's a deeply protective streak in the dragon genes and I can't do much about it."

"Tell your dragon I can fend for myself. As soon as the fae start running their tests on me, they're going to know more about my magic and I'd rather they didn't." I faced Jake. He was so comfortable in his own skin that both of us being naked seemed extraordinarily ordinary. "You always do business without your pants?" I asked.

"Pretty much," he said. "I like nice clothes and shifting into dragon form really fucks up my wardrobe."

At least he had a sense of humor. We were going to need it. I hopped onto the wide ledge and reached for a towel. Ripping and roiling sounded behind me and as I covered myself, three sets of eyes blinked at me from the once placid pool. Jake the wingless dragon hoisted himself out and tore around the rock.

I grabbed another towel and followed him. Nadège and two other male nurses were waiting for us, weapons drawn. Only, their weapons included equipment to draw blood samples. The fae nearest Jake dropped into a crouch and aimed one hand at the dragon's middle head. Long, pointed blades extended from each of his fingers. The dragon lowered to his belly. Four black claws on each front paw ripped at the ground, shredding what little plant matter was left as he shifted into the single headed, very muscley, very naked, Jake.

Panting, he struggled to stand on his knees. "Sorry," he said, holding up both arms. "I thought you were a threat and I couldn't stop the change. If you could give me a ten second warning next time, I can exert better control over my beast."

"Ten seconds?" Nadège made a note.

"Fifteen if you're feeling generous." The nurse didn't crack a smile. And I was certain Jake was lying. Another fae entered behind the trio. I hadn't seen this one before. He was tall, even for a fae, and bulky and held a set of leg irons in one massive hand.

"Hands against the rock," he said. "Spread your legs."

Jake followed the hulk's instructions. I followed the movements of Jake's muscles, bunching under his skin as the hulk snaked the metal rings around his ankles and anchored a long chain to the rock. This chain was slender and flexible. I squinted. It had been constructed from one continuous length of extremely pliable metal. Which meant the chain was packed with fae magic.

Another set of raised lines marked a pattern across Jake's shoulder blades. No tattoos, just scars. Once he was secured, he shook out one leg and the other and faced the group of fae, hands over his genitals. Nadège turned her attention to me. "Drop the towel."

I wanted to ask her which one she wanted me to ditch, the one around my waist or the one I'd wrapped around my shoulders, but I wasn't in a good position to be testing the limits of her sense of humor. I undid the tucked ends at my waist, then dropped both towels. Nadège lifted her device and used it to scan my body as she stepped around me, careful to not muddy her much-nicer nurse's shoes. She spent more time behind me, and then waving the device in front of my lower belly. I could only assume she was taking a good look at my reproductive organs.

"Something's interfering with my ability to get a clear scan," she said. "Something metallic. Have you been fitted with an IUD or are you currently using a magical device to prevent pregnancies—something with metal in it?"

Goddess, she was getting personal, and I was not about to explain my affinity with metal went deep, all the way to the cellular level, and that yes, it probably *was* interfering with my fertility. "No and no."

"What about herbal methods?"

Like many witches, I used herbs in lieu of birth control pills, which had the added benefit of regulating my cycle and banishing premenstrual syndrome. Being a witch had its share of benefits. If Nadège knew to ask about magical devices and herbs, then the fae would test me for their presence whether they thought I was telling the truth or not. "Yes," I said. "I take the same herbs most witches use to control their cycles."

She pointed at me, then pointed at Jake, until I understood she wanted me to stand next to him. She took pictures of us, made more notes on her device, then tapped her ear. "Yes, sire?" Listening intently, she continued with, "No, sire," and "Of course, sire," and when she once again stared at my belly like she was assessing me for breeding purpose, I had to accept that's exactly what she and Lionel were discussing. The timeline for getting myself out of here ramped up from *once I've gathered more information* to *NOW*.

"Jake? Can you shift?" I asked, keeping my voice low and my gaze on Nadège.

"Not sure. The new chain is causing heavy interference."

The hulk wasn't happy that Jake and I were whispering. He stuck out his foot, jerked on the chain, and sent Jake to his knees. Nadège glowered at me and nodded once, sharply. "I think the witch would make an ideal candidate for our breeding program, sire. Once her body has been cleansed."

18

I GOT to leave Jake's enclosure with the help of the hulky fae and his extraordinary people skills. He pulled another coiled section of the same supple chain from the other side of the wards and looped it around my waist. The chain connected to itself, giving the fae a leash by which they could lead me around like a pet. A very naked pet.

The hulk handed the chain through the ward. Whomever caught it jerked me through. Guillaume was staring over my shoulder. He unbuttoned his white lab coat and passed it to the hulk. "Hold this for her."

"But Nadège—"

"I am certain Nadège will not want one of the Imperator's chosen breeders to be subjected to the scrutiny of the other guests. Let the witch cover herself for now."

I slipped my arms into the coat and did up the buttons. I longed to wrap it around me tight and stitch the overlapping sections with my aunt's special needles and threads. Lacking that, I went with the option that kept my arms free and followed Guillaume and my handler along semi-dark pathways, past Sheenah's cell, to a door.

"I'll take her from here," Guillaume said. "The Imperator wishes her cleaned up and dressed for tonight's meal." The magicked chain wound itself around Guill's wrist. He pressed his hand to the touchpad. The door slid into the wall, the vampire pressed his finger to his lips, and up the stairs we went. I counted twenty-four, then lost count once we were inside the multiple halls crisscrossing the ground floor. The tile was cold on my feet, and external cold interacted with the metal inside me. Icy spikes flickered just under my skin and worsened as we neared the open bay and the aerial tram and the alpine air.

We boarded the waiting vehicle. I held tight as it lurched forward. "Can we—"

"No."

I spent the duration of the ride staring at the mountains. After disembarking, Guill led us down another long hall where we encountered more fae, through the rotunda, to the stone-tiled corridor leading to my cell. He unlocked the bars, stepped aside to let me through, then locked it behind us and motioned to me. "This is the only place we can talk safely," he said, once he had triggered the shower.

"I am not getting in any more water, Guill. You have no idea how—"

"You don't have to get in it, Alderose, just stand close enough we can make it look like I'm going for your neck again."

I ran my gaze around the room as Guill secured my hands behind my back with the new rope. If Sidan was here, I couldn't see her. "Sid," I hissed.

Guillaume gripped my jaw, hauled me up against his chest, and deftly maneuvered us so we were between the shower and the corner wall. I couldn't hear anything but water splattering against us and the floor.

"What are you doing?" The vampire bent forward and nuzzled his mouth against my neck.

"I want to see if Sidan is here," I whispered.

"I'm here, Rós." Her knuckles grazed my cheek. "I've had an interesting day."

Guillaume had frozen in place, his open mouth pressed against the side of my neck. He tilted his head slightly. "She's standing next to me, isn't she?" he asked, and when I said yes, he leaned more of his weight against me, pinning me to the wall. "The two of you have got to get out of here. Lionel is pushing everything aside in order to start testing you and Sheenah. He wants the world to see him as a scientist, a...a visionary. If he could run the tests himself, he would—starting tonight. He wants your blood, witch, and I don't think you should let him have one single drop."

"Make it look like she's been taken," Sidan said. "I could bring you close to death, vampire, the fae way. Lionel would recognize the method immediately. He would find it alarming to think there was a killer inside his castle."

The shower had started out lukewarm and was now all cold water. I wasn't going to last much longer. "Can you really make it look like someone tried to kill Guillaume?"

"I am *very* good at providing near-death experiences," Sid said. "The pain is manageable, vampire, but you will be unconscious for at least twenty-four hours."

"Do it," he said. "Then leave. And this time, don't come back until you have an army you can bring with you."

He reached behind and turned off the water. Tugging the blanket off the cot he wrapped me up like a frozen mummy and rubbed my legs and arms. My teeth chattered as I made a visual accounting of my things and what I intended to grab. Sid hadn't given us instructions. I would just...play along.

"Get into bed. Both of you," she said.

Guillaume lay on his back and pulled me on top of him. The rope he'd untied was hidden by the blanket.

"Kiss."

I lowered my head to meet the vampire's and didn't hesitate to bring my shivering lips to his. Freeing my arms, I slipped my hand into the pillowcase and found the vest with the iron pieces and my torc. I slid the torc around my neck, clutched the vest to my chest, and continued to kiss Guillaume like I meant it.

His lips softened, parted, and he threaded his fingers through my hair. I almost believed that what we were doing was pleasurable for him, until his body jerked and his spine arched, throwing me off kilter to the edge of the bed. "Roll to the floor and go limp, Rós," Sidan whispered. "Then just wait."

The terrible sound of someone struggling to breathe mingled with Sid's feet scrabbling on the gritty floor while she did whatever she was doing to Guillaume. I'd rolled onto my belly and was able to get one end off of the torc and a beetle into my mouth and crushed between my teeth before Sidan lifted me up and tossed me over her shoulder.

We were at the bars, down the hall, and through the door before I could swallow. I'd gotten a gold portal stone into my palm. Sid ran us right against the tree. "Do it now," she hissed. I didn't hesitate, just slammed the little ball against the bark and said the first thing that came into my head.

"Home."

Portal travel was horrible when you were naked and cold. I learned that lesson firsthand. A surprise landing in Central Park wearing nothing but a scratchy blanket was worse. My discomfort was ameliorated by Sidan, who was making rapid-fire requests to the wide-eyed portal guide about where we were and could he call us a cab.

"Alderose. *Alderose.* Where do you want go?"

I had no idea. I'd said, *Home.* The portal had delivered us here. Technically, I did live here. I had a New York City address on my driver's license and all the restaurant apps on my phone. "Upper East Side," I said. "Eighty-sixth, between First and York."

The driver summoned by the portal guide wasn't surprised to see two Magicals climb into her car. Nor was she surprised to hear I had no cash or credit cards to pay her and that I couldn't remember my member number. She waved off my attempts. "This is a smart car. Your information'll come up once we're at your door and the charges'll go right to your card."

My condo building had a live-in manager. They had keys. They were also human. During the drive across town, Sidan glamoured herself to look as un-fae as she had the reserves for. The building manager waved off the story I made up on the spot about why I was wearing a blanket and had no shoes, handed me an extra set of keys, and said, "You can't keep those. And you had a visitor. Coulda been your friend's sister. Same height, same bone structure" —she circled her face with her finger— "'cept she had spots on her face. What's that condition called? Sounds like vertigo but I know it ain't vertigo. She wasn't dizzy."

"Vitiligo," I said. I pressed the call button for the elevator. "Thanks, Susi."

Sidan followed me into the elevator. "Who do you know with vitiligo?"

I blew out a breath. "One-Becomes-Three. The disguise she used when she was Jadzia included those pale patches around her mouth and eyes and on her neck."

"Where were you when she showed you that face?

"In the underground cavern. She had Gosia under a spell and together they got me and Clementine tied up and then pushed us into the water. I hate her for so many reasons, Sid."

"We'll find her, Rós. I promise. And when we do, I get a few minutes with her before you turn her over to your uncle. Deal?"

"Deal." We shook on it.

"Let me go in first. I think I can manage a couple minutes of full invisibility."

"My apartment's a one bedroom, Sid. There's no place to hide."

"Doesn't mean there's no place for small creatures brought in from Fae lands to hide. Indulge me. Please. Those ten seconds could save our lives."

"You may go first," I said, giving her a mock bow.

"No talking until I give you the okay."

I made the okay sign with my fingers. Sid stood beside me, our backs to the wall opposite the sliding doors. I smiled at the hazy faces reflected in the polished metal surface as the elevator came to a noisy stop on the tenth floor.

Sid pressed her finger to my lips, motioned for me to stay where I was once we'd stepped out, and walked softly the few steps to my door. She side-eyed me hard when she saw the three locks and had me point out which of the borrowed keys went to which lock. I admired my girlfriend's rear view and had one of those brief flashes of wondering how I'd managed to snag someone who was smart and sexy and funny—and so good with unlocking stuck things like door locks and the deeper recesses of my heart.

Sidan smiled over her shoulder as she tossed the keys in the air and waited for me to catch them. She put her hand on the doorknob, twisted, pushed, and paused.

I saw her spin around as she took a hit to her chest.

I saw the arrowhead protrude from her upper left side.

I watched as she went flying backward. Her body hit the wall to my right. An arrow fletched with sharp black feathers impaled her in place. Blood oozed out of her chest. The door to my apartment hit the stopper and bounced. One light was on—the small lamp I'd picked up in a thrift shop—and the chair I sat in to watch the nighttime cityscape had been turned so it faced the door.

Sitting in that chair was Jadzia, an elbow on her knee and a crossbow in her lap. I dropped to the floor beside Sidan. Her mouth was open wide in surprise and her eyelids were fluttering. More blood oozed out of the hole in her chest, turning turquoise as it hit the air and soaking the nearby blanket, spreading over my hands and arms and knees as I tried to save her, tried to plug the hole, tried to...to fix her broken body. If I could just break the arrow, pull one piece forward, roll her over, pull the sharpened end out the other way, she would have a chance. She would be okay.

I could call—

Jadzia hooked her arm across the front of my throat, lifted me onto my feet, and hissed, "The Imperator does not appreciate it when his *things* are taken from him." She dragged me into the elevator and punched the button for the lobby. I struggled to get free, but her grip was steel. When the doors slid open and the empty lobby loomed in front of us, I tried to run.

She laughed, kept her arm around my throat, and hauled me out the two sets of glass doors and onto the sidewalk. City dwellers were coming home from work or going out for the night, and no one saw us. No one even looked askance. "Go ahead," the fae said. "Try it. No one can see you. No one can hear you. I am invisible to the humans and so are you."

She hauled me in the direction of the river. I couldn't breathe. I still had the torc in my hand and the vest with the iron filigree. I dropped the blanket and pressed the embellished side of the vest against One-Becomes-Three's side. I wrapped my arms around her, sandwiching the iron filigree between my chest and the side of her ribcage. She tried to bat me away with her free hand but I wasn't letting go. She tried hiding us in the shrubs outside a brownstone—and stopped when she saw the matte black iron railings surrounding the bushy plants.

I saw opportunity. Using my weight, I got her off balance and pulled back, stumbling until I could swing myself toward the gingko tree near the edge of the sidewalk. Protecting the base of the tree was another iron fence, shorter and smaller and every bit as spiky. I almost had Jadzia's weight on one leg when she let out a laugh, ripped me away from her side, and released the two other fae in the move I'd first seen at the quarry.

"No one, least of all a common *witch*, tricks me."

I was surrounded by three fae at least a foot or more taller than me. They linked arms, trapping me, and chanted, and as they chanted, changing one word each time, we were transported from one tree to another and another until we ended up at Hangman's Elm in Washington Square Park. The portal guide barely registered our arrival before we were off again.

From there, we landed in France, at the portal tree outside the door at the end of the hall where my cell was located inside Lionel Vigne's castle in Chamonix.

And that entire time, pressed between three bodies with no room to take a breath, all I could see was the shocked look on Sidan's face as the arrow took her from me.

The same hulky fae who'd shackled Jake was waiting in the hall with more restraints and a length of black cloth. "He waits for you," he said, speaking to the fae surrounding me. I stumbled as the three abruptly separated and began to file down the hall. Within a couple of steps, the three became one. Hulky pushed me the rest of the way into the cell. "The vampire lives. The dragon lives. Lucky for you, we all live. The Imperator was not happy. He saw what happened. He sent his best to find you and bring you back."

He backed out of the room, locked the bars, and dropped the

ankle and wrist restraints on the stone floor outside of my cell. "It is my choice whether to put you in restraints. I will let you go the night without them. You have clean bedding and there is a tisane in the thermos. Drink it. Nadège says it will help you sleep."

He left. The room went mostly dark. I was...bereft. Hollowed out and refilled with something as thick and suffocating as the muck in Jake's habitat. I couldn't get enough oxygen into my body, and I could barely stand. I picked up the thermos and cradled it to my heart. I was shaking so hard I couldn't open the cap, and when I looked down and saw my bare feet against the stone, I realized I was still naked.

Clothes had been left on the chair. I set down the thermos, pulled on a nondescript pair of pajama pants and went to button up the top. My fingers forgot how to work a button into its hole; their shaking and fumbling was matched by my trembling lips and all the tears that I'd held back, and when my legs started to go, I gave up. I had to lie down.

The cot had been re-made with military precision, the turned over edge of the white sheet a stark contrast to the dark blankets. I crawled between the bottom and top sheets. Lying on one side with my face to the wall, I drew my knees to my chest and covered my head with the bedding.

I wept for Sidan. If by some miracle she was alive...I couldn't imagine what set of extraordinary circumstances might have led to her surviving. I couldn't wrap my mind around her death. And in my grief, I thought I felt her hand circling my ankle but it was just one of the cats I'd seen patrolling the hall outside my bars.

The weight, the warmth, the throaty purr. The companionship. Grief pinched my gut and started tearing pages from my book of regrets and transgressions and unmet longings, and when I couldn't bear it a moment longer, I willed myself to stop. The cat helped. I centered all of my awareness into the two spots where the creature's front paws kneaded at the blanket and counted in time with its comforting movements.

19

CATS WERE good for a grieving heart. When I came out of a wretched sleep, I couldn't open my eyes and I couldn't move. The heavy weight pressing against my chest matched the weight at the back of my neck and head. Only, that weight was purring. I followed the purr back into sleep. Or, I tried.

Footsteps in the hall said I had a visitor. I ignored the slow slide of a key into a lock, the deliberate stealth as they crept toward the cot, pet the cat, and set something on the bench. I ignored them as they left. But I couldn't ignore the smell of fresh coffee and toasted bread.

During the night, while slogging my way through one ragged dreamscape after another, I decided Sidan was alive. My dreams were all about searching for her, no matter how strange or inhospitable the landscape. I would find her alive. Or I would add her murder to my growing list of deaths to avenge.

I turned to my other side, burrowed my face in the cat's warm fur, and promptly lost my composure. The cat was done providing warmth and affection. It leapt off the cot, stretched, sniffed at the food on the tray, and slipped out between the bars, tail held high.

Softening my gaze, I swept the room. Sid said she had found —or seen—something interesting in here. And Sid being the kind of being she was, she might have left me clues. No, she would definitely have left me clues. Or something. Or a series of somethings. Because from the very beginning, she'd had a bead on me and my next move.

Stay strong, Alderose. Neglect your body at your peril.

Got it, Dad. Eat, then shower. Because I'd been there, done that with the *let me just clean up first and then eat* thing and I'd learned that lesson. I could fight stinky; I couldn't stay sharp without food and water. I brought the tray to the bed, downed the glass of water first, and made myself eat everything. I showered, dressed quickly in the generic undergarments and prison coveralls, and searched for footwear.

My boots had been polished and set under the cot. I felt the leather, knowing the small blades I secreted inside them in Northampton had likely been confiscated. I missed my weapons but having something of mine was ridiculously comforting. Putting on socks after I'd ground a bit of grit into the bottoms of both feet, lacing the boots, and brushing my hair and teeth put a dose of normalcy into a string of abnormal days.

I went back to the cot, pulled a blanket over me, and waited.

I worked on my breathing.

I worked on my magic, teasing it toward the surface of my skin and letting it flow back through my bones and into my marrow.

I worked on visualizing ways out of this mess, and mapping the outcomes I most wanted to see, and the outcomes I'd be willing to accept. I thought about how I could reach Malvyn. Maritza. Alabastair. I wondered if I would see Jake again. Or Sheenah. Or Guillaume.

And when I couldn't dance around it any longer, I thought about Sidan. I pictured her face, her kisses, her body. I inhaled the scent of her naked skin and exhaled into the hand I cupped around my mouth to stop me from screaming. I inhaled again, made a mantra of her name, and shut my eyes to the light.

Sid...An...Sid...An...Sid..An...Sid...

The cat jumped on my chest. Another nameless fae arrived and switched out one tray for another. I didn't bother asking them anything, and they didn't offer any news. What little light was coming in from the high windows was paler and the air was growing colder. Snow was here, or on its way. I curled onto my side again. The cat rolled with me and settled on my hip. I stared at the wall, snuck my arm out from under the blanket and felt along the floor. I'd left two gold portal stones secreted in the grit where the floor met the wall. I could only find one and holding it in my hand gave me one tiny flash of hope.

If I could get out of this cell, I could get to the portal tree. And if I could get to the portal tree, I could get to help.

You're an idiot for thinking you could do this alone.

I know, Dad, I— That wasn't Heriberto del Valle's voice in my head. I grabbed the cat by the scruff and hauled it closer to my face. I'd noticed its collar earlier, only I hadn't *noticed* the collar, as in taken a detailed look at it for signs of magic. I wrapped my arms around the wiggling feline and pulled the blanket to cover us from any eyes that might be in the cell.

"Who is this?" I asked.

"This is Cat." The cat in my arms stopped trying to get away and started scratching at the collar. I changed my grip and rubbed the side of it neck. "I'm Jake's business partner and I've been looking for him ever since his passport was run through a private security firm that deals mostly with Magicals. I'm a witch, by the way, and Oscar's my familiar."

"Oscar's your cat?"

"Yes, she is. And I'd love to chat but I need details. I traced Jake to Chamonix, and last night I was able to get Oscar inside the Clan Vigne fortress. There was a lot of activity around one door in particular, which is how Oscar got in and why she's with you."

"Is there a camera on her collar?"

"Camera. Mic. GPS. I can work everything remotely."

"Where are you?"

"In a chalet not far from the castle."

"Cat, it's bad in here. But before I tell you any more do you have any connections in Manhattan who could go to my apartment and...and check on someone?"

"Sure. Give me the address. I can have an associate there within the half hour. Want to tell me what kind of a scene they're walking into?"

"My girlfriend and I were there last night. She was shot through the chest with an arrow. She's fae. She's amazing. And I have no idea if the shot killed her, or—"

"I'll have two of my best there in under fifteen minutes. What's your name?"

"Alderose," I said. "I'm also a witch. And I've met Jake. And the sooner we put together a rescue operation for the two of us and the rest of the captives inside here, the better."

"Okay. Try not to let anyone see Oscar. Now, tell me who else needs to know you're alive?"

It was a relief to reel off a list of names to Cat, starting with my sisters, then Maritza, Malvyn, James, and Alabastair. "They're familiar with the details. They'll know who to recruit and what to bring." I pinched the bridge of my nose. Oscar had settled herself against the curve of my belly and something about her presence gave me strength. "I fucked up, Cat," I whispered, using the gift of her familiar's fur to act as my confessional. "What's happening here needs to be—"

"Who are you talking to, Alderose?" Lionel's voice froze me in place. His hand caressed the curves of my blanket-covered body, from the side of my head, to my neck, my shoulder, my waist, and hip. There, he ran his hand over my butt and down the backs of my thighs. Oscar tensed, and when Lionel peeled back the blanket, the cat shot off the cot and out into the hall.

Lionel laughed. "You were chatting with a *cat*?"

"Witches and cats go together."

He shifted on the bed. "You haven't touched your food. I chose the soup for you especially and now it's gone cold and there's no time for more because you are due in the laboratory to begin your testing."

Like Oscar, I froze. Unlike the cat, I didn't make it off the cot and into the hall before Lionel had grabbed both my wrists in one of his hands and leaned over to whisper in my ear. "I expect you to pass all of your tests, Alderose. I will be very disappointed if you do not." He let go of me and stood. I continued to stare at the wall and run through my options. Judging by the commotion in the room, I had none. "Nadège, she is ready."

"You have yet to thank me." I assumed Lionel meant the trip from New York back to his castle. How Jadzia knew Sidan and I would end up in the city, at my apartment, was a mystery burning a hole in my chest.

"Thank you," I said, hurrying my pace to keep up with him and the nurse and the fae holding my elbow. Nadège had instructed him to secure me with a lightweight restraint much like the chain used to secure Jake to the rock the second time. "Where is Guillaume? Is he—"

"My beloved Guillaume will survive what was done to him." Lionel's stride hitched. "He is recovering inside the Facility. Given the amount of equipment and medical expertise that would be available around the clock, I had half of the ground floor set aside for treating the castle's staff, as well as family. The vampire is like family to me."

"What happened to him? I—I don't remember much."

"We know you were both attacked by the same fae. We know what she did to him and we know there is no hurrying the process his body must go through to repair itself. He is a vampire and he is strong. I can only hope my dear sister's aim was true."

It was my turn to miss a step. "It was," I whispered.

"Did you say something, witch?"

"You said you sent your sister to rescue me? The face I remember wasn't Linette's."

"That is because I have another sister."

Fuck me. Clan Vigne was the source of the mythical One-Becomes-Three.

I was stunned by the news and terrified that Lionel already knew everything there was to know about me. That he and his sisters had always known, from the moment I'd made the mistake of telling him I was in Chamonix to work with the druid. I hadn't even thought to consider that she might have had a part in this too.

We arrived at the aerial tram terminal before I realized how far we'd walked. The four of us, Lionel, Nadège, me, and my handler, boarded the car and left the car in the same order. Lionel's growing excitement was as palpable as my growing dread. I kept thinking I heard my sisters' voices, or that someone off in the distance was really my uncle or aunt in disguise. Neither of which was true.

When our quartet stopped in front of two doors with reinforced glass windows that opened onto a corridor lined with glass-walled rooms, my belly plummeted. It continued to drop as we passed between two rows of fae wearing surgical scrubs and white coats, as though the generic uniforms had been deliberately chosen to evoke a sense of normal.

Nothing about this was *normal*. Lionel stopped, held up his arms, then pointed to a bed on the other side of one of the glass walls. "There is our jaguar shifter. In the room next to her is our dragon shifter. And here" —he continued down the hall and pointed to a third room— "is where we shall begin testing on the witch. By this time tomorrow, we should know which of the two females will be the best match for the dragon, and once we know that we shall make ready to perform our first official implantation."

He took a satisfied breath and looked directly at me. "Let the testing begin."

Inside my head, the rapture on Lionel's face mingled with the look on Sidan's face when I was frantically trying to do something to help her and failing. I almost believed I was failing again, by virtue of the fact that I wasn't trying hard enough to pull something magical out of my ass and get myself and Sheenah and Jake freed.

Cat, whose voice I'd heard coming from a cat's collar, was sending two of her people to Sidan. Cat, whom I'd never met in person, was within a few kilometers of the castle. Cat and Jake had resources, including being able to connect with my family members even though all I could give her was their names.

I wanted desperately to believe in the disembodied voice of Cat.

Staring into the privacy-free space that was to be my new room, I couldn't believe in Cat. Not fully. Faith hadn't been part of my training. I'd been forced to develop a personal defense system that had nothing to do with magic, and this place wanted to strip me of both.

I glanced over at Jake. The pair of nurses attending him saw me, scowled, and pulled both ends of a hanging privacy curtain around his bed. "This way," Nadège said, ushering me into my room. "Remove all of your clothing."

"Now?"

"Now."

"With everyone watching?"

"No one is watching." Nadège clutched a large notebook device to her chest. I pointed behind her, toward Lionel and the others who were gathering around him. Some crossed their arms. Others consulted devices like Nadège's. Others openly stared at me. The common expression on all faces but Lionel's was bland detachment. The Imperator looked more like a kid given carte blanche at a toy store.

"I beg to differ," I said.

"They are here for the science," she stated. "Remove your footwear and everything else you have on, including your undergarments, and set them on the shelf."

I bent to untie my boots. "Then what?"

"Then get on the exam table." Nadège made adjustments to the table and when I stood to toe off my boots, its forward-tilting angle suggested everyone out there would have a ringside view to whatever testing was coming my way.

I drew a curtain around my guilt and my grief and my shame as I unbuttoned the coverall, stepped out, pulled the stretchy bra over my head, and rolled the underwear down my legs. I turned so I was looking across the table to Jake's room. I let my arms hang at my sides while Nadège fussed with something I could not see. There was movement behind Jake's curtain, an elbow or two bumping into the cloth. If anything was being said behind it, I couldn't hear.

Once I stacked my things, Nadège had me get on the exam table and lie down. I had a brief moment of surprise—I had expected my skin to meet metal. Instead, the material the fae used read more like wood or a composite. While I made an attempt to probe the table at my back, Nadège crossed fae-made restraints across my shoulders, wrists, and waist.

At the foot of the table, she nudged my legs apart before placing straps over my thighs and ankles and flipping up two pieces to support the bottoms of my feet. The number of straps deemed necessary to hold down a five-foot-two witch seemed excessive. But if I was going to get through what I suspected was the facility's version of a gynecological exam, I had to let go of thoughts of my body being an inviolate temple and look at the experience from a distance.

One after the other, each of the fae palpated my abdominal area, some more gently than others, while Nadège lectured them on specifics of anatomy of witchborn females and common variations they could expect to encounter. Only one of those fae bothered to warm their steely hands before touching me.

After the hands-on external exam came collecting my blood and swabbing my mouth. When that was done, Nadège placed her flat screen device over my lower abdomen, had her group gather around, and rolled out the particulars of my reproductive organs. She finished up with reviewing what I explained to her about the herbs I took for birth control.

"Considering what we have gathered, I believe this guest is a perfect candidate for our vision. Once we have removed certain obstacles, she will be ready for implantation."

Lionel heaped praise on Nadège's shoulders as she and the others left my bedside. The glass door slid closed behind them, the lights in the room dimmed, and the Imperator's voice came over a hidden speaker. "You have done well, Alderose. Dinner will be brought to you once the next procedure is over."

I stayed on the bed, unmoving. Nadège's reference to *certain obstacles* chilled my blood. I knew exactly what she was referring to and there was no way those obstacles were going to be removed without a fight—and a great deal of pain. I gripped the edges of the table, closed my eyes, and waited.

And I prayed. I conjured up the vision of the Goddess I had created when I was little and feeling alone, and let her wise eyes and wild hair embrace my fearful heart.

I was floating inside my vision when I saw a group of women in white ceremonial gowns coming toward my room. They stopped at the door. One of them said, "We are here, Imperator."

The door slid open enough to accommodate them entering two-by-two. One of the women stepped to the foot of the table. Two came up behind her, and three behind them, forming a triangle. I lifted my head. Six. They weren't fae.

And they weren't witches.

The women fanned around the bed. Two unlocked the wheels on either side, lowered the raised end of the bed, and rolled it forward so one of them could stand behind my head. That woman leaned over me and held the sides of my head in an unforgiving grip. In sync, four of the women took hold of my arms and legs, adding their strength to the straps already pinning me down. The sixth woman, the one with long black hair who had entered the room first and was still in her place at my feet, removed something from a hidden pocket in her robe.

The stinging sensation in my feet told me that something was a magnet.

It dawned on me with a sudden ferocity why the table I was tethered to was made of wood. The fae had made sure there was no metal within my reach. And without being able to hold a piece of metal in my hand—or even my mouth—I was vulnerable to a kind of magic I had only heard about.

The woman at my feet glanced at each of the others in turn and nodded. As one, the five of them began to chant. As they chanted, their leader swept the magnet over each of my toes, top and bottom, then my calves and my thighs in short, hard, deliberate strokes.

And every stroke removed the metal from my body, taking my magic with it.

I disappeared inside my pain and pleaded with the darkness to take me.

20

THE WHIRLWIND that was life with a Brodeur sister by my side continued. No sooner had we seen Clementine's sister, Beryl, back to health than we were forced to pursue the remaining sister.

Alderose, the eldest of the three, had found out about the attacks on Clementine and Beryl that had happened in the Reformed Realm. Rather than waiting to see if a plan to go after her sisters' attacker was already in motion, Alderose abruptly left for France. And now Clementine and Beryl, and my brothers, Kostya and Iván, and I were trying to determine where exactly in France Alderose had gone.

We were starting at the Brodeur family home in Northampton, Massachusetts. Once inside the commercial building, we filed into the stairwell and headed to the third-floor workroom.

I hit the landing first. The door was open. Inside the spacious room, not much looked changed from the weekend, not at first glance. On the floor, right inside the door, was Alderose's duffel bag, wide open and displaying at least a couple of her knives. Her phone's charger was plugged into a nearby socket and the little light was green.

And sitting in the charger was her phone. No wonder she hadn't answered any of our multitudinous calls and texts.

I opened my arms wide, blocking the entrance, and yelled, "Stop!" Something in the room *had* changed. I sensed it, in no small part because days ago, the first few minutes I spent in this room changed my life irrevocably. Most mortals and Magicals did not forget the moment they met their mates. I would never forget the moment I met Clementine Brodeur.

"Alderose was definitely here," I said, pointing to the obvious clues at our feet. "She left her phone and some of her gear."

"Are her leathers in there?" Beryl asked. "When she's off doing her hunting thing, she always brings her leathers. And she would never, *ever* willingly leave her knives."

I knelt by the bag, shifting my position to allow everyone into the room. "Yes and no. I don't see any clothing, only soft armor. Gauntlets, shin guards, a reinforced vest. And a few sheaths for knives."

"Any of you notice anything off about those mannequins?"

Glancing over my shoulder, I spotted Clementine and Beryl with their heads together. The five dressmaker's dummies, which I vaguely remembered noticing before and which, at the time, had seemed perfectly normal in a couturier's workroom, were arrayed equidistant from one another. All five faced in toward the center of the room. None were clothed.

"Laz, baby," Clementine continued, turning her concerned face to me, "I'm going to put on the mascara. I have to. There's got to be a connection between this...arrangement and the pentagram and candles Alderose left on the floor of the shop."

My gut clenched. Clementine had acted heroically over and over again in the days since we'd met. Most recently, on our trip to the Reformed Realm, she'd held her own with my parents and the palace staff. More important, she'd saved my friend Sheenah's little girl from being taken by Lionel Vigne.

None of us had been able to prevent Sheenah's and Beryl's subsequent abduction—but Clementine had tracked Beryl into the Barrenwood, allowing us to find her sister in time to save her life. I didn't want my mate suffering any more trauma.

That said, holding her back wasn't embracing and acknowledging how strong and clever she was, how utterly willing to do whatever needed to be done to make sure those she loved were safe.

"Go for it," I said. "I've got your back."

Clementine stepped away from her sister. I saw Beryl's cheeks had gotten paler, caught Kostya's eye, and tilted my head in the witch's direction. "She okay?" I mouthed. He pressed his lips together and nodded once.

"Each of the mannequins has a symbol painted on the back of the neck area," Beryl said, accepting the support offered by my brother's chest. "The symbols are the five elements. Air, water, fire, earth, and ether. And the rug's been moved and—" She pulled my brother with her and pointed to the floor. "There's a compass here. Brass. Like the one in the shop, but bigger. Hmm," she added. "Fancier too. Lots more symbols and such. I'll need reading glasses to see what's inscribed on there."

"Okay, mascara's on," Clementine declared. "Can you guys move away from the mannequins and stand closer to the wall?"

"Sissy, hold on a sec." Beryl dragged Kostya toward the front of the room with the four large windows overlooking the street, stopped, and almost collapsed.

"Beryl, what's happening?"

"I moved too fast. I know you guys got a lot of blood into me, but I'm still feeling pretty woozy." She leaned into my brother and pointed to the desk. "Also, that book was *not* there when we were here to look for the fabric for Zazie."

"I'll get the book. Hold on to me." Kostya hefted the album-sized volume under one arm, snugged Beryl against his side, and guided her to the desk chair. "You sit here. I'll find that wool we used before, get you warm."

"You could just kiss me, Kostya."

Damn if my younger brother didn't smile like a lovesick pup and follow up with exactly what Beryl suggested. "Takes one to know one," he muttered as he passed me.

"Laz, can you stand closer? Put your hands on my hips? Helps me to stay grounded."

Clementine's lush curves filled my palms. I dipped my head toward hers and rubbed my nose in her hair. "I'm right here," I said. "Always."

She patted my hand then raised her arms in front of her body. "Rosey was definitely here. She has something of Dad's. And some of Mom's things. And something of...Fen's? A hat? Weird."

She continued. "Curious. She's moving, moving from one mannequin to the next and the next. She's crossing the space, meeting the points. She's meeting the points and she's—" Clementine sucked in a breath and covered her mouth. "Oh, Rosey, oh no, no, no."

My witch collapsed against my chest and covered her eyes with her hands. I held her upright when she said she didn't need to sit, she just needed to process what she'd seen.

"Hey, I have an idea about where she might have gone. Look at this." Iván was by the door, holding up Alderose's phone. "There's a photo in here of a map of the Alps, specifically Mont Blanc, and a valley near Chamonix. There's another photo. Its a close-up, marked with an X. The map looks hand drawn, and I'm thinking it might be in that book on the desk. And she's got a string of messages from a Sidan, forwarded to her via a service that serves as an information nexus between the earth realm and the fae lands."

"Who's Sidan? And how did Alderose leave this room?" Beryl asked. "There's no portal in here."

"The dolls," Clementine said, pushing away my hands. "The big, big dolls. Invoking water, begin with air. Invoking fire, begin with ether. Invoking earth, begin with spirit. Invoking air, begin with water. Invoking spirit, begin with... begin with..."

"Where are the big dolls, Sissy?"

Clementine pointed to the mannequins. "There. Each one anchors a point of the pentacle and together they somehow create a portal. Don't ask me how. I couldn't see how, I could only see one moment Alderose was *here* and the next moment she was *gone*."

"Could she have found something else in this book besides the map?" Kostya asked, showing the sisters the large, plain album. "It sure doesn't look like much."

"Kostya, puncture my finger." Beryl glared at him when he asked why and kissed him as he pressed the tip of his nail into her thumb. "When you're not certain how to wake up a sleeping beauty, you kiss it or you bleed on it. I'm guessing this book requires blood." She smeared her blood around her palm and pressed her hand to the book's cover. When that elicited no reaction, she turned the book around. We all noticed the red-tipped page edges.

"You sneaky, sneaky witch." Beryl squeezed more blood from her thumb and offered it to the unblemished paper. The next third of the page edges reddened as the blood spread, while the cover of the book shifted and changed. We all held our breath as a slightly three-dimensional rendition of Moira's workroom appeared, complete with the compass rose in the center and the mannequins. Glowing lines connected the five standing figures.

"It's a pentacle," Beryl said, sliding her finger between the pages where the dried blood stopped and her fresh blood began.

The book opened to a page with a few lines written in a strong script.

For Beryl. A birthdate was written underneath. The page loosened. Beryl turned it over. Next up was a table of contents. *How to Help Your Sisters* went from black ink to pink, as did *How to Help Yourself.* "Wow, Mom. It's almost like she was expecting us to get into trouble," Beryl joked.

"See what she wrote, B." The book opened itself to the correct page. Alderose's name pulsed and the blank space below it began to fill with words.

The oldest witch carries a heavy heart and will want to lead with her sword. As much as metal needs to be tempered and quenched to achieve a less brittle state, so shall she.

"Alderose had her share of quenching last weekend," Clementine said, stroking the page with her finger. "I'm afraid for what kind of tempering she's going through."

The oldest witch is her father's daughter and will have need of resources that were developed to support his magic. If possible, make the following recipe and see that she consumes it regularly.

Underneath that line was, *For the Scarab Eaters.*

The sisters scanned the page. "Unless Mom kept a supply of these capsules on hand, one of us is going to México," Clementine said. "And what are *Chrysina* beetles? And does anyone know what phase the moon is in?"

"*Chrysina* beetles, also known as jewel scarabs because of the metallic coloring of their shells, are found throughout the world." Ivan read off his phone. "Give me a sec... Okay, *Chrysina gorda* are one of the species found in central México."

Beryl pointed to the ceiling. "The moon is currently a waning crescent and there's one more line you need to hear. *Above all else, love her unconditionally. And forgive her. For she, more than either of her sisters, will know heartbreaking pain.*

"Any of you come across a crystal ball? Because this is giving me the chills. If Rosey's known pain worse than what I just went through?" Beryl shook her head and continued to stare at the page and the lines of pink ink. "Okay, my sister's in trouble. She needs to be love-bombed and she needs these capsules. Which one of you is taking me to México?"

"How about we start with calling Maritza?" Kostya asked. "She may know where to get the soil and the beetles locally."

While those two worked on resourcing what was needed to make the capsules that would strengthen Alderose's magic, Iván studied the images in Alderose's phone. I looked over his shoulder as he opened a mapping app on his own device. "We're going to end up in Chamonix, brother," he said. "Might as well start making plans now."

"What do you think we need?"

"Lionel Vigne, aka the Imperator, owns a castle built into the side of a mountain. And if you zoom in, you'll see the castle has its own aerial tram that goes to a larger stone building in the valley. The design of the structure is based on local architecture, but records indicate that outbuilding's gone up over the past two years. You'll also notice there are no other structures within a wide radius of either, and only one road to the castle.

"I bet they're using tunnels bored into the mountain— maybe ones that were built during the wars—and they're utilizing the portal network. Another interesting thing? Across the valley, see that other castle, the smaller one that kind of rambles around? That belongs to a druidic order. Ni'eve du Blanc runs the place and she's been there for centuries. She's highly regarded, though rumor has it one of her daughters severely tarnished Ni'eve's reputation."

"A bit of intrigue in the Alps?" I asked.

Ivan nodded and swiped to another image. "I want to know where the captured Magicals are kept. In the newer building? Inside the mountain? On the castle grounds?"

"Can we get a drone in there?"

"We could try. But Lionel Vigne is fae and if it's fae magic we're going up against, they're masters at camouflage."

"Personally, I'd like to just show up, knock on the door, and wring his neck."

"You and me both, brother," Kostya said, joining us. "I'm going down to the laboratory with Beryl. Maritza consulted with Malvyn and they've come up with a variation for the capsule formulation that should work. Mal said Alderose dug up some of the dirt from the lab and brought it with her when they all took Zazie back to the island. There were dung beetles in the dirt, only she didn't know until Mal pointed them out. He ran a quick test for us on the soil and said he thinks Moira hauled it up from the different places in México mentioned in the recipe."

"Clever witch."

"And our mates are related to her." Pride suffused Kostya's voice.

"Did I hear you say *mate*, brother?"

"You did." Kostya shrugged out of his leather jacket and turned around. "Feel my back, between the shoulder blades and my spine." Iván and I did, and we both reacted in the same way at the same time.

"Spirit take me, are those *wings*?" Iván asked.

"Those are something, that's for sure. Beryl and I haven't had sex since they showed up a week ago, right as all the shit was hitting the fan."

"Kostya, are you ready?" Beryl waited for Kostya in the doorway. They left. I turned to find Clementine standing outside the circle of mannequins, hands on her hips, staring into the middle of the room.

21

CLEMENTINE

"WHAT'RE YOU THINKING?" Laszlo asked. He'd been speaking with his brothers before Beryl hooked arms with Kostya and left for the cellar. I was bouncing back and forth between being worried for Alderose, wondering about the identity of her girl-friend, and picturing my sister as the invincible warrior witch she'd always been in my eyes. I used to love watching her prac-tice with her swords and knives. She was born to wield weapons, and in her hands, anything could become a weapon.

But she'd left her phone and some of her knives and her protective vest—all of which tipped me over into worried with a dollop of panic on the side. I fought to keep the panic from making me do dumb things. Rubbing my upper chest, I finally answered Laz's question.

"Two of us need to take this portal and see where it leads. I'm ninety-nine point nine percent sure it's currently configured to take anyone who activates it to France.

"What I don't know is where exactly it goes. I'm assuming Chamonix. I want to get us close to Lionel—but I don't want to end up in his living room. Or one of the dungeons."

"Kostya, Iván, and I could do our demon brothers act."

I looked up at my very tall, very handsome fiancé and his slightly taller and freakishly pretty brother. I had the rock that sealed the deal, but Laz and I hadn't had time to design a band, have the ring made, or make a formal announcement in the hours since he gave me the diamond. "You plan to distract Lionel with *comedy*?"

Laszlo laughed. Goddess, it was good to have a light moment. "The Reformed Realm has at times deployed us where size could make a difference in the direction the negotiations needed to take."

"I think we're going to need stealth more than size. Though I wonder about your wings, Laz." An idea was working its way to the front of my brain and when it hit, Laszlo saw it too.

"I *am* a rarity," he said, extending his wings out and up as far as they would go.

"But Lionel Vigne has already seen you," I reminded him. "Maybe not in your full glory, but he's seen you and he's gotten a read on me, so we need a different tactic."

"Call Alabastair. He can portal to the tree in the cellar, assess what's going on with the mannequins and where they'll take us, and send us on our way to someplace near the castle."

The brothers and I gathered up Alderose's things, closed the door behind us, and jogged down to the ground floor. I called Alabastair en route. He promised to gather what he needed from his end and be in the building within thirty minutes. Beryl sent the bathroom elevator up. One minute later the five of us were crowded into Mom's laboratory.

Candles blazed with light, giving us a much better look at the marvelous layout of the room. Cupboards were set into the walls. I hadn't noticed those before. Above our heads, dried herbs and other things hung from a rack attached to the tall ceiling via a pulley system. Beryl was standing on a wooden crate, grinding dirt in the bowl of a large marble mortar and issuing directions to Kostya. He reached up, pulled the racks down to head height, and unhooked a sieve as we explained our plan to utilize Alabastair.

"Sounds good." He set the sieve close to Beryl. "What do you need next?"

"See if you can find another mortar and pestle or something similar to grind the beetles into a fine powder. And I'll need a bowl. Or a tray."

"What can we do?" I asked.

Beryl twisted the emerald ring off her finger. "Laszlo can use this to get Iván to the other cellar, the one with the portal tree, and wait for Alabastair. Have a look around while you're in there."

Laszlo hustled his brother into the bathroom and closed the door to activate the elevator.

"I can't wait for the day we get to explore this entire building without being in a life-or-death situation," Beryl said, wiping her hands on a cloth and leaning against Kostya.

"Me too, B. Me too." Curiosity got the better of me. I reached for the nearest wooden nob and opened a small drawer. Desiccated roots were lined up inside.

"Sissy, use one of the candles." Beryl waved me closer and lowered her voice to a whisper. "I believe there are things in this room that don't like to show themselves in artificial light."

"Isn't candlelight artificial?" I asked.

"Technically yes, but..." She shrugged. "Just give it a try. When Kostya and I opened the door this time, I had the sense the room was waiting for us. That it was... That it's happy we're here. And that it prefers the flattering light of candles rather than the harsh reality of modern technology. No one looks good in that blue tone."

Beryl cracking jokes was a good sign. She was in her element, elbows-deep in magic with people she loved she could boss around. "Oh, you'll find more candles in the cupboard across from me."

I gathered a handful, set them on the table, and lit one. "Kostya, where'd you find the beetles?"

"In a jar labeled Beetles."

"What else does the recipe call for?"

"Rust and gel capsules. And a sacrifice. We found bags of capsules but they were completely melted. The important thing is getting the ingredients ground and mixed together. I can put it into...I don't know, a little box or bag, and we can each carry some of it on us. Why don't you look for containers, Sissy?"

I pointed out the jumble of hand tools and magical implements on the far corner of the table. Kostya volunteered to scrape off and gather the flakes of orange and umber rust lining the knives' and scissors' edges. Which left one question begging to be answered. "Either of you have any thoughts on the sacrifice part of this?"

Beryl's cheeks paled. "I'm avoiding that step for the moment. Maybe because I feel like I've sacrificed enough this week?"

"Let me think about how a sacrifice becomes an ingredient while I find something to put this in." I started at the top of the nearest inset cabinet and opened drawer after drawer. The more I opened, the more I wished there was time to explore every nook and cranny, jar and box and packet. "I got it," I said. "We can use these little Manilla envelopes. They even have a string you loop around a paper button."

"Those are so cute. Don't forget to label both sides."

I returned to mulling over what constituted a sacrifice and which of us should be the one to make it—or would the magic be more potent if we all contributed? Heavy footsteps and the shudder of the elevator settling outside the door announced the boys were back with Alabastair in tow.

"We've got him and he's got ideas."

"Before we head to the workroom, let's finish up here. We have the dirt, the beetles, and the rust. Last step is a sacrifice. Any suggestions, Bas?"

"Blood would be my first guess. Though perhaps Moira's magic was more subtle than that? These capsules were meant for Heriberto, were they not?"

"That's correct," Beryl said. "His magic and Alderose's were —are—similar. They're Unbinders, and they wield metal weapons. My father would make Rosey practice using weapons that hadn't been magically enhanced and without drawing on any of her own magic."

"Water would blend all of those ingredients. Though the particles would remain suspended and separate. Fire would meld them. Start with fire."

"Sacrifice *by* fire?" Laszlo asked.

"Yes. I don't have time to go into detailed theory. Kostya, light the larger burner. Beryl, pour one cup of what you've ground up into a cooking vessel, one with a shallow bottom. Everyone, remove something from your body that is an intrinsic part of you." Once the pan set up on a stand over the flame, Alabastair found a metal spoon and stirred the contents using a precise figure-eight motion. "Quick," he added. "There's no need to overthink this. And no time."

Laszlo handed me his knife. "Take a slice of the membrane. One from each wing, closer to the shoulder area where it's less sensitive." I swallowed hard, affected a clinical approach, and asked him to spread his wings a bit more. "I'll be fine, Clementine."

The knife was sharp and the cutting was over in seconds. I added the pieces to the mixture. Kostya asked for the knife, shaved slivers off his prominent thumbnail directly into the bowl. Ivan asked him to do the same to the tips of his horns. When I finished with the demon brothers, Ivan asked if I needed his help. "Are there any small scissors?" I asked. "And who's got the steadiest hand? I need one of you to snip the ends of my eyelashes where my mother's mascara is the thickest."

Ivàn volunteered. His touch was gentle. He finished with me and turned to Beryl. "You're up, sister," he said.

She extended her arm. "I'll donate blood. What's in my veins came from all of you. Strength in numbers, right?"

"Strength in family. Let me do it, Ivan." Kostya circled my sister's slender wrist with his much bigger hand, kissed her thumb mound, and cut her skin with the tip of his knife. He guided her hand over the bowl and added a dozen or so drops of her blood. Candles added their magical glow to the impromptu ritual.

Alabastair stepped aside. "Now stir everything together while it heats, Beryl. Use your wand."

"I lost my wand in the Barrenwood," she said.

"Here, use one of Mom's." I'd seen a couple of wands in the stack of magical implements moldering at the far end of the table. The one that caught my eye was constructed from numerous strands twisted together in a very organic shape, like it had been cut from living, entangled vines and then dried.

Beryl giggled when I showed her the wand. "I can't tell if the sections are trying to figure out how to get along or doing their damnedest to get away from each other."

"Just like us, B." I side-hugged my sister and left my arm draped around her waist as she cleared her throat, assessed the flames and the bowl in front of her, and took over stirring.

"What chant should I use?" she asked Alabastair. "Did Tía say anything about a particular spell?"

"She did. She also suggested I encourage you to draw from your intuition. If that feels like too much pressure, then I could relay a specific set of words to you."

I shook my head. "You got this," I told her, staying where I was in support of my sister. Alabastair positioned himself across the table.

"What are the properties of metals, Sissy? I'm so nervous I can't remember even *one*."

"Metals are malleable," I said.

"Ductile," Kostya added.

Laszlo, Ivan, and Alabastair joined in one after the other.

"Lustrous."

"Solid."

"Heavy."

"Metals conduct heat and electricity."

"They melt."

"And they make sounds," Beryl said. "Metals are sonorous." Taking in a deep breath, my sister closed her eyes, lifted her chin, hesitated...and started to speak.

"May you bend and stretch and never break. May you channel your powers in give and take." She paused. "May you ground, may you flow, may you bend like a bow. May you shine in the dark. May you sing like a...like a lark."

She smiled, adding, "Welcome to Beryl Brodeur's incantations and poetry slam. Feel free to add your voices as we imbue this mixture of dirt and bugs and blood and bone with the magic bonds of family born and family found."

We all joined in, even Alabastair, until the necromancer declared the mixture fully melded. "Pour it onto the tray," he instructed. "Let it cool. Then break it into pieces and drop those into the envelopes Clementine found. Seal the packets and divvy them up amongst you."

The mixture cooled in record time with the help of Laszlo's ice magic. We followed the rest of Bas's instructions before extinguishing the candles and leaving through the bathroom in two trips. In the stairwell, on the second-floor landing, Kostya mentioned he smelled food. We gathered outside the door to my parents' apartment, all of us sniffing the air.

"You're right," I said. "Could Alderose be *here*?"

"Let's find out." Beryl asked Laz for the emerald ring. She waved her hand in front of the latch and handle. When the lock released, she hit the nearest light switch. "Guys. It's warm and the smell of food's even stronger."

Laszlo announced he was taking the front room. I ducked into the kitchen. Two bowls, two spoons, and two glasses were stacked in the sink. They were still wet from being rinsed—and there was no doubt in my mind that someone, likely Alderose, had been here. "She had company, Sissy. How could we have missed her? Didn't she hear us?"

"I don't know. Though I'm beginning to think the magic in this building is playing with us."

"Let's see if the others found anything."

Ivan, Kostya, and Alabastair had taken to opening all of the interior doors and checking out the rooms and closets. Beryl and I held hands as we walked the few steps to the front room. Kostya was wearing his investigator face and had his hand underneath a lamp's shade. "Vestige of warmth," he said. "On the bulb."

I went to the long, low couch where the imprints of four thighs on the silk and linen velveteen cushions spoke of two recent visitors. I wasn't a sensate witch; I couldn't run my hands over the couch and discern who had been sitting there. "Beryl, can you read objects through touch?" I asked.

"Sadly, no. Why?" I straightened and pointed to the cushions. Beryl glanced down. "What if you were to use the mascara again?"

I sucked in a breath. "I'm wary of over-use. We don't have a recipe for making the compound."

"And we don't have another Clementine if you get walloped again."

"Let's keep going," I said. "We know Magicals were here not very long ago, we suspect one of them was Alderose, and now we've got more incentive to find her."

"Now I feel guilty for lugging her duffel around with us. What if she was here to get her things?"

"That was a group decision, Laz."

Alabastair asked us to wait outside the workroom. He paused in the doorway, taking in his first view of the circle of mannequins. The more I looked at them, the more I wondered why I hadn't seen the circle the first night we were here. Bas walked around the backsides of the dummies, then went to each one, never walking between them in a straight line. "I don't want to trigger the lines," he explained. "Though I can feel them. The residual magic from the portal's recent use lingers."

He studied the rest of the room before walking to a spot near my mother's desk. "Would one of you like to accompany me on a test run?"

"Me." Ivàn took one step forward. "I speak fluent French."

"Je parle aussi français," Alabastair countered. "What else can you do?"

"He's the most skilled fighter of us all, Bas," Laszlo said. "And he's fast. He'll cut down an attacker before you even know they're coming."

"Then let's begin." Alabastair handed portal stones to Ivan and left a handful with me in case things went very wrong on their end. He walked the outer circle, paused, then chose the dummy labeled with the symbol for earth and began to walk the pentacle. As he joined the last line to where they began for the second time, the air around the two of them began to shimmer.

They vanished with a double *pop, pop.*

KOSTYA GRABBED my shoulder and left his hand there a good minute in the aftermath of Ivan's departure with the Portal Keeper. "I travel through most portals as easily as I breathe," he said. "It's different being on this side of it when you don't know what's on the other end."

"Or who's on the other end." I crossed my arms. "Do you think we should stay right here and wait it out?"

Clementine piped in with, "Bas knows what he's doing. Beryl and I are going to sit while we wait." She rolled their mother's chair out from behind the desk, made her sister take it, then popped on top of the desk and picked up the grimoire. "So, this is it. This is Mom's book."

"I think so, Sissy. Took my blood. And that must be Alderose's blood on the pages before mine."

"I want to know what she left for me. But I'm in no rush read it," Clementine said, shaking her head. "I might have been if the lawyer had handed the book to us when he gave us Serena's papers and the set of keys. But not now."

"What if there's something in there that will help us get Alderose back?"

Clementine stroked the cover of the book. "The book will let me know. Or, I'll feel it. Right now I'm just happy it gave you enough to help us find Rosey."

I loved watching my fiancé and her sister. "They're a lovely pair, aren't they?" Kostya whispered.

While we were getting an eyeful of the most important women our lives, the pressure in the room changed, followed by the same *pop, pop, pop*. Alabastair and Ivan were back. A quick check showed all of their limbs were intact.

And that they'd brought along a faun.

"Everyone, meet Larch," Alabastair said. "He's seen Alderose. Twice. According to him, she's a guest at Lionel's castle. Though the way he described it, she's more a prisoner of his fortress and the archaic rules of hospitality he imposes upon unexpected visitors."

We all began to speak at once. Ivàn held up his hand. "There's more. And we're running out of time. Lionel Vigne intends to use Alderose in his breeding program."

"What?" Beryl and Clementine reached for each other's hands.

"And Laz, he has Sheenah."

"Bind him," I ordered. Ivan grabbed the faun's wrists and held them as Kostya pulled handcuffs from his jacket pocket. "Alabastair, did you see anything else?"

"Larch confirms there are very few ways to get inside the castle proper. Our best bet is a single portal tree, which is located outside the section of the castle formerly used to house those captured by Lionel."

Ivàn pulled out Alderose's phone and showed an image to Larch. The faun nodded. "He's confirmed my suspicion that the newer building is where Lionel now houses the captives," Ivàn said. "He's certain that's where Alderose is being kept, if we don't find her in the wing with the cells.

Larch knows for certain that Sheenah is in the new building."

"And how does he know all this?" Kostya asked.

"I keep Lionel's sister happy." The faun grinned. "She and I go way back."

"He's too much of a wild card to take with us. Any suggestions?"

I had to agree with my brother. Clementine slid off the desk and Beryl stood. "We have to go, and we have to go now."

"I will help in exchange for asylum. And I want a guarantee you will do everything you can to protect my portal tree."

"I can set all of that up legally and have Malvyn approve it," Kostya said.

"Alabastair, you're on portals."

"There's still another question. Who's Sidan?" Ivan waggled Alderose's phone. "The two were planning to meet, only Alderose didn't show. The last message says Sidan was planning to come looking for her."

"New York City. Alderose has an apartment—or a condo, I don't remember—on the Upper East Side. It'd be worth it to check that out, especially now that we don't have to drive all the way to Boston to get to the portal."

"I will stay here where I am reachable by" —Alabastair glanced around the room— "every one of you, plus Maritza and Malvyn."

"You might have an ally in the druidess, Ni'eve du Blanc," Larch added. "Her training academy is on the other side of the mountain from Lionel's castle, and rumor has it, he has trapped one of her students. Do any of you know Ni'eve?"

Alabastair swiped the screen on his phone, tapped, and brought it to his ear. "Mari. Lionel has Alderose and Sheenah at his castle. He also has one of Ni'eve's students. We need Calliope's druid." He listened intently to everything Maritza said, then replied, "We have a way to get from Moira's workroom to Chamonix. We also have a portal guide, a faun who goes by the name of Larch. I was going to stay here with him while—" His mouth stayed open as he nodded. "I will bow to your input. Have the druid text me when he arrives in Boston and I will pick him up. Je t'aime."

Alabastair slid his phone into a pocket of his cape and swept his hand over his bald head, ridding him of the hood. "Tanner Marechal is a druid currently living on Salt Spring Island with the same witch who has inherited a clutch of melusine eggs. While that is a story for later, what Tanner adds to our search and rescue is an intimate knowledge of that area of Chamonix. He is an extremely capable ward-maker and he would certainly have a vested interest in freeing the captives. After hearing Larch's description of the tree shifter in Vigne's possession, I can only assume it is Jessamyne du Blanc, Ni'eve's daughter and Tanner's former lover and nemesis."

Clementine went to Alabastair. "Cut to the chase, Bas."

"Your aunt and I want you to stay put until Tanner is here."

Kostya cleared his throat. "While we're waiting for the druid, Beryl and I can go to Alderose's apartment and be back here within an hour. While we're gone, get your rest. Take shifts. Do whatever you need to do to boost your magic." My brother stood behind Beryl, massaging her shoulders. "Ready, Ms. B?"

"Ready. With one stop on the second floor for a coat and a hat and a pair of gloves."

As those two left, I turned to Clementine and Ivàn. "You both should rest. I'll take the first two-hour shift with Alabastair."

My witch yawned and stretched. "C'mon, brother. There are blankets and pillows downstairs too."

Meanwhile, I planned to interrogate the faun further. I wanted enough detail that I could see the inside of the castle as though I had been a frequent guest.

"Will Lionel notice your absence?" I asked.

Larch shrugged. "Perhaps? I have been known to wander off, especially in the spring, but it is October and it is cold. He may assume I'm cuddling with a milkmaid. I've been known to do that too." He patted his thighs. "Do any of you have a cigarette?"

I shook my head and paced. Within twenty minutes, Alabastair had a text from Tanner that the druid was leaving the island. There was nothing I needed to do to boost my magic, aside from having Clementine near me so we could feed into and off of each other. The faun eventually closed his eyes and curled into a ball on one of the rugs. Alabastair turned to assessing the mannequins, then kneeled and brought out a magnifying glass to examine the compass rose embedded in the wood floor. He asked for my knife and used the tip to pick at the area around the disc.

"I suspect the disc is used much like a dial and can be turned to change the destination for those activating the portal. This is classic geomagick, and once we have Alderose safe, I would like to pick this compass apart."

I left the necromancer to his musings and settled my back against the wall. If I went to the second floor, I would want to strip Clementine of her clothing. The constant craving to have her in my arms only softened when I was holding her against my chest. My wings twitched. My other craving, the one that had me itching to climb the stairs to the roof, stretch my wings, and take to the air, was the only craving I hadn't yet voiced to Clementine. Or to anyone.

"Alabastair?" I said.

"Yes?" My voice must have startled him.

"Thank you for all of your help."

He smiled broadly. "The Nekrosine genes contain a strong compulsion to be of service to their community. You and I are now part of a community defined by the women we love and cherish. There is nothing I would not do for Maritza, or for someone she calls kin."

"I feel the same way, Bas. The Demesne has proved powerful in ways I never imagined."

Alabastair extended his arm. I went to shake his hand, when he pulled me to standing and drew me into an embrace. "Let's get Alderose and not lose anyone in the process."

"I'm with you on that."

Bas's phone buzzed. "It's Tanner," he said. "I'm off. Keep an eye on the faun. I doubt he's one for escaping, though..." He shrugged. "They make dedicated, loyal portal guides and they take immensely good care of their trees. I'm choosing to believe what he shared with us."

The necromancer left. I had barely sat down again when I received an incoming text from Kostya. He sent photos of an opened apartment door and a black-and-white tiled floor splattered with blood.

"Nobody here," he wrote. "We're heading right back."

I secured the faun's wrists and ankles to one of the heavy oak tables and tore down the stairs to wake Clementine and Ivan. "Alderose's apartment is empty, but there's blood all over the floor outside her door."

"Now what do we do?"

"We go back upstairs, stay with the faun, and wait for Kostya and Beryl and Alabastair."

"You guys go up," Clementine said. "I'm too anxious to stay in one place. I'll see if there's anything to eat in the kitchen, or..." Her voice petered out. "Laz? I need a recharge."

I spread my wings and offered her my arms. Chanting the words that poured ice magic into my veins, we both watched as the demon lines on my forearms began to glow. Clementine took hold of my wrists, closed her eyes, and started to hum.

I let her take as much as she needed. My well had never been drained, and since bonding with my witch, our magics seemed to feed—and feed off of—one another.

"Thank you," she whispered. She loosened her grip and smiled. "I feel much better. You go ahead. I'll be fine."

"Not until I get a kiss," I said. Behind me, Ivàn groaned.

"I'll see you upstairs, brother."

My wings enfolded Clementine. She lifted her heels, bringing her lush lips within kissing distance. I slanted my mouth over hers and found comfort in the bond between us.

"Don't think for a moment you and the Arkadi brothers are leaving me and Beryl behind," she said, once we'd come up for air. She ran her hands over my demon lines and reminded me we were stronger together.

"You test my need to protect you from harm, my darling."

"I know."

Voices and bootsteps reverberated up the stairwell. Kostya, Beryl, Alabastair, and a dark-haired stranger wearing sandals paused in the doorway to the apartment. "Tanner's here," Beryl said. "C'mon."

We followed them to the third floor and found Ivàn perched on the table, in conversation with the faun.

"Tanner," Larch said, raising his arms. "Long time no see. How's your lovely witch?"

"Calliope is doing well, Larch. And you're staying out of trouble?"

"Never." The faun laughed, then turned serious. "For all that I love a good romp with Linette Vigne, I'll not be sad to see the entire clan brought to heel. I take it you've got a plan?"

"I do," the druid said. "If everyone could gather 'round, I'd like to map out the most expeditious route to the sub-sub-basement of the building Lionel Vigne calls the Facility."

"Rosey. *Rosey.*"

I squeezed my eyes tight against my baby sister's dreamy voice. Clementine was the first to start calling me Rosey, and the nickname had stuck. Though I never felt like a rose, all pungent, soft-petalled, and evocative of romance.

I identified more with the thorns. Because I, too, liked to draw blood.

Blood. Metal. Magic.

Women who weren't fae, and who weren't witches, had combed my magic out of me and now I was hearing Clemmie's voice and dreaming of flowers.

"Alderose Brodeur, *wake the fuck up.* We're getting you out of here."

My eyelids slammed open. Floating above me was a ceiling glowing with squares of bluish lights. My brain registered I was in a clinic. A face framed by a halo of dark, wavy hair moved in from my right side, while another face—this one framed by dark brown curls—came into view on my left. Both popped back out of sight and were replaced by the concerned yet kind face of a man I'd never seen before.

The man was waving a knife. Two knives. They were pretty knives, crackling with lightning-like magic. "I'm cutting your restraints," he said. "We're getting you out of here. Do you understand?"

I nodded. At least, I tried to make my head nod. But by emptying me of my magic, the not-witches had drained me of everything that accompanied that power, including my ability to move on my own. I opened my mouth and tried to explain my predicament to my sisters as the man with the knife hacked at the strap across my belly. Clementine and Beryl each took one arm and drew me up to sitting. My head flopped to one side and the other before my chin slammed against the base of my throat.

I managed to eke out a feeble, "Help." Laszlo, the angelic demon, came to the foot of the table and did something with his ice magic. The straps holding down my ankles shattered, my sisters exhaled, and Laszlo took me into his arms. He even shielded me with his wings. I heard him say, "I've got her."

I tried to tell him he had to get Sheenah.

And that he had to get Jake.

And that if they would just find me some beetles I could maybe, just maybe, begin to build my store of magic...and maybe that other man would let me play with his knives.

Clementine handed me an oily, black cracker. Insisted I eat it as they moved me through the building. I set the bit on my tongue, closed my eyes, and let my saliva do its thing.

IVAN WILL TAKE Sheenah to the Reformed Realm and have her looked at by our healers. She's one hundred percent better now she knows her little girl is safe.

CAT, we're going to help your organization extract Jake.

Jake'll be fine for a while. The Magical world hasn't seen a dragon like him in centuries. If I know him, he'd much prefer we put together an elite crew and blow up Vigne and his operation from the inside out, for once and for all.

Then let's get started.

THEY HURT YOU, *dint they?*

The slightest of touches caressed my cheek. Marsh water wafted into my nostrils.

I warn'd you. I told you they be knowin' all about pain. If I survived, you'll survive. You're a fighter, Alderose. Jes' like your mother. She helpt me, an' now I'm goin' ta help you.

The scent of fresh water left the room, replaced by sleep.

SOFT FOOTSTEPS SHUFFLED on either side of my bed. Or a bed. I could tell I was in a bed and, when I inhaled again, I knew I was in some kind of medical treatment place run by witches or other earth-based healers. The sharp, distinctive smells of healing herbs and antiseptics gave my location away.

"Alderose Brodeur?"

I opened my eyes. A plaster and beam ceiling soared far above me. Two small, firm pillows propped up my head and shoulders and everything else about the bed and the room was clean, spare, and set at precise angles to everything else: the beds, the dividing curtains, the folded-over sheets, and the gray wool blankets.

"Your family is on their way. I was asked to give this to you." A woman in healer's robes slipped a phone into my hand. I pressed the button and brought the phone to my ear.

"Hey. Rós. It's me, Sid. I don't know if you know this yet, but you've got an amazing family. They'll tell you everything, except the one thing they can't—I love you. Where we go from here, I don't know. We both have to heal. But I just wanted you to know I think of you every moment. I'm grateful for you every moment. And I'm so—"

Sidan's voice broke up. I was breaking up too. On the inside. In a good way, even though it felt like Sid was leaving me. Until I noticed my feet were beginning to tingle. I listened to Sid's message again, hit the number to save it, and clasped the phone to my chest.

Looking at the familiar, expectant faces piling into the room, I took a breath and announced, "I think my magic's coming back."

THE END

WHAT'S NEXT?

The first Sister Witches series concludes with

Beguiled, Bewitched, & Broken

(releases August 6, 2020).

PROLOGUE

"Did I die?"

Worried faces studied me from behind clear face shields. I wrinkled my nose at the overwhelming smell of pungent antiseptics and medical supplies and tried to breathe away the banging inside my head. Worry turned to annoyance before one of the hovering faces turned away.

"Please let the prince in before he bashes through the window."

A door clanged against something metal. Kostya materialized at my side. My gorgeous demon stopped just shy of grabbing me, pillows and IV lines and all, and pulling me off the bed.

"Beryl."

"Hey," I said, working to unstick my tongue from the inside of my mouth. "What happened? Where's Clementine?"

I didn't know why I was flat on my back. But I knew with certainty that something had happened to my younger sister. The last memory I had was seeing her talking to a mystery man while a string quartet played in the background.

"She's okay. She's okay, and so is the kid. But you..." Kostya's face crumpled behind his surgical mask.

"But me what?" Relieved as I was that Clementine was okay, I had no memory of a kid.

"You don't remember?"

I went to shake my head, but it wasn't going anywhere. My skull was wedged firmly in place and Kostya's gaze was darting back and forth and up and down like he was cataloguing a sequence of facial fault lines.

"Is there a mirror in here?"

"Why do you want a mirror, Beryl? You just—"

"I want to see what's going on, Kostya. Please." Nothing in his gaze or his tone was instilling confidence in my appearance and my arms weren't cooperating with my attempts to examine the condition of my chin and cheeks. "Because the look on your face is telling me something's wrong with my face."

Another memory slid in. I had been invited to a royal ball. That explained why Clementine was wearing yards of silver brocade. Two demons had done my hair and makeup. I'd been given a gown and shoes and sparkly accessories, including a satin clutch.

"Can you bring me that little purse I was carrying?"

He shook his head. Messy hanks of auburn hair fell forward from where he'd pushed them behind his horns.

"There's nothing wrong with your face, Beryl. It's your neck they're worried about, and I'm not leaving your side for a bloody mirror. Not today. Not tomorrow. Not ever."

Joy blossomed across my chest. Whatever had happened to me hadn't damaged my hearing, and it sounded a lot like my favorite demon in all the realms was proposing. My shoulders sank back into the pillows, and I attempted a grin. Okay, maybe it wasn't a proposal exactly—but it was more of a commitment to the concept of an 'us' than anything he'd said in the past.

Kostya and I were given almost no time to address our relationship parameters for the remainder of my stay in the palace's medical center. Now that I was awake and moderately alert, every moment was taken up by an exam or a consult or another bag of blood. When the healers were getting ready to go, they left the night shift with firm instructions that, if Kostya stayed, he had to let me sleep. I thanked them for taking good care of me and begged Kostya to tell me what happened.

He had a reclining chair delivered to the room. Pushing it right up against my bed, he wrapped himself in a blanket and shared the unadorned details: I had been bitten and almost drained of blood by a male vampire. A different kind of beast—a jaguar shifter who was taken from the palace the same time as me —had likely swiped her claws across my belly, leaving a trio of cuts.

Nothing about the details startled me, which meant the healers had me on painkillers. Not only was I not reacting to Kostya's story, no part of my body hurt. Though the gentle loopiness buoying me almost—almost—masked the faint sensation that something vital was flowing out of a spot to the left of my bellybutton.

Under the cover of my blanket and still holding Kostya's concerned gaze, I made a second attempt to move my arm. It took a few tries to get my hand onto my belly, where my fingertips searched for a way to connect with bare skin. Whatever material the demons used for wound care was thin enough I couldn't feel the edge of a bandage. By following the sensation of leaking magic, I was able to trace three raised ridges I was sure hadn't been there before.

"Did you see the claw marks?" Giddy with success, I slid my arm out from underneath the covers and reached for Kostya. He took my floppy hand in both of his and slowly kissed my knuckles. His eyes were watery when he looked up.

"I did," he said. "I saw the claw marks on your belly and the puncture wounds on your neck, and I vow to never again let anything like that happen to you."

As much as I wanted to ask him more questions about what else he'd seen and what he meant about never leaving my side, the drugs took over and ushered me to sleep.

By the next morning it was apparent to my treatment team that the blood donated by my family, plus the blood products developed by demon researchers, had done an excellent job of accelerating my healing. Once I was fitted with a modest neck brace, given a salve to help with the bruising, and cautioned to not overdo physical activity for at least a week, I was given the green light to leave.

Which was laughable, considering the next bit of news. My older sister had decided to pursue the Magicals whose actions landed me in the medical center in the first place—by herself. The departure timeline from the Reformed Realm was moved from in a few days to as soon as possible. My hope that Kostya and I could have a deeper conversation about the course of our relationship was shoved to the back burner in favor of following Alderose.

CHAPTER ONE

Alderose's solo trip to Chamonix hadn't gone as she'd intended. Though she was in rough shape when we found her in Lionel Vigne's possession, she was now on the other side of the valley, safe inside the walls of Château du Blanc, the home and training center of a renowned order of druids.

Kostya's brother, Laszlo, had carried Alderose from Vigne's experimental facility, through a series of tunnels, and into the druid's rustic infirmary. I stared at the heavy wooden door. No sounds penetrated from the other side. I was shaking from the late hour and the sustained energy our hastily put-together rescue mission had required so soon after I was discharged.

I loosened the neck brace and gently palpated the area where the vampire's teeth had entered. My skin was as numb from the cold as my limbs, and I was beyond ready to become as one with a horizontal surface. All Kostya, Clementine, and I needed was to be shown to our guestrooms. Beds, and privacy, were moments away.

A man about my age approached us. I couldn't tell if he was a druid-in-training or a staff person. Like everyone we'd seen so far, he was attired in a generic uniform of canvas drawstring pants, a sweater knit from natural wool, and felted slippers. His dark blonde hair was long and held away from his face with a leather cord.

"I am the night host." He gestured for us to follow him into a round tower. "Please come with me."

We trudged single-file up narrow, twisting steps that brought us to a dimly lit hall. I was sure I wasn't the only one looking forward to the end of the druid's *Welcome to Chamonix* spiel so I could indulge in a hot shower before collapsing into bed.

"All bathing in the main areas of the castle is cold water only," our guide said, before I could voice my desire to bathe. "Should you prefer hot water, there is a communal bathhouse fed by natural hot springs in one of the outbuildings. Because this is a place of study and worship, we ask that you confine yourselves to our guest wing and the dining hall. Unless you are accompanied by one of our senior staff."

Kostya stopped him from leaving. "Could you give us directions to the bathhouse? This is our first time here."

The druid directed our attention to the hand drawn map on the back of our room's roughhewn wooden door. "Food and drink await you in the sitting room at the end of the hall," he added. "There is always fruit, bread, butter, and cheese available should you become hungry between meals."

I dreaded the answer to my next question. "Is there wine?"

"This is France. There is always wine."

I hugged Clementine once the night host left and waited for my sister to close and latch her door. I took two steps into the room Kostya and I had been assigned and paused. Any other time, spending the night an in ancient castle in the French Alps might have felt quaint. Romantic even. Especially if our hosts had thought to drop a stem of wildflowers into the empty vase on the room's lone table or leave a lit candle in the window.

But right now, with the adrenaline of Alderose's rescue mission retreating, spoiled me was having a hard time accepting the lack of hot water. And the fact that an essential component of my magic-management system might need an emergency repair. I unzipped the leather pants I'd pilfered from Alderose's duffel bag—and worn on the mission for good luck—and lifted the hem of my turtleneck sweater.

The seamless material of my corset hugged my torso as always. Even though I could no longer see two of the claw marks, the center cut hadn't mended completely. Magic continued to leak out. I didn't know if the faint, pale pink mist signaled a dire situation, nor did I know how to return the garment to its pristine state.

The sea witch who made the corsets lived near the Caspian Sea. When we were done here in France, I could ask Kostya to head west rather than east and visit the witch with me. First, I would have to explain to him why I was wearing the invisible garment to begin with.

"Beryl? Come here. I think I can rig up a tub and hot water for you."

I zipped the pants and patted my belly. The situation with my magic wasn't dire...and this I had to see. Tucked into a corner of the bathroom and given a bit of privacy by a half-wall was a white porcelain toilet with an overhead tank. In the opposite corner was an old oak dressing table topped with a matching ceramic bowl and pitcher. Between the toilet and makeshift sink was a beaming, handsome demon pointing to a large copper contraption.

"What's *that* supposed to be?" I asked.

Kostya waved me closer and pointed out the obvious. "It's a *tub*. You sit on the wood slats and a parade of ladies-in-waiting bring buckets filled with water that's been heated over an open fire in the castle's kitchen. Look, there's even a bar of soap. It was probably made by barn wenches from goat's milk and fresh herbs procured by hand on the new moon."

"Are you finished?" I was giggling. It was that, or cry. We'd traversed Chamonix's network of underground tunnels in order to get to Alderose, then again to bring her out. The damp cold had made itself at home in my muscles and joints.

"I'm just getting started. Here," he said, "aim the showerhead toward the tub. As soon as there's a couple inches of water in there, I'll heat it for you."

I could believe in miracles. I hopped to it and let Kostya know the castle had surprisingly decent water pressure. He ducked out of the bathroom, leaving the door wide open. I watched him strip down to his boxer briefs and managed to get water all over the floor gawking at his thick thighs, tapered waist, and lascivious smile.

"How can you *do* that to me?" I asked. "We're in this...this situation and you're practically naked and all I can think about is—"

"Sex?" He placed a folded towel on the floor, sat, and embraced the tub with his legs, chest, and arms. A chant in Demonish fired up the flame-shaped tattoos running along his forearms. Designs I'd never seen in our ten years of knowing each other lit up his inner thighs and the front of his chest.

"Your demon lines come in *so* handy," I said. "Why did I not know about this feature of dating a fire demon before?"

"You've never struck me as the kind of witch who dreams of roughing it." Kostya glanced up at me and chuckled. "In France or in the woods or anywhere else. You focus on filling the tub. I'll focus on heating the water. While you soak, I'll check on Clementine, and if Laszlo's with her, I'll see if he has an update on Alderose."

"Insolent beast." I sprayed him. Steam rose from his chest as Kostya poured more magic into his fiery lines. Keeping an eye on the rising water, my thoughts lingered on my younger sister and her beau.

The Demesne—our family curse, if you could call it a curse at all—had recently paired her with Kostya's older brother. The fact the demon prince had responded to the curse by growing an enviable set of wings was a clear sign their magics were compatible. I hoped their bond would encompass their bodies, hearts, and souls and last their entire lives. I also wished the Demesne had provided *me* with that kind of happiness.

Instead, the Demesne had brought me nothing but trouble, causing me to make a terrible wrong I had yet to fully right, and it had completely ignored my relationship with Kostya.

I turned off the shower, folded my clothes as I undressed, and stepped into the knee-high water. Groaning, I slowly lowered myself onto the slotted seat and leaned back. Kostya removed the neck brace and draped a towel over the tub's rounded back support, providing my pounding head with a deliciously soft cushion.

"Your neck's healing nicely. Remind me to apply the salve when we go to bed," he said, placing a rectangular bar of soap in my hands. "Be right back."

Before the door fully closed, I caught a glimpse of the matching set of raised ridges on either side of Kostya's spine. Those bumps were the primary reason we weren't having sex. When the true mating response arose for demons, a pair of nascent wings appeared. And according to secrets shared when demons got drunk, there was nothing tender about the way the wings ripped through the skin of their upper backs.

Kostya's had begun to appear during our recent whirlwind trip to the Reformed Realm. We'd arrived at the palace and gone straight to his walk-in closet for some wickedly quick sex before making our command appearances at the ball. We stopped midway through our stand-up act when I noticed what was happening on his back reflected in the mirrors.

My big, beautiful demon had withdrawn, thinking abstaining from sex would delay the inevitable and, at the same time, protect me. He never finished explaining what it was he wanted to protect me *from*. With my added uncertainty over how the rip in my corset might affect *my* magic, I swore to whatever goddess watched over me I would lay out all my secrets for Kostya tonight.

Because I knew in my heart it was *he* who needed protection from *me*.

***

www.ingramcontent.com/pod-product-compliance
Lightning Source LLC
Chambersburg PA
CBHW022005170626
46808CB00001B/288